Closing the Circle

Closing the Circle

The Best of Way of the World

AUBERON WAUGH

MACMILLAN

First published 2001 by Macmillan
an imprint of Pan Macmillan Ltd
Pan Macmillan, 20 New Wharf Road, London N1 9RR
Basingstoke and Oxford
Associated companies throughout the world
www.panmacmillan.com

ISBN 0 333 90782 5

1 3 5 7 9 8 6 4 2

A CIP catalogue record for this book is available from
the British Library.

Typeset by SX Composing DTP, Rayleigh, Essex
Printed and bound in Great Britain by
Mackays of Chatham plc, Chatham, Kent

Introduction

by Craig Brown

From an early age, Auberon Waugh had his eye on the Way of the World column. A year after he first joined the *Daily Telegraph*, aged 21, he applied to its creator, Michael Wharton, to be taken on as his apprentice. He was to recall his plan in his autobiography: "I would tend his flocks, polish the shoes of his aldermen, pour sherry for his bishops, tea for his clergymen, whisky for his journalists, sit goggle-eyed at the feet of his Hampstead left-wing *penseuses* and read haikus in Japanese to his captive aesthete down a disused lead mine in (I think) Derbyshire."

But Waugh's application was turned down. "Michael Wharton heard me out with the exquisite politeness of an older generation and, with the same politeness, showed me the door."

For the next 30-odd years, Waugh would continue to nurse this strange ambition. "If it seems presumptuous to have supposed that I could inherit the column," he later wrote, "I knew that the great Michael Wharton himself had announced to our shared friend, Richard West, that he had left a letter, to be opened on his death, bequeathing me the column and all its inhabitants."

However, he was not to achieve his aim without a struggle. In the late 1980s, Wharton announced that he wished to write less. A replacement was needed but Waugh, to his horror, was not offered the job. "In fact, I only learned the job was going when told that Christopher Booker had got it."

For a while, Waugh resolved to grin and bear the sight of Booker "grimacing and gibbering on the sacred ground", even though, as he was to remark, "I cannot believe I was alone in finding his contributions an acute embarrassment." But in 1989, after Booker had rounded on him in the column for making light of the situation in China, Waugh abandoned his charitable forbearance: "I do not think I am particularly thin-skinned, but this high-minded lecture struck me as an unmistakable declaration of war . . . On that day I started a necessarily oblique and tortuous, sometimes crablike campaign to take over the column, the details of which I do not propose to reveal."

His campaign met with victory. On 7 May 1990, he wrote his first Way of the World column. He continued to write it three times a week for virtually the entire decade.

Over the preceding thirty years, in the *Spectator* and the *New Statesman* and in countless other newspapers and journals, but perhaps most memorably and graphically in *Private Eye*, Waugh had assembled his own glorious if unwilling menagerie of grotesques and reprobates on whom to practise his vituperative arts. How uncomfortably they would sit there, chained in the wings, ready to be thrust onstage and poked fun at *pour encourager les autres*.

The menagerie included, to mention just a few, the RSPCA and the RSPB ("screeching busybodies"), bats, Anthony Powell, chimpanzees ("the grossest and most revolting animals, of unpleasant appearance and disgusting habits"), Jeremy Thorpe, Tory Life Peers ("they tend, with very few exceptions, to give off a horrible smell"), Will Self, Cyril Connolly, contemporary poets, road-safety enthusiasts, ramblers, Yorkshiremen, anti-foxhunters ("bitter, power-mad crypto-perverts"), anti-smoking fanatics, Captain Mark Phillips, Shirley Williams, A. A. Milne ("whose loathsome exploitation of his unfortunate son, Christopher Robin, would surely land him in prison nowadays") and, of course, modern architects ("every time a building by Sir Basil Spence is taken down, my heart lifts up").

To most reasonable people, such a cast list might seem admirably diverse, surmounting every barrier of class and education. For every Greg Dyke ("everything he thinks is nasty, stupid and wrong") there is an Alan Clark ("Anybody who went to public school will have recognised Clark as the sort of Old Boy who returns to his old school in some veteran or vintage car to impress the smaller boys"), for every Shirley Williams, a George W. Bush, for every John Pilger, a James Goldsmith. Waugh attacked the police with as much vehemence as he attacked ramblers, reserving a particular hatred for the "punishment freaks" in the Conservative Party. "I am convinced that intelligent, educated and literate Englishmen are neither left-wing nor right-wing," he wrote, "but are bored by politics and regard all politicians with scorn. That is my political creed, so far as I have one."

Yet there is still a small, moody lobby of tut-tutters, led by Polly Toynbee, who believe him to have been beyond the pale. "Effete, drunken, snobbish, sneering, racist and sexist" were just a few of the adjectives Toynbee used to describe Waugh within days of his death – an odd way to repay a man who, some years before, had declared himself so enthusiastic for news of Ms Toynbee's close relationship with "a man who looks like a squirrel" that he even went so far as to argue that their romance should be set to music. It is hard not to feel that, like people resolutely wearing too many woollies when the sun is shining, this band of sad dissenters are suffering for their intransigence. How much more free and happy they would feel were they to read this final, posthumous collection of Waugh's Way of the World columns.

If they do so with their eyes open, they will find themselves in the presence of a master of the surreal, an artist who established a unique comic persona – an omniscient, all-powerful figure, not unlike God, or at any rate a black sheep second-cousin of God. Channelling current events through his strange camera obscura, Waugh creates a parallel world, a world at once more colourful and more grotesque than our own, and, of course, immeasurably funnier.

His plans to reform the world remain relatively modest: a "Nipple Tax" on Murdoch newspapers of a penny per nipple; the dubbing of the television adaptation of *A Dance to the Music of Time*, to make it funnier; an urgent call for Cardinal Hume to ban Roman Catholics from setting foot inside the Millennium

Dome; a blueprint for placing tasteful nude statues of Chris Smith at strategic venues around the country. Though Waugh always billed himself as a practitioner of the vituperative arts, his writing had, in his later years, become increasingly benign: this volume is full of chinks of hope for the world. "It is a glorious moment to be alive," Waugh declares. He is delighted to note that teenagers have "no interest in sex nowadays. Most sensibly decided that they will wait until they are 36." He also views Oxford University Press's decision to stop publishing contemporary poetry as "certainly one of the most hopeful literary developments of our time".

On a visit to Windsor Castle, he is thrilled to discover Her Majesty has placed three ashtrays in a state room: "great actors and artists stood around them, puffing like steam engines". He greets the arrival of the Blairs' baby Leo with joy, convinced that he is the reincarnation of his own Pekingese, also called Leo, who died the day before. "His mother will find him intelligent, affectionate, loyal and utterly fearless," he writes, before adding, "but she might be well advised to keep him away from cats."

His heroes in the present volume very nearly outnumber his enemies. This roll of honour seems to me notably unracist, snobbish, sexist, etc. It includes Sir John Mortimer, Major James Hewitt, the French, the organiser of the Glastonbury Festival, and Sir Elton John ("he can do no wrong, so far as I am concerned").

Of course, few of Waugh's readers would expect to follow him with equal fervour into every nook and cranny of his world view. I would guess, for instance, that those who share his dislike of modern architecture – on a point of etiquette, he once suggested that the correct way to greet an architect was to punch him in the face – would baulk at his disapproval of the police force. Nor would those who applaud his battle against facilities for the disabled ("One day, perhaps, the wheelchair motif will be adopted as our national flag") automatically join him in his stand against capital punishment. And of those who were, like him, opposed to the bombing of Kosovo, how many would subscribe to his proposed National Smack a Child Week? Unlike most columnists, who spend most of their lives sucking up to their readers, Waugh often seemed abnormally keen to ostracise the lot of them.

As Alan Watkins has pointed out, one of Waugh's great strengths as a satirist was his complete absence of restraint and good taste. He was a caricaturist, pointing his distorting mirror at a drabber reality, converting self-righteousness into comedy and bossiness into buffoonery. He also had the prose equivalent of perfect pitch. The most surreal and absurd ideas could be carried on the majestic wave of his prose, propelled from beneath by an undertow of fearless vulgarity.

Explaining his *Private Eye* diaries to a new American readership in 1998, Waugh wrote, "If America can forget a little of its earnestness from reading this book, and learn a little bit of the unseriousness of life, I shall be a proud man. Forget that the characters were ever real people. See through the distortion of truth that life can be a much more interesting place with a tiny bit of effort to transform it."

In his introduction to an earlier volume of Way of the World pieces, he suggested that the density and richness of material might make it unsuitable for prolonged reading. But if you read a paragraph or two upon waking each morning, you will find that the rest of your day is pleasantly transformed, and that, as if by magic, the world has become a funnier place. Though this volume is, alas, the final chapter of Auberon Waugh's glorious day-by-day comic novel – the satiric equivalent of the Bayeaux Tapestry – the world remains a happier place for having been refracted through his vision. Like the children in W. H. Auden's elegy to that other great English comic fantasist, Edward Lear, Auberon Waugh's readers "swarmed to him like settlers. He became a land."

1990

No Kids

At a specially summoned press conference in Community Liaison House, Det Chief Supt David 'Dave' Davey, Community Liaison supreme, introduced a typically British couple, Mikey and Dikey Domingo – he's 17½ , she's a stunning 27 – who had a narrow escape when sick perverts called at their typically British home in Mandela Mansions, Tottenham.

Mikey described how three well-dressed strangers, two women and a man, came to the door and demanded to intimately examine their innocent children, saying they knew the Domingos had 2.03 of them. When asked how he had responded, Mikey replied: "I said, 'No way.' "

Afterwards, he began to wonder whether they might not have been sick perverts from the evil network of fiends, and telephoned the picture desk of a national newspaper.

"I thought there was something odd," explained Mikey, "because although we are a typical British couple, we don't actually have any children. Dikey feels that Thatcher's Government discriminates against single parents who cohabit."

"I hate him, anyway," explained Dikey. "If I could afford to, I would move out tomorrow. I seriously regret having met him in the first place. We make love on average only twice a week."

For once, the fiends seemed to have picked the wrong house. They may not be so unlucky next time.

19 May 1990

Sporting News

An advertisement for British Gas which showed a baby swimming under water has come in for heavy criticism from the Royal Society for the Prevention of Accidents, on the grounds that many mothers will now attempt to teach their babies underwater swimming at a time when insufficient research has been done on the effect of water pressure on babies.

So it looks as if we will have to cancel the babies' underwater swimming race at Combe Florey's Church Fete this year.

Attempts to introduce the new sport of Rottweiler racing at the Crayford greyhound track in Kent have been frustrated by the track's owner, Ladbroke's, who feared it would be bad for their image. The Rottweilers were to have chased an electrically operated baby doll, in place of the more usual hare. The race had to run behind closed doors in Hackney stadium.

Even the tortoise race had had to be cancelled at the Combe Florey Church Fete as a result of this Government's insanely bossy 1982 ban on importing tortoises. Secret plans are being made for a crawling babies race. The babies, when let out of their traps, will be invited to chase after a Pekingese puppy. Now we must expect objections from the new pressure group, Parents for Safe Food. I can only say that during the war, when coal was rationed, we British babies ate odder things than the occasional Pekingese puppy – and, at the end of the day, succeeded in giving Herr Hitler a thrashing from which he never quite recovered.

19 May 1990

Visitors

I write with some authority on the subject of coastal pollution, being an acknowledged expert. A few weeks ago, I received a deputation of loyal burghers who came from distant Taunton to ask my advice about a large oil slick which had been reported on the north Devon coast.

"We hates to inconvenience your lordship," said a trembling spokesman, "but we'm be troubled for knowing what to think about he. There's them as says 'im be bad for fishing, like, but us has been thinking your lordship be mighty in favour of pollution for keeping 'm grackles away."

They watched me anxiously while I pondered the question. Eventually someone at the back saw what can only have been a ray of benevolence pass over my brow, and misinterpreted it: "Three cheers for oil slick. Hip, hip," he piped. A ragged cheer went up, before I silenced them with the merest hint of a frown.

Oil, I told them, was an unpleasing substance of foreign origins. We should not rejoice when it arrives on our beaches. What we Britons expect to find at the seaside is untreated sewage which, with homemade industrial effluent, creates a pleasing bubblebath effect even while it adds colour and pungency to what might otherwise be a dull and inert liquid.

So there was no need for them to ambush or obstruct the volunteers coming down from unmentionable places like Sheffield and Leeds to clean up Devon beaches. Such people were much better ignored, I said, indicating that the audience was at an end.

They thanked me profusely as they were led back into the kitchens where they would be given sausages and ale in preparation for the long journey to Taunton.

30 May 1990

What You Eat

'Dis-moi ce que tu manges, je te dirai ce que tu es' wrote the illustrious Brillat-Savarin in that crowning achievement of the French nineteenth century, *Physiologie du Goût* (1825). The German epicurean philosopher Ludwig von Feuerbach summarised it somewhat brutally five years later: 'Der Dimensh ist, was er isst' ('Man is what he eats') – but nobody could pretend it was a new thought.

Now a Californian criminologist, Stephen Schoenthauer, is advancing what he believes to be the revolutionary idea that criminal behaviour is determined by diet. Cut out sweets and the various toxins contained in junk food, he argues, and the most hardened criminals will take to knitting, tapestry petit point and other benevolent pursuits.

Of course he is right, but like Feuerbach he ignores the influence of taste. However much we urge our children to eat fruit and bran, there will always be those who head straight for a diet of fishfingers, hamburgers, sweets, lighter fuel and other solvents, just as there are babies who will ignore all the nourishing coal laid out for them in the grate and head straight for any elastic bands and dog messes which have carelessly been left lying around on the carpet. Hence our crowded prisons.

25 June 1990

So Intelligent

In the *Spectator* this week we learn of a shocking practical joke played on the Royal Family while it was living at Windsor during the 1939–45 War by the late Sir Osbert Sitwell. Queen Elizabeth was worried about her children's education, so Sir Osbert arranged for a poetry evening, with readings by himself and his sister, Edith. Finally he produced a 'rather lugubrious man in a suit', who turned out to be the American T. S. Eliot, to read *The Waste Land*, and what might have been a most embarrassing occasion was turned into a riot of fun by the Royal Family's excellent sense of humour.

'First the girls got the giggles, then I did, and then even the King,' reveals Her Majesty in a private conversation with A. N. Wilson, the novelist and biographer.

This seems to me a tribute to the Royal Family's education, as well as to its natural intelligence. How many students today could be relied upon to see the absurdity of this gloomy nonsense read by a portentous American in a suit? Nowadays, they would all sit goggle-eyed with their mouths hanging open, trying to look sensitive.

I wonder if I might persuade the Queen Mother to present the *Literary Review*'s Grand £5,000 Prize for Real Poetry in August. It promises to be the main cultural event of the summer.

2 July 1990

Biscuit Days

In all my West African travels, I never had occasion to visit
Cameroon, where French and English are spoken inter-
changeably in the elegant cafés and beer gardens of Yaounde
among the streams and shaded avenues for which the country's
capital is famous.

Why, then, did I find myself burning with sudden
Cameroonian patriotism on Sunday? Why did I cheer every
forward movement of their brave footballers, shining black
against the Italian turf in the World Cup Quarter-Finals, why did
I groan every time they were beaten back?

Odder still, large parts of Somerset seemed to be infected with
the same enthusiasm for Cameroon, even among people who had
never heard of the united republic before – or, if they had, tended
to confuse it with macaroon, the delicious almond-flavoured
biscuit. In London literary and artistic circles I found that
support for Cameroon was more or less solid, with one or two
licensed eccentrics, as was only to be expected, supporting the
other side, apparently called 'England'.

The reason, I suspect, was resentment at the idea that these
sweaty, incompetent louts and their grotesque supporters could
possibly represent the country we know and love and call our
own, the country of Shakespeare and Hardy, of Johnson,
Wordsworth and Chesterton, Barchester, Grantchester,
Wimbledon and *The Daily Telegraph*.

7 July 1990

Baffled

A waxwork of the Duchess of York in a York museum has been sexually molested by so many drunken Yorkshiremen that the curator has been forced to put it behind glass.

We in the South of England can comfort ourselves that Yorkshire is a long way away, and its most famous son, the Ripper, is safely behind bars, but then we read from a survey conducted in Sloane Square that one in eight women walking through that once-respectable area is ready and willing to pay for sex.

Now we learn that the BBC is preparing a film which will show passionate lesbian scenes involving a former gardening correspondent of the *Observer* and the daughter of a royal mistress.

Have we always been a nation of sex maniacs, or is this a new development? Are we being driven to this behaviour by lubricious newspapers and television, or is it our new predilection which shapes our television and press? Which came first, the chicken or the egg?

If waxworks are threatened, can Britain long be a safe place for chickens? When the last chicken has disappeared we may, perhaps, learn the answer to these baffling questions.

19 September 1990

Bald Statement

When I read in last week's *Sunday Telegraph* that a new injection brings hope to dwarfs, that dwarfism may be on the point of being eradicated, I resolved to hold my tongue. I am not a dwarf myself, and it must be quite disagreeable for those dwarfs who do not relish the state.

The fact that I like dwarfs is an irrelevant and selfish consideration. I saw one on the platform at Paddington station on Monday, and the sight made me happy all week. It has long been a secret ambition of mine to decorate one of the rooms at Combe Florey after King Philip's closet in Lepanto:

The walls are hung with velvet that is black and soft as sin
And little dwarfs creep out of it and little dwarfs creep in.

But to obstruct the whole march of science and humane medicine in the interests of a home decoration scheme would be inexcusable. Then I read in Friday's *Telegraph* that a new electro-magnetic apparatus developed by scientists at the University of British Columbia brings hope to the bald; baldness, too, may be on the point of being eradicated.

The time has surely come to call a halt. I may not be a dwarf, but if I am slightly bald I am happy and proud to remain so. These scientists are trying to create a world where everybody is of a standard size and identically hairy. Only neurotics and social inadequates wish to look exactly the same as everyone else. In their struggle, they will destroy all the joy of creation.

24 September 1990

Agony

London this week has been entirely devoted to the State visit of President Cossiga of Italy. I find I have shaken his hand no fewer than four times. It is surprising anyone manages to get any work done.

My own chief anxiety has been whether or not to wear a black silk hat at my son's wedding next week. In favour of the motion is that they are very beautiful objects, there are few opportunities in life to give them an airing and, as with the Crown Jewels, them as has 'em wears 'em.

Against the motion is the fact that very few people still own them – mine is 60 years old, and new ones are prohibitively expensive – and it might be thought ostentatious or, even worse, divisive.

My problem is that I have no one to whom I can turn for advice. On this intimate matter, I can think of nobody alive whose advice I would particularly value. Perhaps the best thing would be to ask the advice of John Pilger, or Karl Miller, or Peter Palumbo, and then do the opposite.

27 October 1990

Have a Good Time

The most terrifying aspect of modern America concerns relations between the sexes. A 27-year-old waitress in somewhere called Oshkosh, Wisconsin, who claims to have 46 different personalities, accepts that one of her personalities agreed to have sex with a 29-year-old supermarket worker, but charged the man with rape after the event because her other 45 personalities had not been consulted.

Much more alarming than this, she found the Oshkosh police prepared to press the charge, and an Oshkosh court prepared to convict. Four of these 'personalities' were sworn in separately, and the court heard different evidence from all four. The wretched man now faces up to 10 years in prison.

Perhaps he can count himself lucky not to be convicted for 45 rapes, for which he could face 450 years in prison. A simple moral from this tale might be for visitors to the United States to avoid anywhere called Oshkosh, but I mention Oshkosh only to illustrate how the madness which we knew to exist in places like New York, San Francisco and Los Angeles has spread throughout the whole country.

I worry for the fate of ordinary English couples who find themselves visiting the United States. The Form of Consent which British law will soon require husbands and wives to sign before each and every act of marital love (or gross indecency, as the law prefers) will not begin to save them from prosecution in the United States, where multiple personalities will be expected to sign separately.

How many personalities are expected to sign? Must every personality of each partner consent to intercourse with every personality of the other? By my arithmetic, this would require anything up to 4,232 signatures before the first amorous advance could be contemplated. Married couples planning to visit the United States would be well advised to insist on separate bedrooms.

12 November 1990

Office Jokes

It is a wonderful thing to find that sense of humour has returned to public life. In Wednesday's newspaper, Sir Peregrine Worsthorne revealed that when a voice on the telephone purporting to be a Miss Simper from No. 10 asked him if he would be interested in the idea of a knighthood, he assumed that it was a practical joke.

"Not surprisingly, I suspected a hoax . . . by Auberon Waugh," he wrote. "The name Miss Simper sounded too good to be true." So he asked his secretary, Susan Small, to telephone Downing Street and check up with Miss Simper.

Practical jokes are cruel and beastly things, and I am ashamed to admit that on this occasion it was indeed I who had telephoned, pretending to be Miss Simper. But it all ended happily. When the telephone rang in Downing Street and a voice said it was Susan Small, secretary to Peregrine Worsthorne, wishing to speak to Miss Simper and confirm the offer of a knighthood, they immediately suspected this was another of my amusing impersonations. The name Susan Small seemed too good to be true.

Entering into the spirit of the thing, they roared with laughter and said of course it was all true. Luckily, the Queen is a kindhearted person. When she saw Perry clanking up to Buckingham Palace in his best suit of armour, she knew what had to be done.

12 November 1990

1991

Not Forgotten

Tomorrow marks the seventh anniversary of the sad death of Mr Fred Hill, the motorcyclist, who died in Pentonville Prison on February 10, 1984 while serving his 31st sentence for refusing to wear a crash helmet.

Hill was a retired school teacher, war veteran and friend of the Sikhs – during the war he had been motorcycle instructor to a Sikh regiment. However, when the Sikhs were exempted by law from having to wear crash helmets in 1976, he started his campaign on the principle of equality before the law.

Motorcyclists all over Britain will remember Fred Hill tomorrow for his opposition to the oppressive and nannyish law which requires them all to wear these helmets. A party from London and the Home Counties will meet outside Pentonville Prison at 1.30 p.m., where it will lay a memorial wreath before driving in decorous and seemly procession to the Department of Transport headquarters in Marsham Street, arriving at about 2.30 p.m.

Fred Hill's actions harmed no one, yet he was treated as a criminal. As another motorcyclist, T. B. Trood, has put it, 'unless we are prepared to act to save our liberty, it will be siphoned away into the bottomless pit of totalitarianism'. The nation's non-motorcyclists should also honour Fred Hill's memory. His sacrifice was on behalf of us all.

9 February 1991

Well Held

Many will sympathise with the Princess Royal and her estranged husband, Captain Phillips, in their reported difficulties over the division of the 1,500 wedding presents which, by convention, are given to couples jointly.

It gives me some satisfaction to think that I have not added to their problems. At the time of the Royal wedding, in November 1973, I could not make up my mind between some transparent oven-proof Pyrex dishes and a slightly more ambitious set of Pillavite ramekins for baking eggs, which were decorated with pictures of baby rabbits.

In the end, I more or less decided on the Pyrex dishes. But, having watched the young couple walk down the aisle, I thought I would hold on a bit and see how things worked out. At times they must have wondered at the long delay.

Seventeen and a half years later, I am glad to see that my caution was justified. I have not only saved myself a considerable sum of money, I have also spared the couple any possibility of further friction at this difficult moment in their lives.

27 March 1991

Save a Princess

As a child, I was constantly faced by the moral dilemma of the Chinese button. Press the button, and a Chinaman drops dead in China. Nobody will ever tell you his name or worry you about the circumstances, but you will receive £1 million in the post next day. Do you press the button?

The correct answer was to say 'no', but even as a very young child, I felt that further and better particulars were required. Was there any causal relationship between my pressing the buttons and the Chinamen dropping dead, or was it merely coincidence? After all, about 35,600 mainland Chinese die every 2½ seconds. Since I started writing this paragraph, with a moment off to refer to population tables, about 500 Chinese in the People's Republic of China have died. It is a distressing thought, but I refuse to take the blame.

I feel rather the same about the Princess Royal's injunction to Skip Lunch Save a Life. On Wednesday, at Dover Town Hall, she refused an elaborate buffet lunch of smoked salmon, prawns, roast fowl and strawberries. All 400 guests followed her example.

Presumably the food was thrown away. Are we to suppose that 400 African lives were saved?

It may well be an excellent thing to give money to African charities, but I fail to see what missing lunch has to do with it. Many Englishwomen have a perverse desire to be thin, but that has nothing to do with the Africans.

These are not matters to be treated lightly. For many Englishmen, luncheon is one of the most important meals of the day. Another challenge might be to go on eating luncheon, and see what effect it has on the Princess Royal.

4 May 1991

Look, No Trousers

Announcing the welcome scheme for a statue of General de Gaulle in London, my friend and colleague Kenneth Rose of *The Sunday Telegraph* ended on an admonitory note: 'I hope the committee will consider an aesthetic point. Monumental statuary died with the trouser, as can be seen in any work put up this century . . . Better stick to a bust.'

This aesthetic point is well taken. It plainly enshrines an important truth which had never occurred to me before. Monumental statuary died with the trouser. It should be set to verse or cast in letters of stone over the entrance to every art college in the country.

Whatever anyone says, trousers look utterly ridiculous on a statue. But it seems rather drastic to restrict all monumental masonry to busts. Perhaps the time is past when we can dress people up in togas and pretend they are Roman senators, but why should de Gaulle not be shown bare-legged? There is nothing ridiculous about bare-legged statues. One thinks of the *Venus de Milo* or Michelangelo's *David*. De Gaulle will be in good company.

I am not suggesting that he should be shown nude. That would be going too far. If he were shown tastefully debagged, it would cover Kenneth Rose's aesthetic point while comforting the anti-French faction in the Conservative party, which might query whether London really wants de Gaulle back, having fought a long and costly world war to the bitter end in order to get rid of him.

My proposal may also reassure Mme Cresson, the Socialist Prime Minister of France, who believes that one in four Englishmen is homosexual. At least the Borough of Swindon is putting up a statue of its distinguished daughter, Diana Dors, wearing a slinky dress. That should satisfy the majority of Englishmen, but it would be a good joke if the de Gaulle monument became a shrine for London's gay fraternity.

19 June 1991

Kutch as Kutch Can

I never knew the last Maharajah of Kutch, whose death at the age of 81 was reported in last Thursday's newspaper, yet he had been living among us, in a modest cottage in the village of Mayford, near Woking, for many years, spending less and less time in his magnificent palace at Kutch.

Although a man of enormous wealth, he despised politics and politicians, confining himself to such patriotic gestures as donating 100 kilograms of gold to the Indian war fund at the time of the Chinese invasion of Assam.

Madansinh Sawai Bahadur was very well born, tracing his ancestry back to the Moon by way of Krishna in a family that had ruled Kutch for more than 1,000 years. How galling it must have been for such a man, in retirement, to find himself frequently asked to lunch at Broadlands by Lord Mountbatten, the European upstart who had tricked him out of his princely inheritance.

Madansinh, whose enjoyment of the *Gadi* (royal couch) of Kutch was so tragically brief, nevertheless became a noted diplomat, as well as tennis player and pig sticker. The Rann of Kutch, we learnt from his obituary, is a desert salt marsh which has traditionally protected his principality from invaders.

It is only from obituaries that we learn such interesting truths nowadays. Those who read modern poetry and criticism will be intensely irritated by the vogue words 'epiphany' and 'epiphanic' to describe any joyous manifestation. But it is surely true that while the plastic and visual, poetic and musical arts have sunk beneath the consideration of intelligent people and vanished from sight, the obituarist's art, drawing on so many strands of shared experience within our culture, is flourishing as never before. It is within our obituaries that our remaining epiphanies are to be found.

5 August 1991

Res ipsa loquitur

It has become a commonplace in Britain to complain bitterly about the state of British Rail – its monstrous expense, its incompetence and its dirt – but an institution which seems to be in every bit as poor a condition is British law.

Almost every day we read of the appalling mistakes it has made – on Wednesday a man was released after 11 years in prison on a false charge of rape. It now appears that there was evidence which may have proved his innocence on at least one of the charges 11 years ago, but it was not produced.

Lawyers are so dishonest that libraries complain they can no longer stock legal textbooks. They are stolen even faster than theological books. And now we learn of a drive by Anthony Scrivener QC, the Chairman of the Bar, to save barristers the trouble of learning Latin: 'We should acknowledge at last that the Romans and their civilisation have gone for ever and their language went with them,' says this firebrand. 'Let the classical scholars argue in Latin or Greek, but let us get on with the language of the people.'

If we despise our lawyers now, how much more will we despise them when they try speaking our language? The truth, I suspect, is not only that they are too ignorant to understand the simplest Latin tags and too idle to learn them – *De minimis non curat lex, Volenti non fit injuria*, etc. – but they also find the commonsense they encapsulate deeply repugnant.

But perhaps the ignorance and intellectual degradation is now worldwide. It was in Ottawa, Canada, that the Princess of Wales had to pretend to be amused by being mistakenly described as the Princess of Whales. Soon, practically nobody in Britain either will be able to distinguish between the blubbery, almost inedible marine mammal it is fashionable to admire and the lovely, maniac-haunted Celtic principality which derives its English name from the plural form of Waugh.

2 November 1991

A Bad Joke

Letters continue to pour in by every post from *Telegraph* readers all over the country agreeing that they had never heard of Freddie Mercury, the alleged singer, before his widely reported death from the American disease a few weeks ago. Some of them are beginning to query whether he in fact existed.

The theory seems to be that he may have been a practical joke played on us all by *The Daily Telegraph*'s learned but skittish Obituaries Manager, Hugh Montgomery-Massingberd – possibly in protest against the constant pressure on all newspapers to print material which might be of interest to the present empty-headed generation of teenagers.

This pressure is misguided, as I never tire of pointing out, because few members of this smelly generation can read, and none has any money. People with serious money to spend are found only in the 50–65 age bracket, by which age people do not wish to read a teenage newspaper. But we are slaves to the lustful fantasies of our incompetent, half-witted advertising industry, stuck in the Sixties, which interests itself only in hip-hugging jeans rather than comfortable tweeds for the fuller figure.

No sooner had other newspapers seen Mr Montgomery-Massingberd's joke in the early editions of the *Telegraph* than they decided they were missing out on youth appeal and started printing even more extravagant obituaries of this non-existent pop singer, saying that he was born in Zanzibar of Iranian parents, that he had landed in a flying saucer from the planet Mercury . . .

The most frightening aspect of the whole phenomenon is that if you see a British teenager sitting vacantly on a wall with its mouth hanging open and ask if it knows about Freddie Mercury, the chances are that it will nod its head and say, 'Yeah.' With their small memory span and almost infinite suggestibility, our teenagers have convinced themselves that there was indeed a singer called Freddie Mercury to whom they once grooved, who was tragically struck down by Aids and died the next day.

Which is all very well, but many teenagers are now so heartbroken by news of Freddie's death that they are refusing to eat or speak or wash themselves. I hope Mr Montgomery-Massingberd is feeling ashamed of himself.

> *His jest will savour of but shallow wit*
> *When thousands weep, more than did laugh at it.*

14 December 1991

1992

Spirit of the Free

Further to my note about Berkshire County Council's decision to celebrate the 40th anniversary of Queen Elizabath II, rather than that of Queen Elizabeth II whom most of us know and love, I have now been sent a photocopy of a High Court writ in which she is referred to as Her Majesty.

It seems that this usurper Elizabath is increasing her kingdom daily at the expense of Elizabeth. Australians who complain at the £750,000 cost of this week's Royal visit should be told quite firmly that they are paying for two monarchs, not one: Her Majesty Queen Elizabeth II, who concerns herself with educated, well-disposed, loyal subjects. And Her Majesty Queen Elizabath II, who addresses herself to those less adept at reading and writing – out-of-door types, perhaps, and swagmen.

Even so, the republicans can point out that no less a person than Michael Jackson, the singer, was able to visit Britain for four days last week at a cost of only £56,000. Michael Jackson may not be officially recognised as the uncrowned King of the United States of America, but nobody can deny he represents the spirit of that extraordinary country, rather as Marianne, the lady seen on French coins, represents the Spirit of France.

Neither black nor white, of an appearance which might indicate questionable gender, living cocooned in a sterile bubble, stupendously rich, earning a reputed £100,000 a day, and buying only children's toys, videos and occasional comics, he represents the *beau ideal* of Mickey Mouse capitalism, more like a god than a monarch in the society which produced him, the great teacher and avatar of the West.

Perhaps the Australians should be given a choice between the

Queen and Michael Jackson for their constitutional head of state. It may be too confusing for those simple souls to accept that we have two Queens, one for them, one for us.

26 February 1992

Gunge-ho for Oldies

The more one learns of what has happened to Oxford University since it started appointing militantly proletarian professors of English, the more one wonders if there might not be a good case for closing it down and turning the colleges into retirement homes for gentlefolk.

The latest practice among the new-style undergraduates, or "students" as they laughingly prefer, is called "gungeing", and involves emptying dustbins over one another. After exams they spend their government grants on bottles of champagne – for spraying over each other, as the *Sun* newspaper has taught them to do, rather than for drinking.

Quite possibly these activities represent no more than the "students"' understandable dislike for each other, but now something called the university's "rules committee" (does this mean the proctors?) has suggested that every college sets aside a "gungeing area" where its members can gunge each other to their hearts' content, leaving the rest of the university gunge-free.

This seems an impractical suggestion. The essence of gungeing is surely to express your dislike by gungeing someone else, not to be gunged yourself. Nobody would go to these gungeing areas for the purpose of being gunged, or on the off-chance of finding an enemy there to gunge.

It would be much more sensible to declare the whole of central Oxford a national gungeing area, where we could all take our dustbins and empty them over any "student" or proletarian professor of English we found.

In this way we would eventually succeed in driving out the "students" and their wretched mentors, leaving all those beautiful quads to be cleaned up and repopulated by gentle, rich, pleasant-mannered oldies like ourselves.

29 February 1992

Ecclesiastical News

We should not be too distressed at pictures of Dr Peter Carnley, described as 'Archbishop of Perth', laying his hands on 10 Australian women, or 'Sheilas' as they are known locally, with a view to turning them, miraculously, into priests. Now he has 10 Reverend Sheilas he can try a little harder if he wants and consecrate 10 Bishop Sheilas, but I don't see that it will make any difference to anything at all.

In Western Australia, around the Margaret River, they make some of the best white wine from the chardonnay grape in the whole continent, but I have never heard it suggested that Western Australians were gifted at ordination. The whole idea of Australians ordaining each other is faintly comical, but none of us who used to play at doctors when we were children should be alarmed.

The sacrament of Holy Orders is not conferred merely by some quasi-magical gift derived from the Apostolic Succession. It is also a question of intention. One day it might occur to me as an amusing thing to ordain my three Pekingeses. As the Rev Leo, the Rev Hyacinth and the Rev Quince, they would have more gravitas and carry greater conviction than many bomber-jacketed clergymen around today.

They are all male and one, I am happy to say, is black (Quincy). But those are really the only qualifications they have. My action would not be invalid just because I am not a consecrated bishop, but because my beloved Pekingeses lack various essential properties of an ordained priest.

In the same way, Dr Carnley can perfectly well go through the motions of ordaining a kangaroo, if that is what he feels like doing. In fact I would be pleased if he did, as it would make the point better than he has already made it. Such an initiative would not hurt the kangaroo, nor would it do any harm to the rest of us, but neither would it have created a new priest to help meet the Church's desperate shortage.

11 March 1992

Threatened Beavers

Further to my note on Monday about rumours of a great drought, I observe that the *Sun* newspaper carried a '*Sun* news special' on the same day, boldly headlined: 'WE'RE IN GRIP OF WORST DROUGHT SINCE 1945: Trees parched and animals dying'.

Millions of families face drastic water shortages in 'the worst drought for nearly 250 years'. I read: 'Thousands of oak and beech trees are starting to die in an area stretching from South Devon to Sherwood Forest. Wildlife such as geese, waterfowl, beavers, otters, frogs and toads are badly hit as streams and rivers turn to trickles.'

I can't speak for the otters, because I have not been looking out for them recently, but my own ducks – mallard and teal for the most part – are in fine shape, and have just been joined by a handsome pair of Canada geese. There is plenty of water and they are all having the time of their lives.

As for the beavers, it's a funny thing, y'know, but I have been around the woods, rivers and hedgerows of England this past half century or so, and I can't rightly recall ever seeing a beaver. In fact I don't think there are any beavers in this country. Whichever 'expert' informed the poor *Sun* reporter that the nation's beavers were being badly hit by this non-existent drought was relying on that newspaper's regrettable ignorance about the natural world and its indiscriminate sentimentality towards animals.

The 'experts' may have been helped by the fact that the newspaper is written in windowless concrete bunkers. Journalists enter them in the dark and leave them in the dark. They never have a chance to glimpse the green fields, the sparkling rivers and streams, the frogs and toads cavorting in the spring sunshine.

They will believe whatever the 'experts' tell them. I still have an open mind about this alleged drought, but I can't help asking myself what sort of drought it is which requires its supporters to tell such whopping fibs to convince us of its seriousness.

25 March 1992

Merrie England

I did not see the London Marathon this weekend, and so cannot complain about it too loudly, but my heartfelt sympathy goes out to those who found themselves confronted by 25,000 runners, all anxious to show how good-hearted they were and what fun they were having.

From photographs I see that some were dressed as chickens, some as rabbits, some as Indian statesmen. Many men wore cushions under their shirts or put on grass skirts and false breasts, whether in emulation or mockery of the gentler sex.

There are those who will argue there is no harm to this, it is all for charity; my objection is not moral but aesthetic. It is not true to say that anything is justified in a good cause: vulgarity, exhibitionism and ugliness are things to be avoided. There is no excuse for inflicting them on your fellow-citizens by saying it is done in a good cause.

The pains of living in an overcrowded island are apparent enough for those who have to travel inside it. But if the torture is to be compounded by organised mass merrymaking, life will soon become unendurable.

When Disney's Euro Park was first mooted I, too, saw it as a cultural Chernobyl and prayed that some mad French intellectual would blow it up. It certainly sounds my idea of Hell on Earth, with no alcohol being sold (as in Fortress Wapping) because as the American organiser explained: 'We want to keep the Magic Kingdom magic.'

Now I feel that the French intellectuals are wrong. There was a time when we might have hoped to educate our Disney-fodder to something better. That time has now passed. The theme for the future is not education but segregation. If hundreds of thousands of Mickey Mouse fans choose to celebrate their preference together in a small area set aside for them in the north of France, then the rest of the country can breathe a sign of relief and head somewhere else.

By the same token, if the London Marathon can be persuaded to run round and round Wembley Stadium, then the rest of us can happily offer to sponsor it.

15 April 1992

Song of Songs

It was civil of Lord McAlpine to attribute the Conservative victory to support from the Press, and it will be good for Tory MPs to reflect on this, as they jostle and climb over one another like so many iguanas in a pit. But McApline stressed the role of the tabloid editors, at the expense of weightier sheets. I would like to think we did our bit on Way of the World.

Over the years I have seen many journalistic colleagues fall in love with the Prime Minister of the day – first with Harold Wilson, then with Mrs Thatcher – and I have always been the first to mock them, denouncing them as toadies and sycophants.

But what are these strange stirrings I feel when I contemplate the blameless countenance of our nice new Mr Major, with his miraculous phantom moustache, his hair like a flock of goats, teeth like sheep that are newly shorn, temples like a piece of pomegranate within his locks.

'My beloved is white and ruddy, the chiefest among ten thousand . . . his hands are gold rings set with beryl: his belly is as bright ivory overlaid with sapphires. His legs are as pillars of marble . . . His mouth is most sweet: yea, he is altogether lovely. This is my beloved, and this is my friend, O daughters of Jerusalem.'

Perhaps it would be premature to describe Mr Major as my friend, as I have not yet had the pleasure of meeting him, but if the daughters of Jerusalem will just wait around . . .

All the editors named by Lord McAlpine have denied their part in the victory, but it would convince nobody if I put in such a modest claim for my own role. There can be little doubt it was the Way of the World column which dragged the nation back from the precipice, and saved the Elgin Marbles for their nation.

Those who suffer aggravation and annoyance from the crowds of their fellow citizens over the Easter break should reflect how much worse things would be if the idiotic Mr Kinnock were Prime Minister.

18 April 1992

Children's Hour

One could easily become indignant about proposals to make it a criminal offence for parents to smack their children, but only if one supposed that anyone would pay the slightest bit of attention to such a law. But apart from its fatuousness, it is a thoroughly bad and oppressive idea.

I can quite accept that corporal punishment does not always prevent children from becoming delinquents, but that is only part of its appeal. Another part is to relieve parents' feelings. Personally, I derive no pleasure from smacking children, but that is no good reason for me to put a stop to other people's pleasures. It is like the hunting issue, which almost certainly lost Labour its fourth general election in a row.

Many parents may have children only to smack them, in much the same way that people keep dogs only to shout at them in a gruff, peremptory way. There are few enough incentives for young couples to have children in our ageing society; we should do nothing to discourage them.

Perhaps anti-corporal punishment fanatics can think of other things to do with small children than smack them. I have heard that babies can be used for netball or American basketball, and this (unlike being smacked) is something they enjoy. But even then the bossy fanatics will probably insist on passing a lot of fatuous laws controlling the height of the goal, etc.

6 May 1992

Greatest Englishwoman

While we are all pondering a suitable honour for Lady Thatcher – should we make her a countess, or duchess in her own right, or Deputy Queen of England, or will life baroness do the trick? – we might spare a thought for Elizabeth David, who died last week at 78.

She achieved more for her fellow countrymen, in terms of improving their standards of comfort, well-being and general happiness, than any woman in my own lifetime, and I dare say in the history of England. She not only revolutionised our approach to food, teaching us how it can easily become one of the principal pleasures of life, she also opened the gates of Europe, teaching a timid and sceptical English middle class the delights which awaited them there. I wonder whether Britain would ever have voted 2–1 in favour of Europe in the historic Referendum of June 5, 1975 if it had not been for Mrs David.

It is against this tide of olive oil, garlic and wine that the Thatcherite lower-middle-class backlash is trying to shut the gates once again. Only those who remember how disgusting most English food used to be before *French Provincial Cooking* (1960) – let alone before *A Book of Mediterranean Food* (1950) – will appreciate quite what these people are trying to do.

In a recent article on reforming the honours system, W. F. Deedes urged politicians to observe the rule 'family hold back' and not grab all the top honours for themselves and their relations. By doing so, they devalue the honours they award themselves.

Mrs David, who saved her country from gloom and despair, received the OBE in 1976 and the CBE, when well over 70, in 1986. This is just a step or two ahead of the award Lady Thatcher chose for her cleaning woman in Downing Street, the admirable Mrs Booker. Yet if any woman has ever deserved a peerage, the Garter or the OM, it was surely Elizabeth David.

I feel Lady Thatcher should wait, like Mr Heath, until she is 75, before being offered further honours. Heath's award is thought to be by way of an apology from the Queen for having called him 'dispensable' on television. I wonder what the Queen will choose to call Lady Thatcher between now and October 13, 2000.

25 May 1992

Lessons of Tennis

June of this year marks the 15th anniversary of the Grunwick riots, when gangs of extremely unpleasant 'workers' from the north of England, led by Mrs Shirley Williams, descended on a London suburb to try to stop some pretty Asian women from working in a photographic processing plant.

They coincided with the Wimbledon tournament, and I remember switching television channels between pretty Sue Barker playing tennis at Wimbledon and the hideous, grimacing faces of Mrs Williams's 'workers' on the news. What a distressing illustration they provided of the Two Nations, I thought. If only Mrs Williams's 'workers' could be persuaded to watch Wimbledon . . .

I do not think we should be too distressed that Mr Murdoch plans to buy exclusive rights to Wimbledon for his own lower-class television channel, now called BSkyB. There can be no question for most of us of having BSkyB in the house. Apart from anything else, it damages property values in the neighbourhood if you stick a 'Rupert's ear' on your roof, and it cannot be long before posses of neighbourhood vigilantes start burning down the houses which display them.

So there will be no more Wimbledon on television, but in truth it has got much duller. Powerful new carbon-fibre racquets mean that the ball moves so fast you can seldom see it, while fewer and fewer services are successfully returned.

Most of us have more important things to do than watch such tedium. What we must all hope is that when Mr Murdoch's 'workers' watch, however incomprehendingly, on their BSkyB machines, something of the gentle spirit of English tennis enters their poor, muddled minds and sweetens their sour temperaments.

27 May 1992

43

All Honourable Women

Amid all the honours being thrown around, the only one which seems to have caused some unhappiness was the honorary doctorate awarded to Jacques Derrida, the French philosopher, by Cambridge University, and that was not the result of an arbitrary political decision but careful deliberation by some of the finest minds in the land.

Derrida's great message to the world is that language is an imperfect vehicle for the communication of ideas because accretions of meaning on words can cause ambiguity and undermine the intention; but even the intention is seldom unambiguous, in any case. So all you are left with is the text, which might be worth a bob or two for an idle academic to take to pieces.

All of which might seem too obvious and too unimportant to be worth saying, but by saying it incoherently enough, Derrida has allowed huge numbers of semi-literate academics to squabble over it. The award should be seen as being in recognition of efforts in the field of academic job-creation.

The only recent honour about which I had some doubts was Lady Thatcher's parting award of the British Empire Medal to her cleaning woman, Mrs Booker. I am not saying for a moment that Mrs Booker did not deserve the BEM. I am sure she did, but then so did many hundreds of thousands of others. One of the cleaning ladies at Combe Florey recently retired after 21 years' service – a good friend, who is sorely missed – and all I was able to give her was a rotten old book. No medal, no ribands.

Why is it thought more meritorious to clean up Lady Thatcher's mess than that of ordinary private citizens? Where is the sense, where the justice, in this?

15 June 1992

Aggiornamento

A correspondent in Kent has been kind enough to send me his weekly parish news-sheet, which includes six 'prayer points'. Here they are:

(a) Praying round the Parish; residents of Whetstead Road, and the commercial properties there.
(b) For the family and friends of Mrs Madge Moon in their bereavement.
(c) For the European Community and the Maastricht Agreement.
(d) For the continuing situation in Yugoslavia.
(e) For dental-health care in view of the proposed cuts in payments to dentists.
(f) For the situation in South Africa.

The most exciting suggestion is that religion should concern itself with dental health, as well as spiritual health. This could be part of the campaign to win converts which was launched in November by Dr George Carey under the name of Spearhead. When members of the Jewish and Muslim communities (already nervous at the prospect of being converted) complained that Spearhead was the name of a well-known Fascist magazine, Dr Carey obligingly changed the name of his great crusade to Springboard.

A springboard is quite a useful thing to have in the swimming-pool, I must agree, although it has few uses anywhere else and it is by no means essential even there. I am not sure that these luxurious swimming-pool accessories really reflect the right image for the Church in the modern world. Perhaps he should change the name of his mighty religious movement once again, this time to Spearmint, after the well-known toothpaste flavour.

Salvation through Dental Hygiene can be its anthem. Many young people today relate to the smell of toothpaste more readily than to the smell of incense. And the old are nearly all concerned about their teeth.

6 July 1992

But Life Goes On

Last week we learnt that the most beautiful house in Somerset – what Christopher Hussey described as the most beautiful sight in the world – has been sold. Brympton d'Evercy has gone to an unnamed English family who seem unlikely to open it to the public when redecoration is finished in a year's time.

All of which strikes me as very good news. It is sad, of course, for the family which has owned it for the best part of 300 years, the Clive-Ponsonby-Fanes, who made a valiant effort to keep it going. But the even sadder truth was that it did not succeed as a showpiece: they had run out of money, the internal decorations were dreadful and they lacked the proper kit to make it look like anything more than a prep school on open day.

So now the most beautiful house in England will be a private family home once again. The historian A. L. Rowse once remarked to me that in the entire history of human civilisation, the most perfect form of existence was that of the English country house in the earlier years of this century.

Without its full supporting cast of indoor and outdoor servants it may be a shadow of its former self, but from my own observation I would guess that even this shadow provides the most agreeable form of life available on this planet.

Others may prefer lying on a Miami beach or watching satellite television on top of a skyscraper in Manhattan, but I would be surprised if there is any greater happiness than that provided by a game of croquet played on an English lawn through a summer's afternoon, after a good luncheon and with the reasonable prospect of a good dinner ahead. There are not all that many things which the English do better than anyone else. It is encouraging to think we are still holding on to a few of them.

31 August 1992

They Can Laugh Now

I suppose we should welcome the news that Marlborough College has appointed a girl as its new head boy – a pretty 18-year-old called Bronte Flecker. It all depends on whether head boys at Marlborough are still allowed to cane their fellow pupils.

Many people believe that public schools, with their strange practice of beating boys on their bottoms, give pupils a taste for being beaten which never leaves them. It was not true in my own case, but who can say what would have happened if the punishment had been administered by an attractive young woman of one's own age?

Marlborough's initiative may yet provide employment for Soho's Miss Whiplashes of the future, not to mention generations yet unborn of *Sunday Mirror* hacks waiting to sneak on them.

However, I cannot rejoice with Mr Kenneth Rose of *The Sunday Telegraph* that the headmaster of Uppingham, Mr Stephen Winckley, has decided to replace the black ties worn by the school ever since Queen Victoria's death with a blue and white stripe. For those of us who have been mourning the great Queen all these years, nothing has happened recently which might persuade us to mourn her the less.

At Downside, the Benedictine abbey school which I attended, we always wore black ties in the winter, with stiff white collars, black coats and waistcoats and hair-stripe trousers, but I do not suppose this was out of any feeling of bereavement for Queen Victoria, or even for Good Queen Mary Tudor.

I think we were simply in mourning for our lives, as they say in Russian plays. A former headmaster, on hearing it said at the Headmasters' Conference that the purpose of public school education was to prepare young lads for life, mournfully replied that the purpose of a Downside education was to prepare them for death.

Revisiting the place last year, I was surprised to discover the boys dressed in garish grey suits and striped ties. Perhaps they have forgotten what inevitably awaits them.

16 September 1992

How Very Sad

The sight of women embracing each other is normally calculated to inspire elevated and sanguine feelings in the male sex. Why, then, do we feel shame and embarrassment at photographs of women kissing and hugging outside Church House, Westminster, on news that the House of Laity had followed the Bishops and Clergy in accepting the idea of women as clergymen?

It is a great cliché of the feminist movement – by definition composed of women who are unhappy in the feminine role – that men who oppose it are misogynists or woman-haters. The truth, of course, is that it is men who love women who are distressed to see them making such fools of themselves.

Men are suited to the role of clergymen – preaching what is good and pure and noble – because men are by nature absurd creatures: bad, impure and ignoble. It is all part of the essential joke of the human condition that men should be chosen for this role. By no means all clergymen appreciate the point, but enough of them do so to keep the show on the road.

Women, by contrast, are by nature nobler and more prone to self-sacrifice. The cult of the selfish woman, however strong in the United States, has not yet established itself in this country to the extent of influencing the ordination debate. Women in religion, lacking any real sense of what it is all about, can only attract the sniggers of the women-haters who put them there.

14 November 1992

Wallowing in Gloom

About 10 years ago I stopped reading the *Economist* magazine, reckoning that it had nothing to tell me about Britain's relentless economic decline which I could not see perfectly well for myself. The subject was not something any of us would wish to gloat over. If the magazine ever has anything of interest in it, *The Daily Telegraph* will tell us.

By this means I learn of a survey in the current issue which looks at the present occupants of what are called the 100 top jobs: head of state, Speaker of the House of Commons, Director of Public Prosecutions, head of MI5, etc. All four of these posts are now held by women, it reports gloomily, only one of whom went to public school.

As if that is not bad enough, the number of public-school folk in these 100 top jobs has suffered an overall decline in the past 20 years, from 67 in 1972 to 66 in 1992, at a time of catastrophic decline in public education. No wonder the country is going down the drain.

There might be some comfort in the news that the 'Oxbridge' element has increased, from 52 per cent to 54 per cent, if we did not know the sad truth behind this figure, which is that for the past 20 years Oxford, at any rate, has embarked on a policy of deliberately choosing the weakest, most 'disadvantaged' candidates in accordance with some mad egalitarian theory or other. So an increase in the number of Oxbridge appointments to the top jobs probably signifies an overall decline in their quality.

Yet it is the bald, unadorned figure of a 1 per cent decline in public-school participation which strikes the greatest chill. If we continue at this rate, there will be no public-school people at all in any of the 100 top jobs by the year 3313. One does not wish to be alarmist about this. Some of those who did not go to public school are among the nicest people in the world and quite intelligent, like Mr Major. But who on earth will tell them what to do, or inform them where difficult places like Ulan Bator and Helsinki are? I do not think I will be ordering the *Economist* again for a while.

21 December 1992

1993

Taste of Honey

A week in the French West Indies – parts of France basking in the sun off Central America where people talk French, eat French food, drink French wine and read *Le Figaro* in blissful disregard of the Great Satan struggling with all its horrendous problems across the water – reminds you that there is more to the European Community than physical proximity or economic self-interest. It is a question of culture.

For my own part, I look to the European Community partly as a defence of the bourgeois civilisation (in which we all grew up) against further encroachment of a proletarian mass-market-led culture from across the Atlantic; partly as a refuge from British politicians and administrators, whose frenetic activities have created more than 3,560 new offences in the past 20 years.

On the aeroplane back, they showed us an American film called *Honey, I Blew up the Kid*, or something of the sort, about a two-year-old American boy, the size of the Empire State Building, who wanders through a city picking things up and dropping them. I did not listen to the soundtrack, which was virtually incomprehensible, but watched the film as Swiftian satire in mime.

The monstrous American kid plainly represented American kiddiehood in all its terrifying ghastliness, holding America to ransom. In the event, I was told by someone who had listened to the soundtrack that the film was intended as a celebration of American parenthood, sentimentality, kiddiehood, etc.

The sad truth is that Europe and America no longer understand each other at all. Mr and Mrs Clinton have proposed spending another $1 billion on a 'Manhattan project' to cure the American disease, but I fear it is too late. Even without the American disease, our European administrators would have to think of some reason for the proposed quarantine regulations on American travellers. This could be even more hurtful for our good friends across the Atlantic who stood up for freedom so nobly until they let their women come out on top.

Returning to an icy England, past rows and rows of grim-faced Customs officers, apparently looking for drugs and terrorists but actually wasting their own time and our money to flatter the self-importance of our politicians, I cursed the British Government for exposing us to all this. Our place is inside a Greater Europe, possibly under Mr Yeltsin's leadership, but preferably under none, its main purpose to keep out American television, American ideas of political correctness, and American kiddies.

3 March 1993

Paisley Old Boys' Net

'Army's snobbish elite wins the war against a classless society,' runs the headline across five columns at the top of one of the *Sunday Times*'s news pages. I am thrilled. Where was the battle fought, and why was I not invited to join in?

I had reckoned without the relentlessness of the *Sunday Times*'s class-war agenda. All it had discovered was a former major in the Royal Ordnance Corps, with the improbable name of Reggie von Zugbach, who has produced a 'study' at Paisley University claiming that the preponderance of senior Army appointments from crack regiments must mean that there is prejudice against those from less-good regiments and support corps.

Major Reggie, who has retired from the Army to take up an academic post in management at Paisley (glittering birthplace of the *Sunday Times*'s brilliant young editor), seems to be making exactly the same mistake as Oxford University when it discovered a high proportion of successful candidates coming from the better schools, and decided this must mean that the system discriminated against less-good candidates from bad schools.

'The old boy network,' claims Professor-Major Reggie von Zugbach, 'is thwarting John Major's plans for a classless society.' Does Mr Major seriously have any such plans, apart from one careless remark?

The *Sunday Times*'s agenda for a 'classless' society, when examined, means supporting the power urges of the New Brits, the nastiest class in Britain – the same incompetent, ignorant and conceited gang which, by wheedling its way into positions of power for the past 15 years, has brought nearly every aspect of British life to its knees: government, administration, health service, nationalised industries, banking and insurance . . . only the armed forces have managed to keep up their standards. No wonder the *Sunday Times* hates the Army, and seeks to impose its own ghastly standards of mediocrity on it.

Nice Mr Major would be well advised to distance himself from the Murdoch agenda, especially now that the American gambler has gone public and distributed four million copies of his Maastricht petition among the British electorate. A sensible way for the Prime Minister to demonstrate that he is not Murdoch's puppet would be to wear a top hat and morning coat on weekdays as long as he remains in office. This would inspire admiration and affection in equal measure.

31 March 1993

Lost its Sting

To a board meeting of *Oldie* magazine, where I find my fellow-directors in a mood of swinish self-satisfaction. The magazine was founded slightly more than a year ago to cater for over-50-year-olds who find their interests and concerns ignored by the youth-obsessed modern media, and above all by demented Peter Pans in the advertising industry.

At the time of its launch, people said nobody would buy a magazine called *Oldie*. Those who had the misfortune to be over 50 did not wish to be reminded of the fact, while those of even more mature years might be prepared to consider a magazine called *Afternoon Sunshine*, or *Golden Age*, but would certainly not identify with anything called *Oldie*.

However, people under-estimated the great hatred for young people which is such a refreshing development on the modern scene, and these whingeing crypto-Americans have been proved wrong. But I am afraid that the success of his initiative may have gone to the head of its editor, 86-year-old Richard Ingrams.

The latest edition carries a new slogan on its mast-head: 'Buy It Before You Snuff It' – which I am convinced will have the effect of alienating not only the morons of the advertising industry, who honestly still believe that teenagers and young adults are the people with money to spend, but also the sensible, prosperous, middle-aged and retired people who might be expected to enjoy the magazine.

However, when I raise the matter before the board, I am contemptuously overruled. The slogan will stay. Perhaps there is a new spirit abroad among the country's maturer citizens whereby they no longer fear meeting their Maker, are half in love with easeful death, if only as a means of getting away from our half-witted teenage society.

3 April 1993

Remember Ethelburga

It was hard not to admire Asil Nadir, the former philanthropist and founder of Polly Peck, for having the courage to face the world with such a terrible surname. Now that I learn he has a sister called Bilge, my admiration for the entire family grows.

Erconwald, Bishop of London in the second half of the seventh century, also had a sister with a ridiculous name. She was called Ethelburga the Virgin. Erconwald founded an abbey in Barking and made her abbess of it. In time, she became known as St Ethelburga of Barking, and it was her church in Bishopsgate that was blown up by the IRA.

The cost of rebuilding the church has been put at less than £2 million, and we must agree that compared to the cost of rehabilitating the NatWest Tower, this would be money well spent. The site of St Ethelburga's (15ft by 30ft) is too small to be of great interest to developers, but there is a certain reluctance to invest even £2 million in building another redundant City church.

In any case, so long as the NatWest Tower stands, it will present an open invitation to bombers, and if St Ethelburga's is to be flattened on every occasion, it seems rather a waste of time to restore it.

Many will decide that the saint would be best commemorated by a vegetarian hamburger bar serving Ethelburgas to the new style of City worker. A small tobacconist's shop might be even more useful.

8 May 1993

Sola virtus invicta

All the best part of England will have breathed a sigh of relief to learn that the Jockey Club has cleared Lady Herries of any alleged impropriety after one of her horses which won a race at Brighton on April 8 reacted positively to a dope test.

Lady Herries, married to Sir Colin Cowdrey, is the eldest daughter of the great Duke of Norfolk whose death in 1975 deprived the English nobility of its greatest adornment. At a time when the monarchy is under fire from demented Australians, and in a week when we saw the next head of the Churchill family, heir to the Duke of Marlborough, carried kicking and screaming into a police van, it is good that nothing has yet occurred to taint the Ducal and Illustrious Howards, described by Burke as standing next to the Blood Royal at the head of the Peerage of England.

Lady Herries explains that she was doping one of her spaniels, called Kandy, and assumes that the dog must inadvertently have urinated on a patch of grass which was later eaten by the race-horse.

My only hesitation concerns the dog Kandy, presumably called after the ancient Sinhalese kingdom destroyed by the British in 1818. As Patron of the Canine Defence League, I do not feel that his guilt should be assumed.

Was Kandy legally represented at the hearing? Perhaps the standard of proof required to find an animal guilty may not be so high as it is for a human: 'balance of probability' may be enough to convict a spaniel where a human conviction would require proof 'beyond reasonable doubt'.

Even so, I am not sure a jury would conclude that the balance of probability favours the theory that Kandy urinated on a patch of grass, and the racehorse chose that patch of grass to eat just before the race.

The mystery of who doped the racehorse remains unsolved: was it an animal rights zealot, many of whom disapprove of horse racing, or was it the IRA, whose cruel hatred of horses has been seen in outrage after outrage, from the slaughter in Hyde Park to the kidnap and murder of Shergar?

16 June 1993

Time to Try Again

As one who missed all the dirty bits in Ken Russell's BBC1 version of *Lady Chatterley's Lover* I might not have the right to an opinion of the whole, but I caught the last episode on Sunday and was amazed by its ineptitude. Much of the fault may have been D. H. Lawrence's for his humourlessness and defective sense of the ridiculous but I have never before seen him so badly acted or hamfistedly produced.

On the subject of the bogus happy ending stitched on the narrative by Russell, Mr Michael Haggiag, the producer, explained: "We couldn't end on a downbeat note after four hours of showing two lovers fighting the class system. If we hadn't changed it, everything would have been left hanging."

I don't suppose that Russell's ending was much worse than Lawrence's, but Russell, like all his generation, is stuck in the 1960s. The class struggle has long since been resolved. The proletarian mass culture finally triumphed in about 1979.

It now spreads its muck and filth over almost every aspect of British life, from *The Times* and *Sunday Times* to the Conservative Party and the Church of England. There is nothing 'upbeat' about celebrating its victory at this late stage.

Under its new Charter, we must hope the BBC will emerge as a bastion of the old humane, bourgeois liberal culture and fight the good fight against the tide of proletarian stupidity and slime. Next time it screens Lawrence's irritating book, I would suggest an entirely new ending.

Lady Chatterley catches a virulent form of herpes from her gamekeeper lover. Covered with spots all over her body, she renounces men and embraces lesbianism. This should recommend my version to the women's movement. As for Mellors, he chokes to death when a shot pheasant falls into his mouth, which he had left hanging open in the manner of his kind. This should recommend my version to opponents of blood sports.

30 June 1993

Much Crueller

Those who hold the Army in affection and respect will have been ashamed to read about the former private in the Royal Regiment of Wales, Mr Anthony Evans, who received £8,500 in compensation after being driven out of the Army by a campaign of racial harassment.

A board of inquiry heard how this descendant of a black American GI was called names like 'Sambo' and subjected to a mock trial by a kangaroo court, at which he was charged with 'being black'.

I had heard of similar atrocities committed against African cadets at Sandhurst in the old days – contributing in no small way to our loss of Empire after the last war. At the time, I attributed it to ignorance. Anyone brought up on Heinrich Hoffman's *Strüwwelpeter* will remember the words of the Great Agrippa:

> For if he try with all his might
> He cannot change from black to white.

Attempts to alter the skin colour of Africans by scrubbing them are not only cruel and impertinent, but also doomed to failure. One would have thought that with all the scientific education which has been going on in recent years, and with the special emphasis on racial awareness and similar topics, this message would have got through. I had no scientific education at all, but before I left school I knew perfectly well that this was no way to tackle what we used to call the colour problem.

The oddest and most frightening aspect of this case is that in all the photographs published, Mr Evans shows no trace whatever of his African origins. He looks like a perfectly ordinary Welshman. Perhaps scrubbing does work, after all.

If so, it is much worse. Mr Evans should receive twice as much compensation for the impertinence and cruelty he has suffered.

28 July 1993

Kiss of Death

Some will be dismayed that the Arts Council has started paying out money to jobless disc jockeys on the "rave" scene, as well as to graffiti artists and "alternative" publications with amusing names like Skunk Comix of Sheffield.

"I was shocked at first that the Arts Council were offering us money to do our thing," explained Mr Iain Oliver, 25, the Salisbury disc jockey. "They sent out these really well-worded forms which said something like 'Do you want £2,000 for nothing?' and we thought, yeah, we want £2,000 for nothing . . . it's brilliant."

Let Ruth Jones, project co-ordinator of the Arts Council, explain: "These are the art forms of the future . . . Who are we to judge what is good and what is bad? The important thing is that there are young people who are doing things."

I feel that Mr Oliver's first reaction was the right one. For the Arts Council to have heard of anything means that it is about 10 years out of date. For the Arts Council to offer money means that it, the recipient, is moribund or dead, has lost all creative vitality and is reduced to a tired repetition of attitudes once thought daring.

It is wonderful to learn that graffiti, the comix and "rave" music are all now thing of the past to be preserved at public expense in the great mausoleum of Modern Studies. When Ruth Jones comes round offering money to the Way of the World column (who are we to judge what is good or bad?) I will know it is time to swim out to sea.

6 September 1993

Not to be Trusted

There is a terrible sermon for our times in the story of the religious education master in a Bristol secondary school who was always cadging sweets from his pupils.

To teach the scrounger a lesson, they arranged for a 16-year-old girl to give him a Fruit Pastille spiked with LSD. The bearded, 46-year-old teacher began hallucinating, dropping books, clinging to walls and asking for help. He was taken to hospital and made to eat charcoal, which is apparently the best cure for LSD poisoning.

With the huge amounts of pocket money they are given nowadays, schoolchildren can easily afford to keep their teachers in Fruit Pastilles if they wish, but that is not the point. They can also afford to poison them. In modern Britain, middle-aged men must learn not to accept sweets from schoolgirls. It is as simple as that.

8 September 1993

Squeak, Squeak

In last Friday's *Sun* I read that "passionate Jane Nottage told last night how she reached 'new peaks of ecstasy' making love with soccer boss Andy Roxburgh".

This was the main news of the day for *Sun* readers: "The love affair will stun the football world and shatter 50-year-old Roxburgh's squeaky-clean image as a caring family man. The father of one has been married to Catherine for 27 years and was awarded an OBE for services to soccer . . ."

Oddly enough I had not heard of Andy Roxburgh. In fact the only Roxburgh who sprang to mind was J. F. Roxburgh (1888–1954), founding headmaster of Stowe, although I'm not sure I would describe his image as 'squeaky-clean'.

If we ask ourselves what possible motive the *Sun* might have to destroy the marriage of this humbler Roxburgh, humiliate his wife Catherine, and upset his only child, we might find the answer in a leader which appeared in Monday's edition of the *Sun*'s sister-paper *The Times*, also published in Wapping.

The Times chose to publicise the claim of an American academic that Benjamin Disraeli had two illegitimate children by two different mothers. It was "the latest sexual scandal to rock the political boat", it said, explaining that the Victorians "kept their gossip private for men of the ruling class in clubs and smoking rooms . . . the difference today is that the media have shone the floodlights into the smoking rooms. So democracy gains what hypocrisy loses."

I cannot imagine that the clubs and smoking rooms of the ruling class would have been much interested in the private affairs of Mr Andy Roxburgh, or the degree of satisfaction recorded by his former girlfriend, Jane Nottage. The *Sun*'s spiteful behaviour towards one of its own kind is typical of the sort of hell the working classes create for themselves when they are given a free rein. Hypocrisy gains what any sense of decency or decorum has lost.

22 September 1993

Beacon of Hope

On Thursday I went to North London to unveil an English Heritage blue plaque to the novelist Evelyn Waugh (1903–1966) in the house called Underhill, 145 North End Road, built by my grandfather, Arthur Waugh (1866–1943), the publisher and book critic of *The Daily Telegraph*, in 1907.

The house is now divided into three flats, and the garden where Waugh filmed *The Scarlet Woman* with parts taken by Alec Waugh, Elsa Lanchester, John Sutro, Terence Greenidge, the Earl of Wicklow and himself has been reduced to a quarter of its size.

Underhill had a profound effect on the novelist in his twenties, chiefly in the desire to get away from it into the elegant salons of Brideshead. Ancient libels recycled occasionally by the journalist Alan Brien insist that Waugh was born in a flat over a dairy in Finchley Road, and that he used to walk half a mile from his home to post a letter so it had a Hampstead postmark rather than one from Golders Green.

I was happy to learn that this second story is also untrue. A kind lady who lives in one of the flats told me that North End Road used to be in Hampstead, and was officiously moved to Golders Green after the Waughs had left. In later life, my father had warm memories of a childhood spent in rural Hampstead, with milk collected in a churn from the local farm, amid bucolic scenes of ploughmen homeward plodding their weary way, lowing herds winding slowly o'er the lea.

Perhaps this recollection was no more accurate than Brien's. There can be no doubt that Waugh was born in humbler circumstances than he later attained. I would like to think that the plaque will act as a beacon of hope to the people of Golders Green, assuring them that with honest effort and application they too can end their days in a West Country manor house.

16 October 1993

71

No Time to Bend Genders

Ludicrous Andrew Neil made some curious boasts about his shameful rag this week. "The readership of the *Sunday Times* is growing and getting younger, more female . . . " he trumpeted across the top of one of his news pages.

Neil must speak for himself. Perhaps he is getting younger and growing at the same time, but few of his male readers will be grateful to be told they are getting more female.

Perhaps they are. I wrote recently about the distressing new fad (no doubt sympathetically discussed in that newspaper's *Style* pages) for men to be castrated and have all other male organs removed – usually at the taxpayers' expense – so that they can pretend to be women. If that is what *Sunday Times* readers are doing, I feel they should be discouraged.

Fortunately, Way of the World sells three times as many copies every week as Neil's horrible ragbag of a newspaper, with all its advertising supplements and comics for moronic American four-year-olds. We must use what influence we can.

Recently I sent a circular letter to selected readers of the *Spectator* bringing the good news that the time had come for them to cancel their subscription to the *Sunday Times* and take *Literary Review* instead. This would save them a lot of money, since the *Literary Review* costs only £22 a year, against £46.80 for Neil's lower-class filth. The telephones in Beak Street have been jammed ever since.

Neil can make his own arrangements. If he likes to think he is growing, getting younger and more female, that is his affair. I promise that reading Way of the World has none of these effects.

10 November 1993

The Sun King

Everybody in my health resort sat up to watch Hanif Kureishi's *The Buddha of Suburbia* on BBC2 after I showed them the front page of Wednesday's *Sun*, denouncing "Porn Filth shame of BBC play. The worst ever full-frontal telly."

"Fury has erupted over tonight's screening of a BBC drama crammed with full frontal nudity, orgies and perversions," the *Sun* exclusively claimed. I do not know where fury erupted, but it certainly was not in Shrubland Hall, Coddenham, Suffolk. Most of the inmates say they fell asleep before reaching the dirty bits, which were in any case short and quite inoffensive.

There is something demented in the *Sun*'s inconsistency which makes it prepared to denounce the "worst ever full-frontal telly" on page one while relentlessly printing immodest pictures of young women exposing their breasts for money on page three. Sometimes bonking is what every fella does to every chick when the coast is clear; at other times, especially if a television actor, football manager or other celebrity is involved, it becomes a vile and wicked act which has to be exposed.

Presumably some of the *Sun*'s oddity comes from the puritanical urges of its proprietor, the strange, debt-ridden gambler Murdoch, in his Los Angeles eyrie. Does he supervise the *Sun*'s manhunts, I wonder. The current one, which is worldwide, is for Michael Jackson, the American singer, who is seeking privacy for personal reasons. *Sun* readers are offered £10,000 for a reported sighting.

The last manhunt was for James Gilbey, an Englishman of respectable family. Backstairs gossip had linked him with some wretched celebrity or other in the public eye. Is it right that the most powerful Australo-American in the world should be able to organise manhunts of Englishmen in their own country? The manhunt for Jackson is conducted with a sadistic relish which only the born-again Murdoch could inspire: "You'll have to strip, my old cock," the *Sun* gloated this week, revealing that "police plan to make Michael Jackson strip so they can see the colour of his manhood".

Jackson is said to be suffering from total nervous collapse and breakdown, which is easy to imagine. Is there to be no pity for this poor hamburger victim?

20 November 1993

1994

Lennon's Death Explained

My note on the dreaded Beatles Reunion next month prompts one correspondent to ask why there has never been a full inquiry into the circumstances of John Lennon's death, as there has been into every detail of the shooting of John Kennedy. Lennon was just as famous as the American politician – he once said the Beatles were more popular than Jesus – and his death was every bit as important. Can anyone seriously believe it was the unaided work of one deranged man?

Where Kennedy's assassination is concerned, the conspiracy theory has become a major industry, but I would be surprised if there was anything in it. Much may be made of the fact that Lee Harvey Oswald once visited the Soviet Embassy in Mexico City. I once visited the Soviet Embassy in Manila, being taken there by my taxi driver in mistake for the British Embassy residence. The Soviet Embassy was holding a reception for the Red Cross, and it was half an hour before I realised my mistake.

There is no need for any conspiracy to explain Oswald's behaviour. The most significant fact about him, which is only seldom mentioned in books on the subject, and never given due weight, is that he lived exclusively on a diet of hamburgers and soft drinks.

Of course the man was deranged. The only surprising thing is that he managed to shoot straight through all the gases swirling around him. Where Lennon's assassin, Mark Chapman, is concerned, I would not be in the least bit surprised to learn that he, too, subsisted on hamburgers and sweet fizzy drinks.

To those who object it is inconceivable that two deranged hamburger eaters would be able to hit their targets within a space of 17 years, I would point out that Chapman was standing much closer to his target than Oswald was. Furthermore, I would not be surprised to learn that Chapman, the deranged CIA operative, had, in fact, missed. His victim, Lennon, also a hamburger and fizzy drink man, expired on the spot, out of fright and inner corrosion.

26 January 1994

Medical Mystery

Many commentators have expressed surprise that no blame appears to attach to anyone in the National Health Service over its employment of the mad Beverley Allitt as a student nurse. She attacked or murdered 13 small children in a Grantham hospital before being discovered.

The incident reinforces an impression among those who still remain outside public employment that the nation's public employees are engaged in a conspiracy not only to grab all our earnings and throttle the economy, but also to cover up for each other on every occasion.

Recently I decided to put this theory to the test. On January 22 I received a letter from a local NHS panel addressed to Mrs Rose M. Kennedy, at my address, inviting her to attend for a cervical smear test. On January 28 I wrote to the Director of the Somerset Family Health Services Authority pointing out that there had been no Rose Kennedy at my address for the past 38 years.

It occurred to me that Rose Kennedy was the mother of a former President of the United States, and this might explain the confusion, just as Fleet Street printers used to invent shifts for Mickey Mouse and Donald Duck in the bad old days. But it would be a pity from the point of view of NHS budgeting, I pointed out, if doctors' panels were to draw money from the NHS in the name of these Mickey Mouse patients.

On February 1 the Patient Registration Manager of the SFHSA wrote back to suggest that the patient must have moved out of the area, and said it had now arranged for her name to be removed from the practice's patient list. On February 5 I wrote back to the PRM of the SFHSA:

"My point was not that Mrs Rose Kennedy might have moved and registered elsewhere, but that she had never existed at this address, at any rate in the last 38 years when we have been living here, and she must therefore be a complete invention. I was alarmed to think that the Somerset Health Authority had been paying for a patient who never existed. She can scarcely have moved out of the area if she was never in it. What was worrying me was whether there might have been an element of fraud involved which, perhaps, you might investigate."

On February 11 the PRM of the SFHSA wrote:

"Mrs Rose Kennedy registered with the —— practice 40 years ago, in 1954, and gave Combe Florey House as her address. I must therefore assume that she lived at that address for a short time before you lived there."

Which, if true, would explain everything – she might, I suppose, have been a housekeeper to the previous owners – except why the local panel should suddenly invite her to a smear test after 38 years' absence. Personally, I feel I have not got to the bottom of the mystery.

16 February 1994

Somebody Loves Them

On Saturday, two days before the feast of St Valentine, the *Sun* sent a special message to those of its readers who were in prison, tipping them off about a baby batterer sent to prison for three years:

"The sentence is an insult. Baby batterers should get a minimum of 10 years. Fortunately, there is still justice in the world. The thug will get a rough time in prison. *Sun* readers in the nick might like to know his name is . . ."

This is an open exhortation to *Sun* readers in prison to beat up a particular prisoner. If Mr Howard, the Home Secretary, had half the courage of a drunk chicken, he would ban the *Sun* from all prisons immediately.

On Monday, St Valentine's Day, also celebrated as National Impotence Awareness Day, the *Sun* addressed its readers again: "Did you get a Valentine card today? If you were forgotten, don't worry. *Somebody loves you. Everybody here at the* Sun."

22 February 1994

Vespal Virgins

It would be a tragedy if nice Mr Major dropped his Back to Basics campaign at this bleak time in our nation's history when it is providing so much laughter and fun for the rest of us.

The surviving hero of the Family Values section so far is still Mr David Ashby, Conservative Member for Leicestershire NW, who chastely shared a bed with his male friend on holiday in France in order to save money.

But Mr Hartley Booth must run them a close second. His four-month friendship with the Left-wing 22-year-old Emily Barr involved no sexual impropriety, although she claims to sleep with a condom on her bedside table and, according to the *Sun*, they would register together in hotels under an assumed name.

A question arises in the councils of the Venerable Society for the Protection of Adulterers (VESPA), of which I have the honour to be the president: whether we should exert ourselves also to protect these non-adulterers. I think we should. Our purpose is to protect people in the public eye from the prurient vindictiveness of the gutter press. Non-adulterers such as Mr Booth (wittily known as Vespal Virgins) certainly qualify.

The time may have come to move our campaign into the enemy's camp. In a circular message from the chairman, all members will be advised, when booking into a hotel with their lawful husbands or wives, to book under an assumed name. Then they should pay with their proper credit cards.

It needs only a tip-off from a hotel receptionist to the *Sun* or the *News of the World* and a successful libel action seems assured. I do not normally advise people to sue newspapers for libel, but until Mr Murdoch drops his dirty habits, we have no choice.

22 February 1994

Only Joking

On Tuesday night we were once again burgled in Somerset, but the burglars were frightened away and did not penetrate far into the house. In fact we have been very lucky – our last burglary was six years ago, despite the best efforts of Somerset County Council to turn the county into a haven for New Age Travellers.

It is an encouraging development that the Children of the New Age turn out to be too nervous and disorganised to make convincing burglars. When they run away in terror, they often leave poignant little souvenirs. If they had penetrated further and encountered some of the practical jokes I have prepared for them, they might have left fingers, hands, whole limbs behind, as well.

The problem will then arise whether to donate these odd appendages, organs and limbs to the NHS, or whether to sell them to hospitals in London which look after visiting Arab sheikhs and their relations. One's first instinct, of course, is to offer them to the National Health.

Unfortunately, there are rumours that after their crackdown on middle-aged and middle-class drivers, the police are planning a crackdown on householders who protect their own property against burglars.

Almost any form of self-protection against thieves is strictly against the law. It won't look good if I turn up at the local hospital with a spare leg or head wrapped in a blanket. But if anyone sees an Arab sheikh driving around London with the head of an English New Age Traveller perched precariously on his shoulders, he will know which way the decision has gone.

19 March 1994

A Tricky Character

Is it wise to bombard the general public with pictures of luxury beyond their means? In Monday's newspaper there was a photograph of a pretty young woman holding a giant egg from the great elephant bird of Madagascar, to be auctioned at Bonhams on Friday. I found myself burning with desire to own it.

Of these eggs, the largest ever laid, only three survive in private ownership, and Bonhams expect theirs to realise between £20,000 and £30,000. Alas, I cannot afford it. This does not seem fair. Everyone should have the right to his own great elephant bird egg, should he not? In this field, the gap between rich and poor, haves and have-nots, is particularly wide, since only three people in the world have a great elephant bird egg, while the rest of us – some five billion people in all – have not.

Brooding on this sort of injustice, as the Archbishop of Canterbury has done, may drive people to desperate acts, like voting Liberal Democrat next month. I must urge them to resist the temptation. The Liberal Democrats include many of the most unpleasant and conceited people in the country. Under their dreaded leader "Paddy" Pantsdown they are committed to closing down all the hunts and banning free Englishmen and Englishwomen from their centuries-old national sport. Whatever he may say, "Paddy" Pantsdown is in no position to distribute great elephant bird eggs among the population. He should be denounced as a liar if he promises to do so.

A correspondent asks why I always put the name Paddy in inverted commas, as if it was not his real name. The answer is that it is not his real name. He was christened Jeremy, just like his predecessor as Liberal leader.

Presumably he asks everyone to call him "Paddy" because he

does not wish to be confused with Mr Thorpe, but this seems a curious way to set about things. Perhaps I should call him Mr Jeremy Pantyhose to make the point. Nobody should believe him, either, if he claims to have seen a great elephant bird in Madagascar. They have been extinct since Napoleonic times.

6 April 1994

Send a Letter

"Prepare ye the way of the Lord," sang the prophet Isaiah. "Every valley shall be exalted, and every mountain and hill shall be made low: and the crooked shall be made straight, and the rough places plain."

These activities are all the more useful if the Lord concerned is in a wheelchair. But Lord Tebbit was spared such a fate, after the unforgettably poignant moment when television viewers watched first his toes, then his feet, then his pyjamaed body emerge from the rubble of the Grand Hotel, Brighton.

It was not on his own behalf, but gallantly on behalf of his wife, an even more innocent victim of the bomb outrage, that Lord Tebbit wrote an angry letter to *The Times* on Saturday:

> Sir, May I suggest that Mr Simon Jenkins should sit himself in a wheelchair and without raising his backside from the seat try to use the telephone in one of the BT red boxes he so admires.
> Yours faithfully,
> TEBBIT,
> House of Lords

Jenkins's crime had been to admire the old red telephone boxes designed by Sir Giles Gilbert Scott, and lament the new booths replacing them throughout the country.

We must suppose that these new booths, although hideous and unpleasant for everyone else, are more convenient for people who have the misfortune to be confined to wheelchairs.

That is a point in their favour, but people in wheelchairs survived somehow during the 60-odd years of the handsome Gilbert Scott design, and I am not sure that their greater convenience is sufficient reason to pepper the whole face of

England with nasty, vulgar plastic capsules.

Above all, I am sorry that Lord Tebbit should seek to advance the cause of the handicapped by adopting the mendicant's snarl, rather than the voice of sweet reason, the appeal to kinder and more generous instincts. Since the philistines appear to have won this battle, as they nearly always do, he might attract greater enthusiasm for his cause by being a little more gracious.

18 April 1994

A Question of Manners

"Made to Crawl by Lady Olga's Tories" was the *Mirror*'s headline under a most unpleasing photograph of allegedly disabled people on all fours on the pavement outside Parliament, wearing rude T-shirts printed "Piss on Pity".

If that is to be the new language of politics, then so be it. The tactics of these protestors, invited to Westminster by Dennis Skinner, are exactly the same as those adopted by North African beggars, who exhibit their amputated limbs and other sores with furious grimaces, as a way of exciting guilt, rather than pity, in the onlookers.

It might work over here, but I am not sure. It would be easy to say that people who behave like North African beggars should be treated like North African beggars, propped against the nearest wall to have the occasional coin tossed in their direction.

I think we are kinder than that, but it is an unfortunate truth that many people who have the misfortune to be confined to wheelchairs become bad-tempered, self-pitying and extremely unpleasant in the course of it. They need – and often find – saints to look after them.

But most people are not saints and, rather than be seriously inconvenienced by the need to flatten every mountain in their path, and fill in every valley, they would be quite happy for the disabled to stay in their bedrooms, or in special institutions, if the money were available. It must all depend a little bit on their comportment.

I think I know what Mr Skinner and the *Daily Mirror* hope to gain by exploiting these wheelchair crawlers, some of whom had to be brought overnight from Glasgow and Cardiff. I wonder if the invalids themselves have any clear idea.

28 May 1994

1995

Secret Society

Tremendous over-excitement has been caused in the secretive ranks of Vespa, the Venerable Society for the Protection of Adulterers, over the Bishop of Edinburgh's announcement that adultery is not a sin, that it is caused by genetic inheritance and should not be frowned upon.

It has been suggested that the Bishop should be asked to become the society's chaplain, but I am not entirely sure that we need one. Our purpose is not to encourage adultery, merely to balance the crazed hacks of the Murdoch empire who seek to spread misery by exposing it.

The Bishop does not have an elegant turn of phrase. Complaining that he had been misrepresented, he told reporters that he had been "stitched up" by the media because he liked to "shoot from the lip", adding: "I wish you guys had a good war to cover somewhere."

This sort of sentiment does not come well from a bishop. Although it is true that vocations for the ministry increase in wartime, it is not often suggested that the Church should start a war for that reason.

When asked about his own experience of the matter in question, he replied: "If you expect me to get personal, get lost."

No, I don't think he strikes quite the right tone to make a successful chaplain. In fact, I might veto his membership. So far the Venerable Society has only one official member, its president. All the rest are secret.

20 May 1995

A Boy for Ever?

When I joined the All Hallows troop of the Boy Scouts I swore on my honour to do my best to do my duty to God and the King, to help other people at all times and to obey the Scout Law. The Scoutmaster who took my oath, the late Joscelyn Trappes-Lomax, believed this promise held for life. Nervously reflecting on this, I sometimes wonder whose life is involved. Not only has Mr Trappes-Lomax died since that awesome ceremony, but also, of course, has King George VI.

The Scout Law is no light matter. As I remember, it required me to be at all times:

> Trusty, Loyal, Helpful,
> Brotherly, Courteous, Kind,
> Obedient, Smiling, Thrifty,
> Pure of Body and Mind.

I sometimes wonder whether anybody with all these qualities would be able to earn a living in journalism. Surely, at 55, I am too old to be bound by a promise made when I was 11, below the age of legal responsibility?

Of one thing I am absolutely sure. If the present Chief Scout, reputed to be called Garth Morrison (in my day it was always a peer, or at very least a baronet), succeeds in removing the oath of loyalty to the monarchy, replacing it with some sort of exclamation in approval of the community and the environment, I shall regard myself as absolved from any loyalty to Scouting.

If any Scout comes to my door demanding a Bob a Job or whatever is the modern equivalent, I shall make lewd suggestions to him until he goes away.

14 June 1995

Too Many Apologies

In the course of his long apology to womankind throughout the ages, the Pope deplored the way women "sometimes continue to be valued more for their physical appearance than for their skill, their professionalism, their intellectual abilities ..." I hope that his Holiness is not suggesting we should ignore feminine beauty, or fail to value it. Some women are beautiful and some less so, it is true, but that does not make it any more unfair to value feminine beauty than to value feminine skill, feminine professionalism, feminine intellectual abilities . . . all these gifts are unevenly bestowed. Who is to say which is more important? At a time when everybody seems to be apologising, the Pope has got off lightly. Jonathan Aitken faces moronic resignation demands from the Rev Don Witts, communications officer for Canterbury diocese, after a woman – how intellectual, skilled and professional I do not know – told the *Sunday Mirror* she had sexual intercourse with him (Aitken, not Witts) 15 years ago. Poor Hugh Grant, struggling to maintain his affability after three weeks of relentless hounding by the world's media, has seen his beautiful friend Miss Hurley reduced to sphinx-like misery. Typically, the world's media blame it on Grant's ludicrously trivial offence rather than their own behaviour. I think the Pope has got off too lightly. He is wrong to make these gestures to Women's Lib, whose driving force is largely destructive, evil and embittered. Perhaps the Church was wrong to burn the ugliest and nastiest of the sisterhood as witches all those years ago, but it seemed a good idea at the time and nothing is to be gained by apologising now. The Pope was not responsible, nor was I, and the only result of apologising must be to give comfort to the new generation of witches about their evil purposes.

15 July 1995

93

Another American Mystery

I was relieved to learn that police investigating the death of Glen Pelmear, 33, in a public lavatory at Ryde, on the Isle of Wight, now treat it as an accident.

Pelmear died instantly when he electrocuted himself on an all-metal lavatory. It was originally thought that malevolent persons had rigged up a connection with the broken 240-volt light fitting.

No reason was given for such an outrage. Like Lockerbie, it might have been designed to argue some abstruse point in Middle Eastern or Gulf politics, or some animal activists might have been arguing the case against vivisection or factory farming or hunting. Or it might just have been mischief for mischief's sake. But, fortunately, it appears to have been an accident. But one mystery remains.

If a 33-year-old builder can be killed instantly on a metal lavatory made "live" because of a broken light fitting, why do the Americans, when they wish to electrocute each other, require an infernal contraption using tens of thousands of volts which causes the eyes to pop out, the blood to boil, and takes 20 minutes to kill the victim? American thoroughness and American preference, perhaps.

We should think of that little electric lavatory seat every time we hear an American call for air strikes in the Bosnian civil war. They will cause a lot of damage, and Americans will enjoy them very much, but I doubt they will achieve anything.

15 July 1995

In Hoc Signo

Some may have been dismayed to learn that the Cross, 2,000-year-old emblem of Christianity, is less easily identified by the public of the capitalist world than the "golden arches" logo of the McDonald's fast food empire. In a survey of 7,000 people in Britain, Germany, the US, India, Japan and Australia, 88 per cent were able to identify the McDonald's logo, with only 54 per cent recognising the Cross.

I do not find this surprising or shocking. Christianity nowadays catches the imagination and inspires the loyalty of a fairly small minority. Even among active, evangelical Christians there is a tendency to play down that part of the Bible story which involves the Cross. Young people, we are told, look to religions for an assurance that life is a feast of generous emotions, and do not find it in the Cross.

In former times crusaders wore a cross on their tunic to announce they were soldiers of the Christian God determined to impose His laws on the infidel. Nothing could be more inappropriate for our soldiers to wear in Bosnia, where their purpose, in so far as they have one, is to prevent the Orthodox Serbs dispossessing the Catholic Croats or the Bosnian Muslims in a civil war that would have been settled three years ago if the United Nations had not decided to send "peace-keepers" to prolong it.

But if Unprofor requires a badge for its tunics, it could do worse than adopt the McDonald's logo. Not only would it be easily recognised by most participants in the struggle, it would also be making a clear statement of the values the UN is fighting for: the global mass culture whose noblest expression is to be found in the jumbo-sized beefburger with cheese and onions, pickled gherkins, and ketchup.

26 July 1995

A Possible Explanation

On August 28 Channel 4 proposes to show a film which claims to show two extraterrestrial aliens being dissected after their flying saucer crashed in New Mexico in 1947.

The story is that a film was made of their autopsies by a US Air Force cameraman who kept a copy without telling anyone what he had done. The figures would appear to be humanoid, but have six fingers and six toes, very large heads and no trace of an umbilical cord.

All of which might be quite interesting, if by any stretch of the imagination we could possibly decide they were genuine. I would be happy to inspect the corpses, if asked. But who wishes to see them dissected? What on earth gave Michael Grade the idea that this is the sort of thing British people enjoy watching in their homes?

The films will be shown all over the world. Either it is a practical joke, which seems to have been gigantically successful, or the result of a terrible misunderstanding. The two figures not only have no evidence of having had umbilical cords but are sexless, with no sign of breast development and no hair on their heads or bodies.

I have a terrible feeling, having examined a photograph in this week's *Observer*, that they may have been a Swedish couple on holiday in New Mexico in 1947 when their car was involved in a terrible crash which knocked it completely out of shape, and suggested a flying saucer to the credulous Americans who found them.

It may not be well known in New Mexico that many Swedes show no sign of having had an umbilical cord after their third or fourth birthday. Everything else can be explained within the allowable range of human diversity.

26 July 1995

Ask Your Barber

The nation's hairdressers are combining through their powerful professional body, the Fellowship of Hair Artists of Great Britain, to demand the withdrawal of an advertisement which might be thought to brand them unfairly. It shows a four-wheel drive vehicle being put through its paces on rough terrain, with the caption: "Hairdressers need not apply."

Among those hurt by the suggestion was Mr Andrew Collinge, vice-president of the fellowship. He said: "I just couldn't believe it. It is just so shocking and offensive . . . We are a major employer of young people and a serious industry."

Sue Clark, news editor of the *Hairdressers' Journal*, agrees: "Hairdressers feel they're being branded as limp-wristed or stupid. They are just as capable of being rugged outdoor types as anyone."

No doubt this is true, but it begs the question of whether people should be permitted to express the contrary opinion. How much freedom of speech should we be allowed? If we are forbidden to express the view that hairdressing is a sissy profession, however hurtful and untrue the opinion might be, the next thing will be that the British Safety Council will be forbidden from showing photographs of the Pope to promote National Condom Week. The poster claimed that the Pope was enunciating an eleventh commandment: "Thou shalt always wear a condom."

Simpler Catholics might have taken this commandment at face value, and suffered terrible physical injury as a result. If the message is intended to be universal, it is a recipe for the destruction of the human race. However it was intended, it was insulting to the Pope and to many of the country's five million Catholics. When a spokesman explained that "the Catholic

Church is directly responsible for the spread of sexually transmitted disease, including HIV and Aids", she was revealing the true depths of ignorance which inspire her organisation. If Catholic doctrine on sexuality were followed by everyone, there would be no HIV, no Aids.

But it is one thing to describe the National Safety Council's message as vulgar and misleading, quite another to ban it. Many think National Condom Week is a good cause. Mr John Major is among its supporters. Obviously, he agrees with Mr Jack Tye, director general of the council, that the Pope is being ridiculous in his attitude to condoms. Some of us may muse about Mr Major's interest in them. I have often wondered whether in some earlier incarnation he might not have been a barber.

7 August 1995

Great British Victory

While the rest of the country agonised over the Japanese apology to Mr Major for outrages perpetrated either before he was born or in the first two years of his young life, the *Sun* brought its readers exclusive news of a signal British victory in Majorca.

"We boot Germans off their Hunbeds," read the headline over a colour picture of three British tourists waving Union Jacks.

"Crafty David James stopped the Germans from grabbing all the sunbeds at his hotel in Majorca – by hiding them in his room. He and his pals were fed up after spending most of their week's hol lying on a lumpy lawn because all the loungers had been taken . . .

"David, 31, a British Telecom manager, said: 'The following morning we marched proudly out to the pool with our sun-loungers under our arms and with all the other Brits cheering. It was great. Julian draped his with a Union Jack towel to add to the patriotic flavour.' "

The quarrel arose because the Germans got up early and reserved the sunbeds by putting towels on them. "By the time we got to the pool there was nothing left. It was just too much so we decided something had to be done. And I don't regret doing it one little bit," said David.

One would hope not, but I am surprised the matter is being allowed to rest there. I should have thought that David, his girlfriend, Joanne, 26, and his mates, Julian, 27, and Lee, 25, could expect an apology from the Germans and compensation from the travel firm which arranged their trip – if Mr Major cannot arrange for the German government to pay it. The Germans have enough money, after all.

19 August 1995

The Serious Side

"We are used to stories about priests, cabinet ministers and air marshals hopping into bed with tarts," exclaimed the *Sun* on Saturday. "But we never thought we would see the head of one of our most prestigious public schools cited in a sex scandal."

Why on earth not? What these wretched people describe as "sex scandals" can be found wherever you look for them. They will be there for as long as the sexual urge survives. The *Sun*'s sermon, under the heading "Serious", continued: "Charterhouse's Peter Hobson has resigned after bedding a call girl. It is all very entertaining, but there is a serious side to this bizarre behaviour. If we can't trust a custodian of vulnerable young people to set an example, who can we trust?"

There is indeed a serious side to this bizarre behaviour of the tabloid press, but it does not concern the standards of our headmasters and headmistresses in the private sector, which is mercifully very high and not in the least bit affected by whatever perfectly legal activities they may get up to in private, outside the circumstances of their work. It concerns the standards of our prostitutes.

Never mind that the prostitute concerned, a 19-year-old with three A-levels, is a refugee from Newcastle University. If she had been bribed enough, she might have continued her studies, since her major interest appears to be money. But we cannot afford to bribe all our teenagers with vast sums in lieu of putative earnings from prostitution. Like it or not, prostitution is going to become a major economic factor and Britain may well be poised to become the prostitution centre of the world. But it is no good saying it is all our young people are good for if they are not much good even at that.

If British prostitutes cannot be trusted to maintain professional discretion – if they shop their clients to the *Sun* and *Daily Mirror* for extra money – they will not have many clients, and foreigners will stay away. One trembles to think how Britain will pay its way. The trade does not require a very high standard of rectitude, but our young people are plainly not up to maintaining even this minimum level.

The only silver lining may be found in reports that the two newspapers which agreed to pay the prostitute are trying to rat on the payments. Perhaps the untrustworthiness of buyers will eventually cancel the untrustworthiness of vendors, but it seems to offer only a tenuous prospect of national survival.

4 September 1995

A Hero for Our Times

Bruce Forsyth, the family entertainer, made a ferocious attack on BBC chiefs last week, saying they attached too little importance to family entertainment. The way the BBC treats its biggest stars, he said, is "shameful and disgusting".

"Family entertainment" can mean one of two things. It can either mean entertainment without sexual innuendo or other filth, or it can be a euphemism for entertainment which is devoid of any intelligent content, aimed at backward adults and exceptionally stupid children. Forsyth, presumably, falls into the second category.

The *Sun* endorsed his sentiments, avowing that Forsyth is "Britain's best-loved family entertainer". In a leading article the following day, it said: "When he speaks, only a fool refuses to listen."

Perhaps he is as well loved as they say, but he is also hated. I distinctly remember that whenever he appeared on our family television set there were groans, catcalls, and noises of people being sick. On top of the distaste of refined folk for anyone whose performances are so vulgar, stupid and affected, there is the traditional hatred by *Sun* readers of anyone who is successful or makes a lot of money. National Lottery winners complain they are treated like lepers by their neighbours.

So perhaps our Brucie is indeed a national hero, after all. We have been searching high and low for one to put on the empty pedestal in Trafalgar Square. To be a popular entertainer in modern Britain is probably the bravest thing anyone can do. Let us see what the pigeons make of him.

11 September 1995

Unfair to Our Dumb Chums

A kind reader, knowing of my interest in the latest theological developments, has sent me a cutting from the *Chipping Sodbury Gazette* which shows on its front page a colour photograph of the Rev Donna Dobson eating from a tin of Pedigree Chum in the Chipping Sodbury Baptist Church.

There might have been many lessons to draw from this spectacle – the need to make sacrifices for the poor of Rwanda, support for the Muslim cause in Bosnia (the dog food was chicken-flavoured) or a general mortification of the flesh. But the Rev Donna's sermon was slightly different.

"I was trying to make the point that Jesus rose from the dead and walked about for everyone to see him. But people would not have believed if they had not seen it with their own eyes . . . A lot of people asked me afterwards if it really was dog food. They didn't really think I would do it, but it definitely was. I just hope it got the message across."

The message, as I understand it, is that we would not believe that a priest (or priestess) would eat dog food in the pulpit unless we had seen it. But in this case we would have been wrong to disbelieve it, ergo we would be wrong to disbelieve in the resurrection of Christ, merely because we had not seen Him walking around, ergo Jesus rose from the dead.

This classic example of feminine – or Toynbee – logic should be included in all the textbooks, but what worries me about the new method of preaching is the effect that it might have on any dogs in the congregation.

Far from confirming their belief in the resurrection of Christ, the spectacle might turn them against all religion. I wonder if the Rev Donna Dobson has thought this one through.

18 September 1995

Another Dead-End Job

John Birt, 50-year-old director general of the BBC, has apologised to the City of Liverpool, its inhabitants and, above all, its football supporters for a tasteless television trailer advertising the police drama *Backup*. In the course of this trailer, skinheads were seen dressed in the Liverpool FC supporters' uniform. A voice-over said: "When football hooligans are about to clash . . ."

The inference was obvious: that among Liverpool's football supporters – who are among Liverpool's most respected citizens – there are some who might be, or might have been, or might be about to be noisy or disruptive in their behaviour.

It would be hard to imagine a fouler libel against a city which may have produced a few geniuses in its time – John Lennon, Albert Einstein, even John Birt himself – but has certainly never produced a single football hooligan.

It is this sort of libel which is responsible for the general sense of despair on Merseyside. As we all know, Liverpudlians are the best workers in the world, but the constant drip of snide, satirical comment creates unemployment and explains why comparatively few Liverpudlians ever become seriously rich. Andrew Neil, the Glaswegian "meritocrat", may not be a Liverpudlian, but he is the sort of person who could easily be one.

John Birt himself is a typical case: Liverpudlian born and bred, he finds himself at the age of 50 stuck in a dead-end job, apologising to these tearful, whingeing, unemployable football hooligans when he could be playing ping-pong for England.

21 October 1995

Very Interesting

People often complain that there is little of interest in the Sunday newspapers, but a fascinating correspondence has been running for several weeks in the *Sunday Telegraph* on the subject of aged parents.

Mr R. J. Buckstone, of Emmer Green, near Reading, reveals that his paternal grandfather was born in 1802, and wonders if any other reader can claim a grandparent born in the eighteenth century. William Court's father, who fought in the second Afghan war, was born in 1848.

G. C. Williams, who lives in Winchester, had a grandfather who met a man who saw Bonny Prince Charlie's army cross the border in 1745.

This seems to me far more interesting than all the rubbish about the Beatles, or the new James Bond girl, or Bill Gates the computer king, with which other newspapers fill their pages. I wonder if anybody will be interested to learn that as a boy of five, I wandered into a bathroom in my grandmother's house and saw my step-great-great-grandmother with no clothes on.

Granny Grace, as we called her, was the widow of the 10th Earl of Wemyss, who was born in 1818. She survived my sighting of her in the nude by only one year, dying in 1946 at an unknown age. Her husband, my great-great-grandfather, who married her at 83 in 1900 as his second wife, and died in 1914, would be 177 years old if he were alive today.

It may be hard to know exactly what record I have established, but I am sure there is one there. There are those who say that the nudity aspect is irrelevant, but this sort of thing makes a profound impression on a young boy. It may explain why, at the age of 55, I still smoke cigarettes from time to time.

15 November 1995

Too Much Falstaff

Nice Mr Major was quite right in his instinct that the whole country is suffering from a dangerous level of Soames fatigue. Nicholas Soames, Minister for the Armed Forces, is a genial soul, affectionately known as "Fatty" among his intimates. One would be as happy to buy a second car from him as one would from any other Old Etonian who had come down in the world, but I am afraid that as leader of the Prince of Wales's heavy mob, he lacks the honeyed eloquence to convince us of the justice of his cause.

Many people in Britain, understandably suspicious of anything they see on television, and on their guard against being manipulated, were deeply shocked to hear the clear voice of undiluted truth when the Princess of Wales spoke about her recent history, her hopes and fears for the future.

It was unacceptable, they felt, for anyone to bare her soul (or, as they preferred, to wash her linen) in public. Never mind that much human communication is taken up with presenting a case, otherwise known as persuasion. We expect people to lie to us, to have a hidden agenda on television. Jane Austen's *Persuasion* should be renamed *Manipulation* for the modern reader, and served up as a textbook for our stupid, suspicious age to be on its guard.

Then Fatty Soames appeared on the screen – he has scarcely left it since – and restored the status quo. It was evidence of "the advanced stages of paranoia" of the Princess of Wales that she believed there was a heavy mob waging a campaign against her. He found her performance "toe-curlingly dreadful". She must either work inside the system – Fatty Soames is the system – or she must shut up and go away.

I do not think that the Prince is well served by his heavy mob, nor does it reflect well on his judgment that they should rely on the misogynist rhetoric of ex-public schoolboys to explain his marriage difficulties. Before he comes to the Throne, he must emulate Prince Hal in *Henry IV, Part Two* and send Falstaff packing. The sight of a Prince cowering behind these overweight minders is not an inspiring one.

25 November 1995

Britannia Indisposed

Few will be surprised to learn that beefburgers have been identified as a possible cause of Creutzfeldt–Jakob disease (CJD), the human form of the incurable mad cow disease, bovine spongiform encephalopathy (BSE). It would appear there are few ills which may not be explained by the hamburger habit.

In Amble, Northumberland, recently, an unemployed man, Philip James, who was warned by police to leave the Tavern pub in Queen Street, was fined £150 plus £40 costs for throwing his burger at a police car. This final debacle was plainly caused by the hamburger, but we must ask ourselves whether its fumes might not have been responsible for his earlier unruly behaviour. Need he, even, have been unemployed if he had not fallen prey to this noxious addiction?

Even now, when we can see its appalling effect on our manners and morals, we seldom ask ourselves the right questions. Last week, two highly respectable Englishwomen were each jailed for five years after being extradited to the United States to face a charge that 10 years ago they discussed plans to bump off a local official among their branch of the Oregon Bhagwan Shree Rajneesh cult. Some Britons protested at their being extradited in this way. We none of us asked if, in their earlier life in America, they had been subjected to hamburgers, whether by primary or secondary, "passive" ingestion. Many newspapers were fiercely critical of Nicholas Soames, the normally genial Army minister, after his intemperate attack on our lovely Princess of Wales, but only one reproduced the old photograph of him, as Food Minister, forcing himself to eat a hamburger in the line of duty. History may yet judge him a martyr.

Of all the evidence which points to our national decline, most can be laid at the door of the hamburger and its associated gases. The tragedy is that nobody can see it.

4 December 1995

Tipping's Law

Happy the man whose wish and care
A few paternal acres bound
Content to breathe his native air
On his own ground

Alexander Pope wrote his famous 'Ode on Solitude' before the Ramblers' Association arrived on the scene. Under draft legislation to be presented in the new year by a Labour MP called Paddy Tipping, Ramblers can march in gangs of 20 or 30 on anyone's private land, subject to a few prohibitions, making as much noise and looking as ugly as they please in their terrible multi-coloured apparel. Under the Paddy Tipping rule, the only place where a poet will have any prospect of solitude will be in the lavatory. This may explain some of the disgusting rubbish already being written in the name of poetry.

No doubt these Ramblers think Paddy Tipping is a fine fellow. They will drink his health in condensed milk from tin mugs, banged solemnly together before they pull up their shorts and start rambling anew. But for every Rambler who is made happy by being empowered to stride over someone else's land or along someone's stretch of river there will be at least one small landowner who, with his family, will be dispossessed, at least one country dweller whose favourite spot is invaded by these unpleasant gangs of strangers.

The more that townspeople force their unwelcome presence on the countryside, the more hostility they will encounter. Already the police are finding it hard to recruit spies to inform on their neighbours in the countryside. Informing on neighbours used to be a major country sport, but increasingly the law is seen to be on the side of the enemy: animal activists, urban environmentalists, Ramblers and busybodies of every sort.

"The real requirement by the police is good intelligence, good information on who exactly is committing the crime," says Supt Keith Akerman, a divisional commander in Hampshire. "If people themselves are not interested in helping, we might as well pack up and go home." Quite so.

16 December 1995

Starvation in London

In the glut of information available about every aspect of our national life in every newspaper and magazine, it is sometimes hard to believe we are all living in the same country. Mary Killen, writing in one of the Murdoch newspapers, solemnly proclaims the death of the dinner party. Instead, people nowadays give supper parties, sitting down at 9.45 p.m. to little more than a leg of lamb, a Thai chicken, some jelly and cream.

She explains that they are taking advantage of the great national mood of exhaustion to hide the fact that they can't afford anything better, having lost all their money on Lloyd's. But the exhaustion is genuine, too. In the Nineties, she says, people are too exhausted to meet new people. They are physically and mentally reduced by their days at the office. They can only meet old friends. "New people just drain your energy and we have lost the skill of coping with bores. The dinner party is dead. Enter, *faute de mieux*, the age of the supper party."

Does Mary Killen live on the same planet as the rest of us? Everybody I know in London or the country sits down to a five- or six-course meal every evening. They start at half-past seven and end at 11.30 sharp. Increasingly, these meals are attended by foreigners whom nobody could possibly have met before. I think this may be something to do with the European Union. Where Killen might have a point is that many people nowadays no longer eat a proper luncheon. This may explain their exhaustion in the evening. Is it not time the Government did something about it?

20 December 1995

1996

Holiday Planning

At a time of year when everybody is thinking where to go for their summer holidays, several obvious choices seem determined to rule themselves out. New Zealand, one of the pleasantest spots imaginable, with good food, friendly, comprehensible natives and some of the best wine on earth, seems to be going through a silly phase politically.

There is talk of abolishing knights and dames from the New Zealand social scene. One meets many more of them in Australia and New Zealand than one ever does in Britain, and although we tend to laugh at knights in this country and pinch their bottoms if we get a chance, there can be no question that people in the former colonies enjoy a title.

To withdraw from this benign system suggests a more general retreat from conviviality and humour into pomposity and self-importance. This may not be the best moment to go.

Similarly, the south Malaysian state of Johore, which many of us may have been thinking about, has suddenly announced that any Muslim caught committing adultery or cohabiting will be caned. That is all very well, but if, on holiday, one suddenly fancies the idea of committing adultery, one does not necessarily wish to be caned for it – nor to have to convince some imam or other that one is not a Muslim.

Perhaps the best thing is to stay in Britain and go to the seaside. A new competition among English resorts for the most polluted beach has been won this time by a cove at Silverdale, Lancashire, with 166 items of litter per metre. By comparison a long stretch near Bideford, Devon, has fewer than one item per metre.

One of the problems about filling a beach with refuse is that seabirds and mammals – including dolphins, whales and sea turtles – will come and eat some of the best litter or take it away.

One defence might be to poison the sea first. This would dispose of all the seabirds, dolphins, whales and sea turtles. Then we can lie down and sunbathe in our own little area of rubbish, surrounded by drink cans, sweet bags, crisp packets and plastic cups.

10 January 1996

Dishy Days

Travelling east out of London on Wednesday I could not help noticing how many of the poorest, ugliest and dirtiest homes had been further disfigured by the presence of a satellite dish aerial, often stuck immediately above the front door like some sort of armorial achievement.

It was explained to me that people needed these ugly objects in order to watch sport on television. They were not proudly announcing that their household was uneducated and un-cultured, although they plainly invited others to reach this humiliating conclusion.

Under the circumstances, Robert Atkins's call for a £5 levy on the BBC licence fee to pay for sport might seem humane and sensible. He was speaking at a London conference on the future of television sport. The only contribution from other Labour and Conservative MPs present was to accuse sports administrators of financial greed in selling television rights to the Murdoch-dominated satellite channel BSkyB. They suggested it was somehow unpatriotic not to sell them for less money to the BBC.

But why should sports lovers be forced to watch Murdoch's other rubbish, and disfigure their homes with his horrible emblems? The £5 sports levy on a BBC licence only makes good sense if those like me and my dear wife who detest sport can opt out of paying it, otherwise it becomes a simple case of extortion.

People should be able to devise a television set which does not receive BBC sport. By the same token, on a system of levies, people would be able to exclude all BBC programmes about pop music, politics, the Royal Family, modern art, the north of England, all American thrillers and love stories, and so on according to taste.

At one time we used to watch the Grand National, the Oxford

117

and Cambridge Boat Race and the Wimbledon finals, but one grows out of these things. Television without sport would be a distinct improvement, but if they plan a compulsory levy on the television licence, they would have to build an enormous number of prisons to accommodate all the women who will refuse to pay.

20 January 1996

Leadership Qualities

My experience of watching television is too small for me to pontificate often on the subject, but I was interested to read a review of a new quiz show called *Carnal Knowledge*, described as "possibly the single worst programme in the history of British television".

"It is hard to come up with a comparison to make sense of quite how cretinous, vulgar, amateurish, adolescent and mind-bendingly boring this new quiz show is," wrote Matthew Norman in the *Evening Standard*, explaining that it consists of four unattractive exhibitionists talking dirty, while everybody shrieks with laughter.

I am afraid I believe him. The great question is why anybody makes or shows this dismal rubbish. Have Britons degenerated so far that they now prefer it? My own guess is that they would be equally happy to be shown something much better. These programmes are made and shown because the educated middle-class has lost control, the yobs have taken over.

Some of the blame must attach to the country's leadership. Although nice Mr Major is fast becoming a love-object on this column – his beautiful manners, his kindness, his patience and common sense – he fails the Way of the World leadership test, and fails it dismally. This is determined by whether the candidate would look impressive as a Roman or Greek marble statue in the nude. Major would look absurd. He has no leadership qualities.

Only one figure in public life seems to have the necessary grandeur. When we were both younger and he was Prime Minister, I used to see Edward Heath as a petulant, chippy little fellow. I used to mock him and throw packets of peanuts at him to emphasise his humble origins.

Now, as he approaches his 80th birthday in July, his stature has grown with him, until he has become a giant on the political scene. Everything he says is true, everything he writes is well written and wise. He would make a splendid nude statue in Trafalgar Square or anywhere else. I hope it is not too late to ask him to lead us into a United Europe, into a new spirit of pride in our achievements and confidence in the future, greater fecundity among our women and a higher sperm count among our demoralised males.

19 February 1996

Resist the Hairless Future

The scientist who has discovered a laser beam which offers men the prospect of never having to shave again may suppose he has made a significant contribution to human comfort.

Professor Marc Clement, of the Swansea Institute of Higher Education, accidentally exposed his arm to laser light, and later noticed that the area remained completely bald, the hair never growing back. A laser light, tuned to the correct frequency, will fry the hair follicle in a way that is thought to be permanent.

Shaving is not a particularly enjoyable occupation, although it has become less tiresome since the invention of the electric shaver. Its essential function is to remind the shaver of his gender, of his function in the scheme of things – to cherish and protect his womenfolk. A man who does not shave or grow facial hair will soon degenerate into a whimpering, childish thing, expecting to be coddled and protected by his women. This will add to nobody's happiness in the long run.

The treatment is also said to offer women the promise of silky smooth legs without discomfort. Is this really what they want? Perhaps they do not agree that a lower leg without any touch of prickle is like champagne without its spritz. It all seems to be leading to a general attack on hair. Before long they will announce that hair is insanitary, germ-ridden and dangerous.

The thinning head can be most attractive, I agree. My colleague and friend, Christopher Booker, would not look nearly so distinguished without a certain lofty elevation to his brow, and Gerald Kaufman would be unrecognisable if he suddenly grew hair again.

But as Trollope remarks in *Ralph the Heir* (not *Ralph the Hair*): "There is a baldness that is handsome and noble, and a baldness that is peculiarly mean and despicable." Can we not leave it at that?

26 February 1996

Sheep Opportunities

Many wise old heads were shaken over the news that scientists have managed to produce two identical sheep by cloning. When applied to humans, we are assured, this will surely lead to a fascist dictatorship, rather than produce a new breed of attractive, amiable, intelligent, healthy people.

Before we decide, I feel there are many experiments, not to say practical jokes, which should be tried on these two sheep. At present they look pretty well alike, but would they look the same after they had been in a field for a couple of years? More particularly, would they be the same after they had been put in different fields?

All arguments about the rival influences of heredity and environment will be settled if one of these sheep is sent to live as the pet of a duchess, frisking on the lawns of some stately home during its holidays from Eton, while the other is sent to live in a rundown council estate in Liverpool.

Will the Scouse sheep develop unexpected musical talents, or have motivational problems in school? Will the Etonian develop a charming, self-confident manner and a certain vagueness about whose turn it is to pay for the next round of drinks? I feel we are on the verge of great discoveries. This is no time to turn back.

9 March 1996

Try Almost Anything Once

Many people will have been shocked by the story of Philip Hall the ornithologist who made a long trek to the banks of the River Niger in search of the incredibly rare rufous fishing owl, only to be shown the remains of one which had been eaten by villagers the night before.

I hope he took the opportunity to ask if he could nibble at the remaining leg. Ornithology is a respectable science, and gives many people pleasure, but gastronomy is the more important of the two, affecting, in its way, the whole human race.

If the rufous fishing owl proved exceptionally delicious, it might be worthwhile to mount an expedition to secure a pair and breed them up for the table. Somebody always has to try these things first or we would never know, for instance, that rabbits are good to eat, rats are not.

Being a bird-lover should be no impediment. It may not be completely true that every man eats the thing he loves, but I, who am Founder, President and only known member of the Dog Lovers' Party of Great Britain (and a patron of the Canine Defence League), once ate dog in Manila. My attempts to eat giant panda in China were frustrated, and I caused grave offence once in Adelaide by asking where it was possible to eat koala, but I think one has a duty to try everything.

The answer to our present beef crisis is obviously ostriches.

I ate ostrich several times in South Africa, and liked it, while mentally taking off my hat to the person who tried it first. Another suggestion is that we should eat alligators from Florida. I ate crocodile once in Cuba – it tasted halfway between lobster and pork – but am not sure I would welcome its cousin from Florida. There are times when we have to allow health considerations to come first.

25 March 1996

Unsound Neighbours

The latest idea for treating violent young offenders is to give them vitamin pills. I wonder if it would not be as good an idea to give them large doses of margarine, now once again thought by the "experts" to be better for us than butter.

On Saturday we read about Mrs Kay Potts, a mother of ten, who was finally evicted from her home on a council estate in Wythenshawe, Manchester, after the family had amassed 500 complaints from the neighbours.

Community leaders who organised the protest were presented with bouquets by the council "for standing up against a nuisance which has caused so much misery".

Poor Mrs Potts is now homeless with her ten children, who were accused of burglary, vandalism and threats to kill. They were rudely described in the County Court as "neighbours from hell".

Nobody at any stage offered them extra vitamins or margarine. Mrs Potts may reflect bitterly that her face did not fit, she was considered unsound.

Many people have suffered from this, among them the great Sydney Smith (1771–1845), essayist and wit, appointed Rector of Combe Florey in 1829. He is the subject of an article in the current *Spectator* by Paul Johnson, the distinguished historian and polemicist.

Johnson reveals that he, too, has suffered from being thought unsound. This may explain why he has never been offered a job in the Cabinet, as his talents undoubtedly command. He now lives in Somerset, only a few fields away from the village of Combe Florey, where my family lives. He has never burgled or threatened to kill any of us, nor have any of his children, although it is worrying that he continues to boast of his unsoundness.

"I am all for unsound men, not least because they are nearly always right," he wrote of Sydney Smith. "All my own life I have been dismissed as 'Oh yes, he's a clever fellow, but not sound, you know.'"

Perhaps we should send him some vitamins. That would be a neighbourly gesture, and safer than margarine.

15 April 1996

Whisper Who Dares

No child has ever been so cruelly exploited as Christopher Robin Milne, who died on Saturday at the age of 75. I never met his father, A. A. Milne, creator of the fictional Christopher Robin who has sickened generations of English boys since his first appearance in the Twenties, but I believe him to have been an exceptionally unpleasant man.

A. A. Milne led the pack against P. G. Wodehouse during the war, denouncing that gentle, kindly soul as a traitor after he had been tricked into making some innocent broadcasts on German radio. When Milne died in 1956, he left the copyright on his ghastly oeuvre – *When We Were Very Young, Winnie the Pooh, Now We Are Six* and *The House at Pooh Corner* – to be shared between the Royal Literary Fund, Westminster School and the Garrick Club, with only a quarter going on the death of his widow to the only son, whose life he had ruined.

As a result Christopher Robin Milne, who might have been very rich, lived a life of comparative penury as a bookseller in Dartmouth. I do not know whether it occurred to him to sue the estate. Whatever A. A. Milne may have owed to Westminster School or the Garrick, he would have been nothing but a minor hack on *Punch* if he had not discovered the poor young boy to dress up in frocks and exploit.

A modern six-year-old would probably have dialled 999 and had him arrested for mental abuse as soon as *Now We Are Six* appeared in 1927. For once, I feel that modern youth would have been right. If Christopher Robin Milne had beheaded Winnie the Pooh, garrotted Eeyore and pulled Tigger's tail off, he might have been better prepared for life's vicissitudes.

24 April 1996

Banquo's Ghost

It was not a good idea for Buckingham Palace to publish the guest-list and seating arrangements for the state banquet on Tuesday night to welcome President and Mrs Chirac.

Although there were one or two stars present, the guests were for the most part a dreadfully dull lot. It must be a depressing thought for the younger generation that at the top of the ladder in this country, nothing awaits one but boredom.

My own complaint is more specific. Seeing that I was not on the list of those attending, many of my friends assumed I must be ill. All this week, my telephone has been ringing with their tender inquiries and condolences. Others observed that the Princess of Wales was absent, too, and supposed I was dining tête-à-tête with her. Would that it had been so.

No, the simple truth is that on Tuesday evening I dined quietly in my club, perhaps brooding about an empty chair only a few hundred yards away in the Palace ballroom. It is a sad day when we can't even organise a state banquet without the invitations going astray.

At least they did not make the president eat beef, as a loutish gesture. What people in this country do not realise is that the French are genuinely worried by Stephen Dorrell's hedging on the question of BSE's transferability to humans.

The European ban is entirely the result of Dorrell and his "expert" adviser, Professor John Pattison. It has nothing to do with French hostility to Britain. My own abiding memory of President Chirac's visit (not having been at the dinner) is how well the French tricolour and Union flag looked fluttering side by side in Whitehall.

18 May 1996

Unfair Advantage

Oxford University has been alarmed to discover that women undergraduates' examination results, across all degree classes and in almost all subjects, are poorer than men's. It has launched an official inquiry.

The same phenomenon has been observed at Cambridge. Dr Margaret Spear, who is to conduct the study, said: "Among the theories that have been put forward are that women are less intelligent than men, they cope less well with the stress of final exams, and have lower expectations of themselves and their careers."

My own theory is that the women are distracted by a hopeless yearning for male company, and cannot concentrate. Men have been so terrified by all the feminist and politically correct propaganda from America that they now shut themselves up with their work, and do even better at exams as a result.

Some women have become so desperate that they have taken to playing golf as a way of meeting members of the opposite sex. Even there they are mocked by men who have had sex-change operations to be like women, and who thrash them at the game. Now they have changed the female handicap to favour only those women who were female at birth.

Dr Spear says she is looking for factors which can be changed "so that women have an equal chance of securing a first-class degree". I suppose this will mean some form of positive discrimination. Even there they may be frustrated by male undergraduates who wilfully undergo sex-change operations in order to compete on more favourable terms.

27 May 1996

New World Problem

The new fashion among American churchgoers for taking their communion in hermetically sealed individual plastic containers – one for bread, the other for wine – is apparently prompted by health anxieties. They are nervous of catching diseases from a shared chalice, with the wine, or from the priest's hands, with the bread.

This neurotic terror of disease, which has developed as a major feature of the American culture, does not suggest any great degree of confidence in the promise of an after-life. Instead of awaiting their Saviour's call with joy, they spend most of their time and vast amounts of money fighting against it.

Twenty-five million of these special containers are being distributed to churches each month. The spectacle is bound to raise the question once again (among those still interested in such things) of whether Americans can be said to have immortal souls. If not, they might be seen as disposable, like their own plastic communion cartons, or paper handkerchiefs.

The question is then bound to arise: when an American sneezes, which should be thrown away, the paper handkerchief or the American? To the extent that a sneezing American represents a serious health hazard to his neighbours and to the community at large, the only responsible answer must be: both.

10 June 1996

A Good Idea

Taunton, county town of Somerset, has been made virtually unvisitable by the ruling Liberal Democrats, who are turning the centre of the town into a gigantic shopping precinct with traffic reduced to a single file, permanently blocked.

Bypassing it on Friday afternoon, I found myself stuck in a traffic jam for 20 minutes beside the car of Mr "Paddy" Pantsdown, the world statesman.

My dear wife and I were going to stay with some friends in Gloucestershire; Pantsdown, with a grim-faced female chauffeur, was no doubt headed for his home in the sink of depravity called Yeovil. He spent all 20 minutes rapping orders into a mobile telephone.

It occurred to me that these people who have taken over the old Liberal Party have nothing whatever in common with old-fashioned liberalism. They are bossier, as well as stupider, than any other political party has ever been. Perhaps they are part of our general decline.

This is not a subject we should dwell upon. What we need is some natural catastrophe, such as has happened to the Spanish in Madrid, which has been invaded by millions of large moths from North Africa, soon to be followed by billions of giant caterpillars. Crowds of moths enter homes every night, covering television screens, blacking out street lights and pursuing cars. A challenge of this sort might at least take our minds off Euro '96.

17 June 1996

No, But Seriously

I could spot only one journalist among the 1,041 names on the Queen's Birthday Honours list. An MBE went to Dr Thomas Stuttaford, the medical correspondent of *Oldie* magazine, and it couldn't have gone to a nicer man. A former MP, he believes that smoking even one cigarette cuts off much of the blood supply to the male genital area. If true, this would suggest a solution to the notorious Westminster sleaze factor that is preferable in every way to the alternative suggestions being considered. These involve compulsory castration of all MPs.

Otherwise, it has been a wonderful week for journalists, with the editor of the failing *Independent* writing a letter to the editor of *The Times* complaining about *The Times* having lifted an article from the *Daily Mail* criticising an article in the *Independent* which attacked the *Daily Mail* for considering running an article about the private social arrangements of Miss Polly Toynbee, social affairs correspondent of the failing *Independent*.

Frank Johnson, in his wise and witty account of it all in Saturday's newspaper, suggested it was time for Toynbee to shut up and stop telling us about her close three-year relationship with a man who looks like a squirrel. Speaking for myself, I can't hear enough on the subject. It should be set to music. This is what Andrew Marr, editor of the *Independent*, wrote to *The Times*:

"I was disgusted but unsurprised that the editor of the *Daily Mail* chose to punish her [Toynbee] in this way; but I was genuinely saddened and very surprised that *The Times* has seen fit to follow. Was this really fair play?"

On a more serious note, it occurs to me that if journalists are regularly to feature in sex exposés – no doubt the public is as happy to read about the sex lives of unknown hacks as the sex lives of unknown MPs – proprietors may decide to take action. They do not want their newspapers reduced to the level of the House of Commons by these allegations of sleaze. They should insist that all journalists in their employment smoke cigarettes, as they always used to do in the good old days, when everybody knew his place.

17 June 1996

Unfair Advantage

The British Medical Association is to debate whether doctors should be permitted to have sexual intercourse with their patients. My own feeling is that it would give an unfair advantage to doctors. Not only are they held in an absurd degree of reverence, not to say awe, by their patients, who see them as God-like figures possessing the powers of life and death. But there is another reason.

A doctor can always suggest to a patient that she removes her clothes, and she will nearly always comply readily. That is what I mean by an unfair advantage. Of course, nothing I say applies to attractive young women doctors. They should be free to do what they like. That is what the sexual revolution was all about. That is what we mean when we talk about consenting adults.

But where male non-doctors are concerned, the business of persuading women to undress, or be undressed, is often half the battle. We can always pretend to be doctors, I suppose, and suggest they take their clothes off for medical reasons, but I believe it is a criminal offence to impersonate a doctor in this way.

If the BMA decides to change the rule at its annual meeting in Brighton tomorrow, it must also see to it that the rules are changed that forbid private citizens to pretend they are doctors. Otherwise, health fascism will have gone too far, and Britain will scarcely be distinguishable from Nazi Germany.

26 June 1996

Those Potty Exams

Those of us who have held driving licences for the best part of 40 years could not help smiling to read that future applicants will be expected to sit a written exam on the theory of driving. Those who came out of the first tests this week were smiling broadly, saying they were a doddle.

Perhaps these people do not quite realise what is being done to them. The exams are arranged on the "multiple choice" system, now almost universal in the United States, whereby candidates are asked to choose between one of four answers as the correct solution.

There can be no argument that the solution designated as correct is the correct solution. A book of 600 questions liable to be asked is available at £9.99, with the correct answers supplied.

What the system ensures is that the candidates are brain-washed into accepting the "correct" answers, whether they agree with them or not. If they give an incorrect answer they risk failing the test.

This imposes a degree of conformity that would be un-acceptable to any liberally educated person. It also explains the extraordinary gullibility of our American cousins and the whole sad phenomenon of political correctness. The liberal European would find it repugnant that there should be a "correct" answer to every question. The liberal American mind can see no alternative.

At least the system is now worked by self-conscious liberals. If the question were: the American Negro fails to excel in academic examinations because (a) he is kept back by the weight of inherited racial prejudice, (b) he is intellectually and morally inferior, (c) he has too much sugar in his diet and takes too much dope, or (d) he has no ambition – there can be no doubt that the correct answer would be "a". But it needs only a small shift in the power structure for the correct answer to be "b". What is slightly frightening is that people who now tick "a" would be equally happy to tick "b" if they thought that was the answer expected of them.

6 July 1996

Honouring Benjamin

Some have been tempted to mock the councillors of Aldeburgh who expressed a preference for a birdbath over a statue to commemorate their greatest citizen, the composer Benjamin Britten, who died in 1976.

No doubt they are mindful of Kenneth Rose's dictum that modern dress (especially the modern trouser) is not suitable for commemorative statuary. A frequent solution is to show the person to be commemorated undraped, but this may not be suitable here. The councillors of Aldeburgh could feel they have no curiosity to see Benjamin Britten in the nude, and I understand their point of view.

A commemorative birdbath has possibilities, but so fickle are the masses, and so short is their memory, that it would probably soon be known as the Benjamin Birdbath monument, inviting confusion with Peter Simple's equally famous genius, Julian Birdbath. So far as I know, they are not related.

Various compromises have been suggested. Britten could be shown clad in those wondrous new underpants we have been reading so much about, called Waist Sculpt. I fear that in 20 years' time we may have forgotten about Waist Sculpt, and wonder what on earth he is wearing.

I think a compromise is the answer – a nude statue with its modesty protected by a discreetly positioned birdbath.

That should please everybody.

5 August 1996

Give Him a Chance

Many years ago, in the mid-Fifties, when Lord Beaverbrook wished to persecute my poor father – in those days, novelists were thought worth persecuting – he sent one of his employees, the late Nancy Spain, to harass him in his Gloucestershire home. Spain telephoned to ask for an appointment, and when this was refused, turned up at the front door with a tall, gangling young man whom she introduced to the butler as her friend Rufus Noel-Buxton. One assumed she had bought him on *Daily Express* expenses.

When they were refused admission, an altercation ensued, which brought my father out of his library, red in the face and quivering with rage. Had they not seen the notice in the drive, he demanded, "No admittance on business"?

It was at this point that Noel-Buxton produced a rejoinder that was to echo down the years. "I am not on business," he said. "I am a member of the House of Lords."

And so he was, the son of a Labour minister for agriculture raised to the peerage by Ramsay MacDonald in 1930. The notion that no member of the House of Lords could be refused admittance to anyone's home had a profound effect on social thinking in the 1950s and 1960s.

Now we learn of Rufus's son, the third Lord Noel-Buxton, that after becoming a solicitor, he lives in a Battersea charity flat with a regular income of £47 a week, signing on for income support once a fortnight. He has achieved fame at the age of 55 by almost managing to live on the welfare provisions available for single males – he is separated from his third wife – and the measly expenses allowed by the House of Lords on the few days of the year it is in session.

Of his father, Rufus, the friend of Nancy Spain, who described himself as a writer and painter and once worked on the editorial staff of *Farmers' Weekly*, we learn that he died of alcoholism, destitute, in sheltered housing, in 1980. That, perhaps, was only to be expected.

But the third Lord Noel-Buxton, who has been fighting the good fight through Alcoholics Anonymous, is plainly a most amiable person, part of the rich reserve of well educated, intelligent, well-mannered Britons we all ignore.

I wonder if he would like to be *Literary Review*'s talent scout in the House of Lords. We don't pay much, but not everyone in this country is yet entirely eaten up with Thatcherite greed for money. I suspect there are many well-educated, intelligent, amiable people in that place, feeling rather left out of things.

31 August 1996

Saving the Koala

News that London is emerging as one of the richest places in Britain for wildlife – not just rabbits, hedgehogs and deer, but rare creatures such as water voles, dormice and marsh warblers – must have some social significance. In the old days, these animals were caught and eaten by the poor. Just show a water vole or a marsh warbler to your average old-fashioned Cockney, and he would pop it straight into his mouth.

This may seem cruel, but at least it kept the numbers down. Nowadays we are constantly told that under nice Mr Major the poor are poorer than they have ever been, so I can attribute the present plague of water voles and marsh warblers only to the fad for vegetarianism.

Australia is facing a similar problem with koalas, whose numbers have increased up to ten times in some places, threatening the survival of the very eucalyptus trees whose leaves are the only thing they eat.

One proposal, to cull 2,000 of them in South Australia, created an outcry from animal lovers. Now the State of Victoria proposes to vasectomise as many as possible of the males, but I am doubtful about this. Roger Martin, a research fellow at Monash University in Victoria, points out that vasectomy won't work because "koalas are highly promiscuous animals. You only have to miss one and he will fertilise all the females right through the summer."

Strangely enough, it never seems to have occurred to anyone to eat them. On my first visit to Adelaide about 12 years ago, my hostess asked if there were any Australian delicacy I fancied. I said I would like to try a koala. They all fainted in horror.

Now they know that koalas are an ecologically responsible thing to eat, the Australians should produce them at official receptions for visiting grandees like the Prince of Wales. This might produce an incentive for those of us who really want to know what they taste like to work a little harder and try to get invited.

23 September 1996

Interpretation

Further assaults on our ability to understand anything are launched daily by the advertising industry. Thursday's newspaper featured a poster advertising the new Harvey Nichols store in Leeds. It showed the ugly double photograph of a bald model with a dog's collar attached to a lead round her neck, over the legend "Harvey Nichols Leeds (Not Follows)".

The women's committee of Leeds City Council is protesting on the grounds that the poster is an insult to women, tending to dehumanise them or showing them as passive, degraded victims. My objection, apart from the ugliness, is that I cannot understand the message. Why should that ugly picture and silly legend persuade anybody to shop at Harvey Nichols?

Why, in particular, did the model shave her head? I have often gallantly maintained that women do not really need hair, and we would love them just as much without it. On the other hand, like single motherhood, it might be seen as a condition requiring sympathy and support, rather than as one to encourage as an end in itself. Perhaps it is intended to reassure rather than mock such people as Princess Caroline of Monaco who have the misfortune to lose their hair. I do not know, but I feel it is in questionable taste.

Doreen Lewis, deputy "chair" of the women's committee, said: "Showing women in dog leads gives the message that women are not even human and that they need to be kept under control."

I am not sure. It might also be an attempt to attract dog-lovers. The dog-lovers' vote is something which politicians neglect at their peril, as Jeremy Thorpe discovered in North Devon in 1979, and as Mr Major will discover when he is thrown out at the election for not having abolished our cruel quarantine laws.

Women and dogs can both be delightful, but in entirely different ways. It is foolish to confuse the two. Why can't they just say: "Please shop at Harvey Nichols . It is a very good shop." That, I think, is what they are trying to say.

12 October 1996

All-American Potato Man

George Pataki, the Republican Governor of New York, sets us a puzzle when he insists that the new doctrine on the Irish Potato Famine of 1845–1849 (as an example of British genocide) should be taught in all New York schools.

"The great Irish hunger was not the result of a massive failure of the Irish potato crop but, rather, was the result of a deliberate campaign by the British to deny the Irish people the food they needed to survive."

Never mind that this is rubbish. The famine was a result of potato crop failure and Britain voted an unprecedented £10 million – almost the exact equivalent of £1 billion today – to help the Irish in their plight. Between one and two million used the money for assisted emigration to the United States.

Quite a few of the Irish Americans in New York and Boston are descended from these migrants. I can well understand that they should feel bitter against the British to find themselves in a country of lethal hamburger gases and filthy food when they could be breathing the pure sweet air of Ireland, eating her delicious pigs' trotters and potatoes.

As I say, we can understand the bitterness of Irish Americans, but what of George Pataki? His name suggests Greek descent, and the Greeks have no particular reason to hate us. Perhaps his sensitivity to the potato problem derives from his surname. The Greek word for potato – *patata* – becomes *pataki* as an affectionate diminutive: "my little potato".

It may be this which has driven him to the strange conclusion that potato failure has nothing to do with the presence of so many Irish in New York.

19 October 1996

Such a Very Pleasant Man

Wednesday of this week marked the first meeting of a new secret society, composed for the most part of influential journalists and broadcasters. Called the Penal League for Howard Reform, it will continue to meet, as it met on Wednesday, in the private room of a Soho restaurant, for members to compare notes and make plans for the future.

It is committed to ensuring that no opportunity is lost for making jokes in public about the Home Secretary, Mr Michael Howard. Some will complain that this is not fair, that it will foster feelings of persecution in the Home Secretary which might be dangerous.

Others will argue that Howard is not a fit subject for jokes, as he spends another £3 billion of our money and proceeds towards his ultimate goal of a National Register of Suspected Masturbators, with life sentences for persistent adulterers.

Some seem to feel that Howard is the devil incarnate. Recently, when my godfather Lord Longford was addressing the F. E. Smith Society in the House of Commons, Howard came up and introduced himself, in the pleasant manner he has, despite a long history of violent criticism from the aged Labour statesman. Longford, instead of offering his hand, made an elaborate sign of the Cross.

Despite an unbroken record of deferring to the police, giving them helicopters and submachine guns, more money and more powers every time they ask, his name was jeered and booed by Metropolitan Police officers on Wednesday. But I am sure the best and kindest way to treat the Howard phenomenon is to see him as a joke. That is how we won the war, and built the bridge over the River Kwai. My terror is that he will find out about our secret meetings and somehow infiltrate one of them, possibly jumping out of a huge steak and kidney pie to shake us all by the hand.

2 November 1996

Baldies Unite and Fight

Much has been made of the revelation by Jon Snow that when, at the age of eight, he discovered his mother was bald and wore a wig, he suffered from a sort of post-traumatic stress syndrome which turned him into the horrible person he has become.

The revelation is made in a fascinating new book, *Sons and Mothers*, edited by Victoria and Matthew Glendinning (Virago Press, £16.99). Snow blames his mother for his inability to form close relationships, and reveals that when she had to be put into a home, he was "ruthless in his refusal to make sacrifices for her".

His brothers have complained that this is no way to write about a mother, but nobody has queried the suggestion that parental baldness can have this effect on a sensitive child. Is there no organisation of baldies prepared to put him to rights?

It is one thing to insult your mother in public – Mrs Snow, a bishop's widow, is still alive at 85, although in no position to answer back – but quite another to insult a group of fellow citizens who include many of the hardest-working and most respectable people in the country.

When pretty young Mr Blair comes to power, I hope he will make baldism a punishable offence, along with racism, ageism, heterosexism and all the other -isms which indicate persecution of a harmless minority. Snow obviously has an obsession about hair. He says his only really happy memories of his mother were after he had had his hair washed, and claims that his great pleasure now is to have his daughters run their fingers through his hair.

The sentence of this court is that Jonathan George Snow be taken to a place where hair is cut and have all his hair shaved off, and that he shall not be permitted to let it grow again for so long as he may live.

4 November 1996

The Unanswered Questions

Standards are slipping in West Sussex where the market town of Horsham has decided to honour the poet Shelley, born nearby in 1792. He was the son of the local Tory MP but disgraced his family and the whole neighbourhood by becoming a libertine, a socialist – and worst of all, a poet! Many writers are disagreeable enough, but poets, as anyone who has had dealings with them will know, are an abomination.

For more than 200 years the people of Horsham have hidden their shame. This week they are distributing 2,500 gingerbread men in their primary schools and unveiling a huge monument which involves a fountain and fibreglass sphere in constant motion. What has this to do with Shelley? What have the children of Horsham done to deserve so much gingerbread? Why has the grocer Sainsbury decided to pay for it all?

It would make more sense to explain that the gingerbread is designed to comfort the poor children for the horrible years ahead of them while the monument will serve as a salutary warning not to take their armbands off when swimming.

Shelley, of course, drowned in the sea. That is probably all he has to teach them. But this is not really the time to put up monuments, least of all to a poet who left some perfectly good verse for us to remember him by.

6 November 1996

A Taste of Old Europe

When I was a young man on the Peterborough column of this newspaper about 35 years ago, I conceived a great hatred for the City livery companies. Junior reporters were expected to dress up in dinner jacket (or sometimes white tie and tails) in the late afternoon to watch elderly businessmen in similar fancy dress proposing toasts to each other and acting out a charade of gracious living which had no relevance to anybody's life at that time. It was at one such function, sitting next to a distinguished old judge (long since dead), that I learnt what judges wear under their robes. Whatever Mr Justice Hooper of the Queen's Bench division of the High Court will say on BBC2 next week, they mostly wear crotchless ladies' tights, obtainable only in one or two Soho sex shops. That is why you see so many distinguished old gentlemen queueing outside. Then and there I decided to go to no more City events, as representing the wrong sort of old England. However, on Wednesday, I found myself in Drapers Hall, Throgmorton Street, for a reception organised by the City wine merchants Corney and Barrow to fete Christian and Cherise Moueix, makers of Châteaux Petrus, Trotanoy, Latour de Pomerol and half the best wines from the right bank of the Gironde. The Drapers have an absurdly magnificent hall. Of the 80-odd guests, all the men were in dinner jacket, and many were probably businessmen. We drank '82 Trotanoy and Latour de Pomerol, '79 Petrus. M. Moueix turned out to be witty, clever, well informed, modest and unbelievably amiable, his wife a vision of loveliness. I even met some pleasant lawyers. Elsewhere, no doubt, English and French fishermen were squabbling about fishing rights. In Drapers Hall, we celebrated the liberal, humane, bourgeois European culture which still survives, somehow, in our wretched proletarian society. Even the judges in their crotchless tights are our only protection against Mr Howard. I shall never be rude about these people again.

7 December 1996

All Guns Blazing

It was when William Rushton asked to be excused from *Literary Review*'s monthly captions conference on December 3 that I felt the first twinge of alarm. In anyone else, it would have been inconceivable to expect an appearance between two visits to hospital and a dash north to entertain the masses, but for 10 years he had nearly always attended them.

The normal form was for one of the younger members of staff to hold a picture in front of Willie's face. There followed a stream-of-consciousness session: puns, malentendus, twisted quotations from Shakespeare, obscenities, clever, oblique references to popular songs and famous television advertisements which were completely unknown to me. All this was delivered in his perfect enunciation, the product of a clever, well-focused mind working at full speed. From this burble of sound the perfect caption was born.

I think he must have quite enjoyed these occasions, although it seemed strange for anyone to take so much trouble for a small magazine. He already illustrated the covers, never missing a deadline in 10 years, and always for a pittance. You could call it professionalism, although his attendance was unpaid. In fact, he needed a serious reason to miss one.

Then, just before he went into hospital last Monday, he expressed doubts about whether he would be up to illustrating today's Way of the World and did an extra drawing, which I hope to use next Monday. Otherwise, the shock was complete. It was a rascally way to go – even if, in time, his friends will learn to be grateful that he went down with all guns blazing.

14 December 1996

A Bad Time

The days between a man's death and his funeral are not the moment to celebrate his life, to tell Willie stories and remember the good times. Eventually, as I say, we may be thankful that he decided to leave us at the height of his powers, with a suddenness which took everybody's breath away, but not yet. These days are a time of bitterness and loss, a time for anger, even, as we contemplate the cruelty and horror of death. The one comfort is to discover quite how widespread is the affection in which Willie was held.

The reason he was universally loved was not because he was so funny. In fact, there is often something disconcerting about people who are as funny as that. The real reason everybody loved him was for a basic warmth of character, a total benevolence which no amount of mocking buffoonery could ever disguise.

I have described how he detested *The Times* newspaper, but there was no malice behind his hatreds, only amazement. His jokes and drawings could appear merciless. It is only when you study them at length that you realise how the driving force behind his work is simple enjoyment. He loved the human race, not despite its aesthetic, moral or social failings, but because of them. And the human race loved him back.

14 December 1996

1997

The New Chivalry

Modern society came in for a bit of a bashing last week from Sir Cliff Richard, the Christian thinker, after the death of Dean Marvin, 34-year-old son of Hank Marvin, the legendary guitarist. Dean's body was found in a hostel for the homeless where he had been living for the past five years. Father and son were estranged when Hank decided to become a Jehovah's Witness some 10 years ago, and according to the keeper of the YMCA hostel where Dean lived, "the only thing he was very proud of was the fact that Cliff Richard was his godfather". Richard had not seen his godson since the late Sixties, but issued a statement just the same: "It does not matter who the victim is, it is a sad indictment on society when people die in this way." An even newer knight, Sir Paul McCartney, the multi-millionaire animal lover from Liverpool, reacted angrily when he thought he had been criticised by a BBC programme for preventing the widow of his former road manager, Mal Evans, from selling a scrap of paper on which he had scribbled the words to "With a Little Help from my Friends". Evans was shot by police in Los Angeles 20 years ago. His 60-year-old widow, Lily, hoped to raise money by selling the scrap of paper, now thought to be immensely valuable, but Sir Paul brought an injunction halting the sale. He explained: "They were never Mal's lyrics and therefore any relative of Mal's, such as Mrs Evans, does not have the right of ownership of these lyrics." I suppose he knows what he is talking about, but one can't help wondering whom Mr Major will think of knighting next in order to endear himself to the nation's pop music fans.

13 January 1997

New Hope

Whoever it was who had the brilliant idea of opening another Harrow school in Bangkok may have started something that will save British education and, with it, the whole country, as it begins to fall about our ears. Bangkok, as most readers will know perfectly well, is the capital of Thailand, an enchanting country whose people are highly intelligent, attractive, hard-working, cheerful and witty. But perhaps their most important quality, in this context, is that they have the most beautiful manners of anyone in the world. They smile through every misfortune, and regard any sign of irritation or bad temper as a tremendous loss of face. They are pious in their attitude to their Buddhist religion and deeply respectful towards their king. It is this emphasis on good manners and respect which is missing from young people educated in England. Even before we learnt that A-levels in our private schools have been improperly upgraded in order to give private pupils an advantage, many British parents must have worried about the prospect of educating their children in a country where the rudeness and violence of the pupils cause most good teachers to seek early retirement. The Harrow International School, which opens in Bangkok next year, will teach traditional subjects, such as classics, and lessons will be in English. My own children are all grown up, and my five grand-daughters are too young (as well as being excluded, at present, by their sex) but it seems the best solution for those with children of school age. I hope that all the major public schools follow suit.

13 January 1997

The Three Topics

In my continuing search for material that satisfies the nation's passion for stories about slimming, the Royal Family and journalism, I think I might have found one which contains elements of all three. The Duchess of York, the slimming expert who was last reported to have landed a £1 million-a-year contract with Weight Watchers International to teach us all how to slim, has now accepted a £300,000 contract to conduct six interviews for *Paris Match*, the French magazine. These are not normal rates for a journalist. The money must come from the slimming aspect. I was interested to read in *The Times* that when W. F. Deedes, the distinguished *Daily Telegraph* columnist and former editor flew out to accompany Diana, Princess of Wales through the minefields of Angola, he was sent economy class. When I was a young man on this newspaper's Peterborough column with Deedes 35 years ago, there was an absolute rule that even the most junior reporters went first class, even on a day trip to Brighton and back. Now that he is 83, a former editor, a member of the Privy Council, a former Cabinet minister and a life peer, he is sent economy class. These are bad times for journalists. However, since I can spot no slimmers' angle to this story about a member of the Royal Family and a journalist, I shall not pursue it.

22 January 1997

Dangers Ahead

As the threat of a general election draws near, perhaps it is time we stopped moaning about the gang of uneducated and disagreeable young men who have taken over the Conservative Party. We should concentrate on the horrors in store under Labour. Labour councils will definitely abolish the grammar schools, despite Mr Blair's pledge to let parents vote on the issue. As I never tire of pointing out, we should not look at Blair's pretty little chihuahua face. We should watch the hideous wolf's tail wagging him from behind. Graham Lane, chairman of the Association of Metropolitan Authorities, explains: "Once we have a Labour government, we will begin the procedure." The problem will be what to do with the unemployable school-leavers who emerge from the procedure. My guess is that they will all be taken on the public payroll as counsellors. Then the government will have to raise further vast sums in taxation to pay for them. The resulting despondency will create the need for even more counsellors. This may be one of the happiest and most successful areas of the New Britain. The real worry comes when people such as Glenda Jackson are put in charge of harassing motorists. Jackson, who is already shadow minister for road safety, appears to have accepted all the misleading figures produced by the Associated of Senior Police Officers, to suggest that there was more drink-driving this Christmas than last year. She is completely sold on the idea of giving them unfettered discretion to stop and humiliate drivers for no reason, and reduce the permitted alcohol limit so that they can make more arrests and claim that the problem of drink-driving is getting worse. Police motives in all this are either imponderable or too worrying to contemplate. Labour motives may be something to do with a traditional preference for public over private transport, for rail over road. Jackson is warmly remembered in many quarters from the scene in a film about Tchaikovsky, called *The Music Lovers*, where she is seen on a train, hanging naked from the luggage rack. An interesting and unusual sight, I agree, but scarcely the basis for a national policy on road safety.

22 January 1997

Historic Choice

Nobody will have been surprised to learn from the latest NOP survey that fewer than half of Britain's children aged eight to 16 can place London on a map in Britain. Nearly one in eight was unable to find Britain on a map of Europe. We probably should not be too perturbed by this. Does it really matter whether they know where they are? The only thing which does alarm me slightly is that three out of five do not know what language is spoken in Tokyo. As the Europhobes of the New Tory party make it less and less likely that we can continue as members of the European Union, we are going to become more and more reliant on Japanese investment for the jobs we all prize so much. Last week alone we learnt that Toyota was taking on 600 more workers at Burnaston, near Derby, bringing its workforce there to 3,000. This followed Nissan's announcement of 3,500 new jobs in Sunderland with a £215 million investment. Yet all week we have seen an anti-Japanese undercurrent in the news. British employees of Japanese firms in this country keep suing for racial discrimination and wrongful dismissal. One had been sacked for allegedly inadequate command of written English. A female employee who was awarded £81,000 for wrongful dismissal from her job with a Japanese firm explained that she refused to adopt the "servile" manner of Oriental female colleagues. It is true that they are polite, cheerful and friendly – a terrible thing to expect of British women at work. But if we expect these people to give us jobs, we must adjust to their ways. One newspaper article claimed that a significant proportion of Japanese males – if not most – have their first experience of sexual intercourse with their mothers. Against this, I learn the stupefying fact from my friend Bryan Appleyard that 50 per cent of German funerals are unattended. It is all very worrying. We must simply decide which we prefer.

25 January 1997

The Sixties Remembered

Michael Howard has been forced to drop his plan to prevent prisoners from watching television in their cells – not because his proposal was judged fatuous and sadistic, but because prison officers warned it would cause riots. Personally, I would riot if I were forced to watch television. Perhaps Howard, in his search for ways of making prison more unpleasant, might divide prisoners into those who would suffer most by being denied television and those who would suffer most from being forced to watch it. Then we could all riot together, and a new solidarity would be born. On Friday we switched on our machine to watch an old programme from 1962, *Betjeman Revisited*, hoping to discover whether it was as bad in those days as it is now. The old boy took us to Sherborne in Dorset and Sidmouth in Devon. I thought he might have tried a little harder with his poems in Sidmouth, but the effect was deeply moving. Schoolgirls in baggy uniforms walked in groups, and old men wandered around looking for church bell ropes to pull. That is exactly how I remember the Sixties. Nothing to do with Jean Shrimpton or dancing the twist, just a lot of old people wandering around looking for bell ropes to pull. Where have all the old people gone? Some are packed into trains and sent backwards and forwards between their grown-up children as the cheapest way to keep them out of sight. Others spend all their days watching television. Oh dear.

29 January 1997

A True Giant

It is a sad time when the only item to feed the public's insatiable appetite for news about journalists takes the form of an obituary. Colin Welch, whose death at the distressingly young age of 72 was reported this week, founded the Way of the World column in 1950. Lt-Col M. B. Wharton, who wrote it with him, continues to write his Peter Simple column weekly in this newspaper at the age of 83. When Colin gave up this column in 1964 to become deputy editor, I told him he was making a great mistake to follow the power urge against his vocation as an artist. Executives may seem to exert power, but they don't really. However, I was plainly wrong, because 16 years later he was still deputy editor, before leaving *The Daily Telegraph* to become editor of a magazine called *Chief Executive*. He was a brilliant parliamentary sketch writer, who later practised his art for many years on the *Daily Mail*, a sad loss to this newspaper. His last active years were spent on the *Independent*, where I thought his talent was a little wasted. He told me, at the time, why he was leaving the *Telegraph* after 30 years, but I have forgotten the reason. He was unquestionably one of the few original giants in a profession which prefers to inflate pygmies. I wonder why he left.

1 February 1997

Under the Iron Heel

Having moaned on this page for some time about how we are liable to a fine of £2,000 if we annoy or frighten a particular winged mammal, £5,000 if we kill one, I now learn from the *Western Gazette* that we face a further fine of £5,000 if we publish details of where it lives, or even mention its existence. The newspaper discovered that a building being considered for redevelopment housed a certain species of wildlife. It was told by English Nature that it could not identify either the form of wildlife or the site, under Section 9 of the notorious 1981 Wildlife and Countryside Act. The newspaper checked with its lawyers, who confirmed the situation. The result was an article with the name of the wildlife societies and site replaced with the word "censored" in capitals, thus: "The problem revolves around plans to develop an old building at CENSORED which is home to a colony of CENSORED." The planning office manager for South Somerset District Council described the paper's coverage as "sensationalist". David Villis, species protection officer for English Nature in Taunton, said he had received complaints from local people, who claimed they could identify the site from the details which were published. We await further developments.

8 February 1997

The Wife-Beating Option

Since my note on the elections in Pakistan, where local chieftains decreed that any woman who used her vote should have her home burnt down, I learn about women voters in Egypt. According to Agence France Presse, when 7,121 married Egyptian women aged between 15 and 94 were polled, 69.9 per cent agreed that a husband could legitimately beat his wife for refusing to have sexual intercourse, 69.1 per cent said women who talked back at their husbands deserved a beating, and 27 per cent said a wife who burnt her husband's dinner should be beaten. It occurs to me that in this country, where women have an undisputed vote, there is no opportunity for them to express preferences of this sort, if they happen to hold them. Nowhere within the Blair–Major programme, nor within Pantsdown's statesmanlike prospectus, is there the slightest suggestion of a wife-beating option. In an election when many people have no enthusiasm for either of the main parties, there must be room for another single-issue party, to accompany the disintegrating Referendum Party and the new Pro-Life Party, which plans to contest 70 seats. Perhaps a Pro-Wife Beating Party would steal many of its votes from the anti-abortionists, but politics is a tough game.

10 February 1997

How to Win

It would be a terrible thing if the politicians and their journalistic running-dogs succeeded in driving us all mad with boredom between now and the election. Practically nobody in Britain is interested in politics, as I never tire of pointing out, but those who are interested in it are temperamentally unable to understand how much politics bores everyone else. Some years ago I proposed a nipple tax, whereby newspaper publishers would be required to pay the exchequer 1p for every picture of a nipple they printed. Mr Murdoch was destroying the mystery and allure of femininity, I decided. Perhaps readers would be prepared to pay the extra. I do not know. What is certain is that very few would be prepared to pay for photographs of Mr Major, Mr Blair, Mr Howard and the rest of them if such a tax were imposed. But of course it never will be. Our lawmakers like nothing more than to see pictures of themselves in the newspapers, even if they threaten to destroy the newspaper industry in the process. I feel the nation's editors should agree to have no mention of any of these people until the election has been announced. The latest threat is to identify the floating voters and send them a video of pretty Mr Blair giving his five election pledges. This is madness. If Blair seriously wants our votes, he should send us videos of Mrs Blair doing slimming exercises, preferably in the nude and with a member of the Royal Family.

24 February 1997

Sale of the Century

Reading Robert Hardman's description of the Prince of Wales at the British design exhibition in Bahrain earlier this week – it looks as if he might have succeeded in selling a new MG motor car to the Bahraini Prime Minister, Sheikh Khalifa – I was struck by the most appalling thought. If ever it occurs to the small-minded, mercenary people who run this country that they have an extraordinarily valuable property in the Prince of Wales, they will almost certainly try to sell him. One can imagine the Arabs bidding recklessly for this idealistic young man, his enthusiasm, his probity, his devotion to duty, his quiet, English good looks. A final insult might be to put him in the June sale of the Princess of Wales's cast-offs, when all the big bidders will be present. Conservative England may be appalled at the thought of selling off the heir to the throne, but we must suppose it is better than paying higher taxes. Perhaps it would be a kind thought to throw in his faithful old friend Nicholas Soames for company, as part of a job lot. Soames cannot hope to stay in the Government, after allowing his officials in the Ministry of Defence to deceive him for so long about the consequences of the weedkiller they poured on British soldiers throughout the Gulf war. It is all very well for "Fatty" Soames, as he is affectionately known among the tiny body of Etonians left in government, to say that he has no intention of resigning, that it is all the fault of his officials, but it is one of the sustaining myths of our democracy that ministers are responsible for their departments. Without the pretence of ministerial responsibility there can be no importance attaching to ministers, no pretence of power, no fun. Fatty will have to go, alas, but nobody wants a loose cannon of that size rolling around in the House of Commons. When he is safely in the Gulf with the Prince of Wales, he will be able to make himself useful, by teaching the Arabs how to talk public school English. They appreciate and respect fat men in those parts.

1 March 1997

Frontiers of Science

Readers of this column will not be at all surprised to learn that scientists now believe there is nothing particularly wrong with our sperm counts. The scare originated with some Finnish scientists who were not very good at counting. The explanation for our declining fertility in the West is to be found in the water. For many years now the public water supply has contained a high proportion of oestrogen from contraceptive pills, maliciously urinated into it by female onanists. This has the effect of making men grow breasts and women grow moustaches. In some areas, fluoride is also added to the water by scientists. Its apparent effect is to mottle the teeth of children who still have teeth left to mottle, but when I was in America I learnt from a conservative magazine that this dangerous poison also has the function of destroying that part of the brain which makes it resistant to the false blandishments of Marxist dialectic. Now half a million people in the South of England have been told to boil their water in case it contains a parasite called cryptosporidium. I very much doubt whether cryptosporidium, or any other parasite, could survive in that water for long, but boiling it might have the effect of concentrating the chemicals. Nobody with any sense would drink English tap water. Good Catholic households might permit its use for washing their cars, but they would certainly not use it to water any garden where vegetables were growing. The only debate is whether we should drink white wine or red wine instead. So far as scientists talk any sense on this subject, the consensus seems to be that whereas white wine may be less harmful, red wine is more beneficial. Bad wine is not to be recommended. I wonder if this explains the epidemic of diarrhoea that has closed five primary schools in Barnet.

8 March 1997

Punishment Corner

As fewer children take any exercise, fewer are killed on the roads. In fact road deaths among young children have fallen by 34 per cent. Most people, I hope, would regard this as good news, but the *British Medical Journal* points out that this lack of exercise has produced a degree of obesity which will mean they risk dying in middle age from health problems. I don't suppose the threat will make them change their habits. Elsewhere, we have read of children refusing to eat green vegetables. The new thing is to tell them they will catch cancer if they don't eat their greens, but that doesn't seem to work, either. I do not know whether all this adds to the case for reintroducing corporal punishment in our schools, as recommended by Judge Daniel Rodwell QC at Luton Crown Court, or whether it detracts from it. The judge seemed to think it might discourage young children from harassing their neighbours and setting fire to their house, but I am not sure. No other country in the world feels the need to cane its children. There is a robust school of thought which maintains that young Anglo-Saxon males are unique in requiring to be whipped, just as pekingese require to be brushed, ponies shod, etc., but I don't think it has any effect on their behaviour. When my older son, who is now 33, was five years old, I told him that he should not refer to some white horses as "white". For some reason, they are always called grey. He fixed me with a steady gaze. "If I call a white horse white instead of grey, do I go to prison, or to hell?" he asked. There must be something to be said for the cane as a middle course.

10 March 1997

Message of Hope

Whenever people tell me they fear that Sir James Goldsmith may have secret designs to take over the country in some sort of Benito Mussolini role, I tell them to watch Sir Jocelyn Stevens.

Stevens was appointed by Michael Heseltine as chairman of English Heritage in a aggressively philistine gesture which was also like the abolition of Net Book Agreement, entirely gratuitous. "All I know about English Heritage is that it stinks," he told Heseltine.

Since then, he has taken over what is left of the GLC's Historic Building Division to promote his plan to destroy what is left of London and put up mad, unpleasant buildings like the American Libeskind's sugar-lump extension to the Victoria and Albert. "Well-known architects are piling in," he exclaims excitedly. "No one has any idea what's happening." I wonder if any spin doctor in New Labour has been keeping an eye on this man. "Whatever party wins the election, there will be new ministers, and if I were them I'd appreciate our views," he says.

No doubt he would. I would like to think that under New Labour there will be no money for putting up any new buildings until everything built between 1945 and 1975 has been pulled down, with medlar and quince trees planted in their place, perhaps the occasional cherry. That should be our message of hope and renewal this Easter, as we grimly await the election.

29 March 1997

Disillusioned

There are various explanations why foreign tourists wish to come to Britain in the first place. Few of them seem interested in our beautiful country churches or rural domestic architecture, or in listening to the excellent readings organised by the Royal Society of Literature in Bayswater. According to Sir Jocelyn Stevens, they wish to inspect our hideous modern architecture, but the Tourist Board thinks they wish to admire the creativity and verve of our young people, listen to their amazing Britpop music, and possibly share a glass of their celebrated "alcopops" beverage in a dive. Then they go away again, possibly leaving a foreign disease or two behind. All this seems unlikely. Our architecture is terrible, and although I have never been exposed to a full-blown Britpop, I have now tried alcopops. A neighbour kindly sent me two bottles of teenage Hooch, as it is called. The blackcurrant flavoured alcopop was pretty poor stuff, but the lemon flavoured one was delicious. On the other hand there seems to be little point in coming all the way to Britain to drink them since they can be drunk equally well abroad. Another suggestion the Tourist Board might make is that Britain is a wonderful place for gays. I am not sure why this should be so, but they seem to be making much of the news nowadays. On Thursday we read how a novel describing homosexual acts between two males had won the Romantic Novel of the Year award. On Wednesday, we read of an 11-year-old schoolboy up before a judge at Nottingham Crown Court accused of having raped a 12-year-old schoolboy. The alleged rapist was 10 at the time. The day before that we read that Dr Carey had decided he did not approve of marriage between clergymen of the same sex, but on Sunday we read of a senior Jesuit, the Rev. David Birchill, director of the Loyola Hall Spirituality Centre on Merseyside, who is advertising four-day seaside retreats on the Internet for homosexual or bisexual priests. They will be offered prayer workshops, discussions of sexual orientation and massage. Father Birchill, I should explain, is a trained masseur. So that would seem to be the score: massage but no marriage. It might attract a few foreign visitors, I suppose. We will need new faces to replace the tens of thousands who are heading for South Africa since Tony Blair announced he will vote for a ban on foxhunting. He is not a nice man. At this late stage, I can see he is not even very pretty, although others may disagree.

19 April 1997

A Major Decision

The most distressing result of the election to date has been its effect on the *Observer*, a newspaper I have taken faithfully for many years, ever since it printed a civil review of my first novel in 1960. One cannot complain about its rejoicing over the first Labour victory in nearly 23 years. It is the babyish gloating which I find offensive.

"We are a nation reborn" was the main heading, across an entire page, to introduce 15 pages of election analysis. This was not offered as opinion, but as news, under a most unpleasing photograph of three ugly women – presumably *Observer* readers – grimacing together.

But it is the front page which causes greatest distress. This shows a photograph of Michael Portillo with a price of £1 mysteriously stuck to his jacket under the caption: "Adios Portillo. It was the Obs wot done it! See page two". In fact there is nothing about him on page 2, but on page 25 there is a major article headed "How the Observer sank Portillo". This deliberate cribbing of the *Sun*'s style in "The Paper for the New Era" as it now calls itself is sad enough. The rest of the page is even more shaming. Ninety square inches at the top of it, normally devoted to the main news headlines, are occupied by the two words "Goodbye, xenophobia". By way of explanation, in coloured print underneath, we read: "The Foreign Office says Hello world, remember us?"

Is this news? Is it comment? Or is it just explosion of babyishness, marking the first surrender of a quality newspaper to the moronic or kiddies' culture of national television? The text promises, among other things, that the Foreign Office will show "a new professionalism; an end to the country house tradition of policy making".

The country house tradition of policy making went out nearly 40 years ago, much to the nation's loss. Committees nearly always make the wrong decision. Many excellent ones have been made and continue to be made, in country houses. Among them, in a country house in Somerset this weekend, I have decided to cancel my order for the *Observer*.

7 May 1997

Creating Waves

Those of a suspicious turn of mind may see something sinister in the fact that the Security Service known as MI5 should choose the *Guardian* for the first open recruiting advertisement in its 88-year history. They will wonder what sort of intention lies behind the mysterious slogan: "Use it to create waves and prevent repercussions."

My own objection is not that the advertisement's placing is sinister – MI5 is now chiefly concerned with drugs, child pornography and paedophile rings like everyone else in government – but that it may have been a waste of money.

"We are not discussing why the *Guardian* was chosen," said a Home Office spokesperson, drawing attention to a subsequent advertisement allegedly placed in one of the throw-away sections of Murdoch's *Times*. "The sort of people who might look for jobs in those newspapers are the sort of person we are trying to attract."

Among my friends, I have noticed that those who read the *Guardian* are generally those most afflicted by social and intellectual insecurity. There is nothing wrong with that, of course. Some of them, especially the women, are the most delightful people in the world, and should certainly not be excluded from working for MI5, if that is what they want to do. They also tend to lack curiosity, imagining they know all the answers already.

Perhaps MI5 reckoned that readers of *The Daily Telegraph* are more likely than not to be fully employed: they might have a better chance advertising their seedy jobs in the *Guardian*. My own experience does not support this. A year ago, a friend kindly produced some money and suggested we should advertise *Literary Review* in the *Guardian*. We bought an entire quarter page in the books section, paying the enormous sum of £1,586.25 for it.

The advertisement was irresistible, and had already reaped scores of subscribers from the *Spectator*, *New York Review of Books* and elsewhere. From the *Guardian* it brought in precisely two new subscribers at £22 each. Perhaps MI5 does not really want new recruits at all.

24 May 1997

Rejoice, Rejoice

Lord Rothermere is a genial soul, as well as being immensely rich, and I don't see why, at the age of 71, he should not be allowed to sit down on the Labour benches in the House of Lords if that is where he wants to rest his legs. No doubt the company is preferable on that side of the Chamber. Tory life peers in particular tend, with very few exceptions, to give off a horrible smell. It is a shame he should choose to celebrate his great new love for Tony – we all love him a little bit, if we are honest – with some silly, Old Labour remarks about the hereditary element in the House of Lords. I am not sure Tony would agree with them. "I am a democrat," says Rothermere. "I believe in democracy and the world moves forward . . . nobody has the hereditary right to govern." Of course the world moves forward. He may not have noticed it, but we are no longer governed by the House of Lords. In exercising a mild, restraining influence on an all-powerful House of Commons, the hereditary element is the only truly democratic part of the whole system. No longer exclusively representative of the rich or landed classes, or those with a stake in society, it includes some members who are rich, some poor, some clever and some stupid and provides a genuine cross-section of the country, randomly selected. The House of Commons, by contrast, attracts only those who wish to exert power over their fellow citizens and establish some sort of superiority by bossing everyone else around. They are social and emotional cripples even before they become power maniacs. We must not be seduced from this perception by the fact that some of the new Members have nice faces. An appointed or elected second chamber would be little better than the first. We should rejoice in the House of Lords as it has evolved, and Rothermere, of all people, should rejoice with us.

26 May 1997

174

Anger at Last

There are those who complain that our New Labour Government is showing itself too bland, too suave, too consensual. Real anger emerges for the first time in an interview with Frank Dobson, exciting new Health Secretary, which appears in the current *New Statesman*.

Dobson calls for "horrendous action against alcopops and the people who promote them". At last, someone is talking about the real issues in our society – and talking tough, the way we like to hear it.

For my own part, I tend to share his doubts about whether these sweet fruit drinks are the best way to introduce children to the delights of alcohol. My own introduction, at the age of about six, on my Father's knee, was to teaspoonsful of crème de menthe and minute quantities of wood port. Unfortunately, crème de menthe is appallingly expensive nowadays and good tawny port is hard to find as more and more people concentrate on the greatly inferior "late bottled vintage".

My own children were started at the same age, possibly younger, on inexpensive French wines from the Languedoc, mixed with water. All still enjoy their wine, and none of them has yet turned into an alcoholic. I doubt whether alcopops provide quite such a satisfactory introduction, but I would not take the threat to their future pleasures quite as seriously as Dobson. "The alcopop effort is just to get children hooked on booze," he says. "Anyone who says that it is not so is a liar."

Oh dear. I wonder what "horrendous" punishments he proposes. Something rather odd seems to happen to politicians whenever children are being discussed.

14 June 1997

The Ticket Inspectors

In the new war against "fat cats", a name for anyone who does better than anyone else in life's struggle, the first person to single out Sir Desmond Pitcher as an object of public loathing was Ian McCartney, now Tony's exciting new Minister for Industry. Sir Desmond, who was born on a council estate in Knotty Ash, and has deeply offended New Labour voters by working hard and earning a lot of money, was the victim of a firebomb attack over the weekend by someone denouncing him as a fat cat.

Last year, Mr McCartney said: "Sir Desmond Pitcher has taken over the throne as king of the fat cats. Every time anyone in the country turns on a tap, puts the television on or has a cup of tea, they are paying out resources to feather the nest of a few fat cat directors".

McCartney has at least had the grace to dissociate himself from the firebomb attack on Sir Desmond's home condemning it outright. The *Independent on Sunday* was slightly less generous in its response. Under the heading "Fattest cat has whiskers singed", it commented: "Fat cats do not come much bigger than Sir Desmond Pitcher, victim of an arson attack at his Cheshire home yesterday. Nor do they come more unapologetic about their wealth."

Recording that "he lives in a mansion in Cheshire and has a house in one of the most exclusive parts of Surrey and a yacht in the Mediterranean", it concludes: "Yesterday's attack may shake him but it will not shift him."

The same newspaper carries a long account of a "new United Nations report" claiming that UK poverty is the worst in the West, our rich are the richest, our poor the poorest, this "devastating document" complements an earlier one proving that Britain is "the most unequal country in the Western World".

When our intelligentsia occupies its time with such rubbish as this, the only sane response must be to call in the Belgian ticket inspectors.

18 June 1997

After the Rump . . .

Harrow School should not be dismayed to learn that, for the first time in more than 270 years, there are no Old Harrovians in the House of Commons. The school that produced William Deedes, Winston Churchill and others should be proud to have dissociated itself in good time from whatever the future may hold for this sorry collection of failed primary school teachers, animal welfare experts and hygiene enforcers.

"Blair's rump" is the title that history will probably give the last British Parliament on the old pattern. By then the time will have come to stop smirking and talking about Tony's rump, as if it was something rather sweet and endearing, something to be patted if not actually stroked or fondled. Blair's rump will be seen as the final point in a 50-year period of national degradation when, under the unfamiliar influence of mass advertising, a cowed urban proletariat was allowed to entertain the illusion that it could determine our culture and run our affairs.

On Sunday we read that the BBC had turned down a sequel to Frederic Raphael's classic Seventies drama, *The Glittering Prizes*, because executives decided that modern audiences do not wish to learn about an elite group of Cambridge graduates. As part of a deliberate policy of "dumbing down", they can only be shown dramas about the dimmer elements of the unreconstructed urban working class, talking to each other in regional accents.

We must watch the rump and wait. It may be good news that its New Labour members, for all their odious puritanism in relation to other people's pleasures, have already taken to drink. They have drunk the House of Commons dry. Even the Strangers' Bar, normally well stocked, has run out of lager beer and bitter, and another bar has had to be opened to cope with the scramble.

One shudders to think what will happen to them eventually. If they are lucky, they may end bobbing up and down in the Thames. Perhaps history will judge that their biggest mistake, when they arrived on the scene so full of truculent stale ideas, was to declare war on rural England. In the country, you meet a different kind of Briton to the cowed urban specimen, happy to be told when it can smoke and when it must wash behind its ears.

Whatever happens, I hope that not too much blood is shed, and that nothing is done to harm Charles Barry's magnificent building – something in which future generations of Britons can still take pride.

18 June 1997

Elastic Band

Pray God I shall never become a republican, but I made a principled decision to boycott the Duke of Gloucester's investiture as Knight of the Garter in Windsor on Monday. It is inevitable that every family produces at least one sheep of a somewhat duskier hue than the others, and in the normal course of events one would have nothing but sympathy for any family if a younger member suddenly announced that he was going to become a British architect.

There must be worse disgraces than that, but where her young cousin the Duke of Gloucester is concerned, it seems to me that the Queen may have allowed Lord Melbourne's famous quip – "I like the Garter. There's no damned merit in it" – to go to her head.

Since 1974, Gloucester has been Patron of ASH, the anti-smoking organisation which started as a good cause, aimed at spreading information about the health risks in smoking, and now threatens to take over the whole country.

Like many pressure groups, it is dedicated to preventing other people from enjoying something its members do not themselves enjoy, but it has been much more successful than most. The removal of smoking carriages from trains, the banning of smokers from vast buildings like Birmingham New Street Station – all these may seem to prove no more than the traditional British delight in disobliging customers. In fact they spring from a profound and all-embracing misanthropy. That is the true explanation for nearly everything that happens in this country, especially when it passes as philanthropy or a tender care for children and wild animals. How I yearn, in revenge, to ban television, football and cricket – all on heath and safety grounds, with particular reference to the danger to kiddies. But I will not expect to be given the Garter as a reward if I succeed.

21 June 1997

Incomprehensible

New South Wales has decided to outlaw the serving of raw prawns and lobsters. The measure has been introduced on cruelty grounds – Asian restaurants in Sydney are said to be serving them live – but the punishment of two years in prison still seems excessive, and it will be very sad news for Barry Mackenzie fans in this country if raw prawns disappear from the Australian menu. Mackenzie, I should explain for the benefit of those who don't already know, is a fictional Australian hero who created a cult for Australia in this country, and endeared our Australian cousins to an entire generation of Britons. In Sydney, they take rather a dim view of the man, whose conversation was always peppered with mysterious references to raw prawns. These did not refer, as many seem to think, to the wife's best friend, otherwise known as "Percy" or "donger". They referred to the likely contents of a technicolour yawn. The expression "do not come the raw prawn over me" was effectively a request not to chunder over the speaker. Raw lobsters did not feature so much in the mythology of the time. Although many will remember that Peter Cook had great difficulty extracting a live lobster from the actress, Jayne Mansfield, there was nothing specifically Australian about his quandary on that occasion. But it will be a sad day for Anglo-Australian relations if raw prawns are removed from the language. How will visiting statesmen like Mr Howard discourage us from chundering over them?

28 June 1997

Shandong Candidate

Photographs of young Britons floundering in mud at the Glastonbury Festival in Saturday's newspaper reminded me irresistibly of the Great War, about which I find myself brooding most of the time. Nowadays people seem most interested in the number of people executed for cowardice, many of them deranged by terror and exhaustion. I doubt whether there were many executions for cowardice at Glastonbury, although a number of the participants may have been mentally confused enough to qualify.

The main significance of the First European War was that it marked the end of European civilisation. Everything had been getting better until August 14, 1914. Then it all stopped . . . the saddest thing that ever happened.

Perhaps Michael Eavis, the amiable organiser, was making the same point when he invited Mark Fisher, New Labour's Old Etonian Minister for the "Arts", to wallow in the Somerset mud. Certainly most of Somerset will have felt affronted by the presence of a member of the Government which proposes to end hunting. I don't know. Fisher may be a source of general embarrassment, but he scarcely qualifies as a national disaster.

Even if this year's Glastonbury festival did not represent any major milestone in the decline of British culture since the First World War, the pictures certainly provided a suitable backdrop for today's handover of Hong Kong to China.

Many were puzzled when Margaret Thatcher decided to give Hong Kong Island and Kowloon as a sort of present to the Communists in 1984. The Chinese government has no claim whatever to legitimacy beyond force of arms, but it might have had some nebulous arguable claim to the New Territories on the expiry of an unenfranchised 99-year leasehold. At the time, I attributed her generosity to the fatal compulsion in so many politicians to leave something permanent behind.

Lady Thatcher will be remembered with gratitude for having defeated the unions, and possibly for having driven Argentina out of the Falklands, but of course the unions were coming back already, and it can only be a matter of time before some British statesman has the bright idea of winning a little local immortality by giving the Falklands to Argentina. Lady Thatcher's gift of Hong Kong to China looks like being pretty permanent. Can that have been her motive? The Chinese in fact claim that she was born in China. If you visit Weihai on the Shandong peninsula, about 1,200 miles north of Hong Kong, 400 miles south-east of Beijing, they will show you the house where they say she was born, daughter of an English general. It is something of a shrine among the Chinese.

Her own office sticks to the story that she was born in Grantham, daughter of a Lincolnshire grocer. I don't know. The Weihai story is certainly most interesting.

30 June 1997

Question of Maturity

On Thursday I attended a lunch party to celebrate the 100th edition of *The Oldie*, the monthly magazine designed to celebrate the joys of middle age and keep young people in their place.

The 100th issue, which is now out, carries the usual delightful reminiscences – "In the bath with Evelyn Waugh", "In bed with Ned Sherrin" – and a powerful article by Leo McKinstry arguing that the under-forties must be banned from Parliament: "If William Hague is the answer, what on earth is the question?" it begins – memorably and, I think, unanswerably. Everybody should read it, most particularly the 92 members of the surviving Tory rump in the House of Commons who voted for him.

Perhaps we should all ponder this question in the days before Thursday's great showdown when up to two million people will pour into London from all over the country.

Is our existing democratic system in danger of falling apart? If there is no credible alternative to Tony, where do we turn? Lords Longford and Deedes are old enough, so are Dame Barbara Cartland and Naomi Mitchison, but which is sound on hunting, gummerisation and young people?

5 July 1997

Not the Answer

The British Medical Association's annual meeting in Edinburgh this week, which predictably enough called for tougher laws on alcopops, heard Dr Tim Webb, a GP from North Clwyd, complain: "Now as I wander round the town square I am blinded by the clouds of teenagers' smoke as I trip over their discarded alcopop cans and bottles."

The danger of blinding and tripping up GPs as they wander round the town square is not the end of the peril. Vivienne Nathanson, head of the association's science and ethics division, warned that an epidemic of liver disease was possible within 20 years if teenage drinking trends continued to increase.

For my own part, I find myself a trifle sceptical about this epidemic of liver disease. Many people are rather more disturbed by the prospect of a generation of teenagers – let us not call it the Euan generation – which is ineducable, unemployable and violent, as well as drunk, eventually being in charge of the country.

As Somerset slowly returns to normal after the depradations of the Glastonbury Festival, I was interested to hear the officer in charge of policing it, Chief Insp Mike Greedy, explain: "What is different this year is that we have had organised gangs of youths from Merseyside stealing and ransacking tents."

Nobody will be surprised that gangs of youths from Merseyside came down to steal and ransack the tents. What is much more surprising, and what gives pause for serious thought, is the suggestion that they were organised. In a sense we should be happy that Merseyside youths have learnt to organise themselves. In another sense, it produces feelings of dread for the future. Should they not have been given a little more alcopop before they set off?

Somerset must soon come to terms with the problem of what to do with these visitors from other parts of the country and from abroad. The current issue of *Which?* magazine declares that much of the food served in Britain's main tourist attraction is riddled with bacteria. Only one in seven food outlets passed hygiene tests, and one in five sandwiches was poisonous.

Each of these tourist centres received more than 750,000 visitors a year. It seems rather a drastic solution to poison them all, but the least we can do is to advertise the dangers.

5 July 1997

Important Item

The news that William Hague and his fiancee shared a bedroom at the Mandarin Hotel in Hong Kong – and that the beautiful, efficient Ffion Jenkins has moved into his flat – broke like a thunderclap over Combe Florey.

It is all very well to say that we country bumpkins have no business to know about such things, let alone talk about them. I shall certainly think twice before discussing the matter with anybody else. But once we have been told, it is jolly interesting. Of course it is absolutely normal for young people to behave like this. Mr Hague is to be congratulated on being so normal. We must resist the temptation to see it as a desperate attempt to attract the younger vote, because teenagers have no interest in sex nowadays. Most have sensibly decided that they will wait until they are 36. However I am saddened by the lack of response from the Conservative Party's family values group.

Gillian Shephard, the shadow leader of the House, has made vaguely supportive noises – "I don't see why anybody should mind it" – but why have we not heard from Ann Widdecombe? She has something to say on every other subject, and remains the Tory party's official expert on family values as well as royal marriages, with her memorable observation, delivered in the course of an interview with Petronella Wyatt – "Sex? Yuk!" Has Widdecombe been silenced by this development?

Still, I suppose they are doing their best. None of us need be bothered if teenagers have lost all interest in sex. It just seems rather sad, and a little unfair, to think of William and Ffion working away at it so hard.

9 July 1997

Older or Younger

It cannot be a coincidence that the Government should choose the same day to announce its intention to raise the age at which young people are permitted to buy cigarettes, and reduce the age at which young people may be seduced into a life of homosexuality. Homosexual acts will be legal at 16, instead of 18, while buying cigarettes will be legal only at 18, instead of 16.

I do not share the hatred of male homosexuals which runs so deep in certain elements of English society, and number many among my friends. It may seems a pity that they should decide to turn their backs on the female sex, when women are so delightful, as well as being purpose-built, as it were. But I agree it is none of my business, and can well imagine that some confirmed homosexuals would find 16-year-old boys even more tempting than 18-year-olds.

If that is what members of the Commons want, let them have it. But I am appalled at the suggestion that these 16-year-old boys, being seduced for the first time, will not be allowed a cigarette to help them through an ordeal which may be painful as well as unfamiliar.

A nauseating leader in Monday's *Times* – "Stub it out: changing the law could curb smoking" – seems to accept that public policy is designed ultimately to prohibit smoking. Under these circumstances, the writer found it perfectly reasonable to raise the age for buying cigarettes to 18.

It is true that within the anti-tobacco lobby there are countless zealots working for a total ban, but the function of an alert and responsible press is to keep these bossy fanatics down and protect the people from weak, vain politicians who will always respond to them.

16 July 1997

Images

Was it wrong of us to be more interested in the menu provided for John Major's last supper with his former Cabinet than in the list of people attending it? We know it cost £50 a head at the Berkeley Hotel, but nobody can be seriously interested in what they had to say to each other, and most will have been depressed to be reminded of their names.

In fact, they ate prawn salad and fillet of beef, followed by something called warm pear and apple jalousie. This last dish is unfamiliar to me. The French word jalousie means "jealousy", as any privately educated schoolchild knows, but there is an English and French word, jalousie, describing a particular type of window blind or shutter. This derives from the old French gelosie, meaning a lattice-work screen.

What, exactly, was the former Cabinet eating? Was it wise to choose a little-known foreign-sounding dish that can only infuriate the Euro-sceptics and puzzle everyone else? Perhaps they had no choice; some new Euro-regulation may have insisted that they ate foreign shutters on this occasion. But I don't think it will help any of them to be re-elected. They have a long way to go.

The occasion provides a good opportunity to observe how things have changed. If ever nice Mr Major posed for a photograph, we never had to read about what sort of make-up, how much rouge and how much lipstick he wore to make himself more agreeable to the voters.

Perhaps he wore none, which may explain why he led his party to such a terrible defeat on May 1. Modern voters expect their leaders to make a bit of an effort. Eating warm pears and apple lattice-work was too little and too late.

The new official photograph of William Hague, complete with

playful smile and twinkle in the eye, is terrifying enough, but perhaps younger Britons enjoy being terrified in this way. This would explain the abiding popularity of horror films, but I am afraid the choice of portrait tells us more about Hague's self-image than it tells us about juvenile tastes and preferences. If I were still a Conservative, I would be deeply worried.

The new portrait of Tony Blair by Snowdon is even more worrying. It tells us little enough about Tony Blair, whom we are beginning to know rather well, but it tells us quite a lot about Snowdon. I am in nobody's confidence, and have not even heard any informed gossip on the subject, but I am prepared to bet that Snowdon was overjoyed when New Labour won the election. His portrait shows us what these people are still hoping for.

26 July 1997

World at Their Feet

In the general tumult of medical advice, one can sometimes hear a little old-fashioned common sense. In Sunday's newspaper Dr Hugh Rushton, the eminent authority on hair loss and Fellow of the Institute of Trichologists, revealed that one of the best ways to stop going bald is to drink to excess.

With such a distinguished surname, Dr Rushton might be suspected of playing a practical joke, but he was supported by no less an authority than Dr Malcolm Carruthers, the consultant andrologist who associated the hairiness of heavy drinkers with a lower testosterone level. Pictures were shown of such well-known drinkers as Jeffrey Bernard, Oliver Reed and George Best. All had plenty of hair. Comparing them with my own slightly thinner top, I cannot help wondering exactly how much one must drink to achieve the desired effect.

Further good news on the health front is to be found in a report from Exeter University Schools Health Education Unit. Our teenagers are altogether healthier than they were 10 years ago. They are watching less television, paying more attention to personal hygiene, brushing their teeth more and having fewer fillings. They are also smoking more, although the researchers do not necessarily adduce this as a reason for their better health.

More boys and girls consider themselves regular smokers by the age of 15 than in 1986. I think that the reason for all this optimism and self-assurance is that for the first time in years there is some prospect of employment for them. Police are now recruiting vast numbers of teenagers to inform on their friends and acquaintances – and paying large sums of money for the service.

Now they learn that if they drink enough alcohol they have a good chance of keeping their hair, and they can see that the world is at their feet.

30 July 1997

A Terrible Doubt

People in London seem to be suffering from a memory crisis epidemic. Wherever you go you see them stopping in the street and beating their heads as they try to remember a word or a name. Things have been made much worse by NatWest staff believing they had found the ancient mummified remains of a dead pygmy in a safety deposit box in one of the bank's City branches. The discovery was said to have been made only because flooding from a water main caused the so-called mummy to start decomposing. This resulted in a most unpleasant smell. It is a terrible thought, but we must all look at each other with wild surmise. I am almost sure I have never left anything like an ancient mummified body of a dead pygmy in any bank vault. So is everyone else with whom I raise the matter. Yet we may have forgotten. NatWest say they have now contacted the owner of the box and there isn't a body in the vault. But how can they be sure? Someone else may have left one.

2 August 1997

Bright Future?

It is very good news indeed that John Keegan, who is not only the world's foremost military historian and this newspaper's Defence Editor but also an occasional and very welcome contributor to *Literary Review*, has been chosen to give this year's Reith Lectures. His subject – the future of war – is one that should preoccupy us all. Members of the generation slightly older than mine, who experienced the second German war as adults, tend to look back on it as the happiest period of their lives. Post-war existence has been insipid by comparison. Even so, one must admit that modern war, which involves wholesale destruction and civilian dislocation as well as the killing of soldiers, is probably the worst thing that could happen. It would be nice to think that war has no future. I read somewhere that the British government now employs more counsellors than soldiers. We must all agree that counsellors do a tremendous amount of harm especially among young people, in making them boring, self-obsessed and unemployable. Even so, it seems rather a drastic remedy to put them in uniform and tell them to kill someone. There can be no doubt that young British males need something to harness their aggressive instincts. The precision bombing of weaker, Third World targets from a safe distance, as we saw in the Gulf, will do nothing to improve anyone's character. Perhaps Mr Keegan will show us a way out of this problem. There are those who assume that in order to rediscover our martial virtues we should declare war on Sweden. I am not sure this would be justified. Very few Swedes smoke, even if it is true that most of them are deaf by the age of 16 through playing their Walkmans too loudly. On the other hand, Mr Keegan must say something about the future of war, or his lectures will be tremendously dull. Silence is always agreeable, but people expect more, and he is a very good speaker.

2 August 1997

A Vote-Winner?

As president, chairman and only known member of Vespa, the Venerable Society for the Protection of Adulterers, I find myself deluged with letters as accusations of adultery are thrown around like confetti at a wedding. Anybody in public life nowadays risks being exposed as an adulterer. This strikes me as odd. Adultery, like any form of sexual activity, is essentially a private matter. Nobody knows about it except the two people involved. Nobody has any obligation whatever to confirm or deny or answer any charges, as in a libel action, where the plaintiff is assumed blameless unless the defendant can prove, on the balance of probability, that he isn't. The libel law might have been invented to counter public accusations of adultery, yet it is seldom used. Mere fornication – where neither party is married – is more complicated. We are told that William Hague and Ffion Jenkins share a bedroom in London, that they shared one in Hong Kong and that they propose to share one in Blackpool. This information invites us to assume that they fornicate. But perhaps fornication – unlike adultery – is nowadays quite acceptable to public opinion: a vote-winner, rather than a vote-loser.

9 August 1997

Health in Florida

A week of bliss spent in southern France confirms my view that there is nothing wrong with that magnificent country. I hope Tony Blair drew the same conclusion from his stay in the neighbourhood. Intelligent Frenchmen are proud of their unemployment and the current drop in investment, seeing it as a useful check to the gummerisation of their countryside and the Americanisation of their culture.

Englishmen who are made to feel inferior by the French, or are terrified of France, often cite the mosquitoes to be found there as good reason for avoiding the country. In fact, they are easily held at bay by the simple expedient of smoking cigarettes. For some reason that has never been explained, mosquitoes react to cigarettes in much the same way as American feminist academics react to them.

This point does not seem to have been fully appreciated in Florida, where anti-smoking campaigners have persuaded a guilt-ridden tobacco industry to pay $11.3 billion (more than £7 billion) to the state government towards its treatment of those allegedly suffering from illnesses caused by tobacco.

One might imagine that everyone in Florida was having a big party, except for some terrible news on the health front. Central Florida, where Disney World is situated, is on a mosquito "red alert" after being invaded by swarms of these dangerous insects.

Needless to say, they are not just old mosquitoes that have decided to invade the most sacred shrine of American culture. These ones carry a strain of encephalitis that is particularly deadly to humans, unlike the mild and benign variety that improves the taste of English beef.

The Florida state health department – the same body that has just received more than £7 billion from the tobacco industry –

advises no one to go out of doors at dawn or at dusk, to avoid being bitten by mosquitoes. The symptoms of encephalitis, which attacks and destroys the body's nervous system, as the department helpfully explains, are headaches, a stiff neck, high fever and constant drowsiness. Even a cigarette is of no relief in its later stages.

30 August 1997

Further Medical Notes

My call for British Telecom to be renationalised without compensation to the foolish "investors" gains strength from the news that it is developing a telephone that will enable wives to trace the exact location of their husbands to within 20 feet, thereby revealing whether or not they are engaged in an adulterous assignation.

As President of Vespa, I might react pompously by demanding that further telephones should be developed that would enable husbands and wives alike (straying wives also come under the society's amiable protection) to disguise their location, and put tabloid hacks on the wrong scent.

But the truth of the matter is that it is all too sordid. So long as the telephone system is in the hands of these greedy incompetents, we should try to avoid the instrument as much as possible. There is mounting evidence that excessive use of the telephone can cause CJD, the dreaded Creutzfeldt–Jakob disease which threatens to wipe out the entire human race in the course of the next few years.

This should be our major preoccupation, rather than the present obsession with alcopops. So far as I know, there is no evidence whatever that alcopops cause Creutzfeldt–Jakob disease, yet it is the alcopop that has been banned. Listen to the *Daily Express*:

"We hail a significant victory. But the war will not be won until all alcopops are gone, destined to become a shameful footnote in the history of drink and marketing."

What nonsense. The great thing is to get "kids" off the telephone.

30 August 1997

What is Left

The impact of Diana, Princess of Wales's death on the world stage rumbles on. Now it is more often compared with the impact of President Kennedy's death than with that of Princess Grace of Monaco. Does this make any sense? Perhaps there is a feeling that Britain will never again produce a figure of comparable international standing. Certainly there is no one in the horizon. The Spice Girls lack the necessary gravitas, and even George Harrison, the 54-year-old former Beatle, somehow fails to make the grade as senior world statesman with his solemn guidance to the rest of us: "My advice is to plunge into meditation which gives the keys, making God's signs comprehensible in order to open the door to understanding."

Oh dear. Even less can we suppose that Robin Cook has got what it takes, with his Ethical World Tour of the Far East. Although he is plainly an amiable fellow, and looked quite pretty with his bearded head sticking through a floral necklace in Indonesia, even then he lacked the necessary sublime beauty.

He lectured the Malaysians on the human rights in Kuala Lumpur, declared war on the international drug trade in Jakarta and assured the Filipinos that he would punish any Briton taking advantage of the child prostitution available in Manila. His hosts were too polite to tell him to mind his own business, but I would be surprised if he receives a tremendous number of invitations in the years to come.

His decision to sell no arms to any country which might use them for unethical purpose is admirable enough, but rather hurtful to the governments concerned, and it is hard to think of any very ethical purpose for arms nowadays. If they are used to shoot squirrels, there will be a world outcry.

Worse than any of this, he neglected to call on a dying

Indonesian radical who had been prepared for a visit. Muchtar Pakpahan was waiting to be touched, or whatever it is that radical politicians do to each other on these occasions, but Cook never turned up. This will not do. However, he seems happy to make a fool of himself, and that is probably the best we can hope for in the modern world.

3 September 1997

So Farewell

Jeffrey Bernard, the gifted comic writer, has been dying for some time now. In the 25 years I have known him, he always struck me as a gloomy fellow. That was part of his charm. From the Middlesex Hospital, he has been inviting readers of the *Spectator* to share the experience with him, but it is not a tempting invitation.

A celebrated smoker and drinker, he claims to have been denied the comforts of smoking as he awaits death because the Middlesex has declared itself a "no-smoking" hospital. He says they did not even allow a glass of Guinness to a friend in another ward on the day before he died of cancer. As Simon Jenkins pointed out in *The Times* last week, even condemned murderers were once allowed such consolations.

After my comments in last Saturday's newspaper about the new NHS attitude to painkilling drugs, I was interested to learn that Bernard has been prescribed 50ml of pethidine. When I was in hospital as a gravely wounded soldier in the late Fifties, the usual dose was 100ml, and you did not need to be terminally ill to receive it – just in pain. But when the dying Bernard asked for relief, a nurse refused to give him more than 25ml because "in her judgment" that was enough. No doubt she was acting according to the rules, but what has happened to the NHS? Has it, like the National Trust, been infiltrated and taken over by the wrong people?

I do not know. If Bernard's account does nothing else, it might remind us that we must all die one day. Somebody called Brandon Tartikoff died the week before last in Los Angeles at the age of 48. I never met him, but he achieved wealth and fame as a television tycoon who understood popular tastes in America. At 25 he caught Parkinson's disease and had to attend conferences in a wig with false eyebrows taped on his forehead. He was much respected in his profession.

3 September 1997

A Different England

While the entire country plans to shut down this morning as a sign of respect, members of the Sydney Smith Society have been in urgent debate about the propriety of holding a planned reunion this evening in Combe Florey, Somerset, where Smith was rector after 1829.

The likely attitudes of two people seemed relevant: the Princess, and Smith himself. After some deliberation, we decided that the clergyman and wit who tied pineapples on the trees in his rectory garden to celebrate the Somerset weather would have laughed at us if we cancelled our little celebration, for which people are coming from all over the country. And so, of course, would the Princess. At least one of them might have been appalled by elements of mass hysteria. But the nation's grief strikes me as the most surprising manifestation of our popular mass culture as it has evolved since the war, and one of the most likeable. At last, it seems, we all – or very nearly all – have a genuine emotion in common.

The mass culture is less amiable in nearly all its other manifestations. A few miles down the road from Combe Florey, Butlin's proposes a gigantic refurbishment of its old holiday camp, part of a £139 million programme to bring three of them up to modern requirements.

Noddy and Big Ears will be star attractions, under a £3 million licensing agreement signed with the Enid Blyton organisation. All three of the new holiday centres will feature franchises of high-street burger chains, fish and chip shops and ice-cream manufacturers. The idea is to encourage English holiday makers down to Minehead who have been finding Torremolinos on an Airtours trips was actually cheaper, as well as warmer.

As the new Englishness asserts itself, all our talent and wit seem to have settled in a new sort of television doll called a Teletubby. Or so I have been told. I have not seen one yet, but am patriotically convinced they are excellent. Even so, this morning, we may remember that we once had different reasons to be proud of ourselves as a nation.

6 September 1997

Rest of the News

Through the monomania of this past week, a few items of news have broken through. Surveys continue to be published. To add to our knowledge that we in Britain have the most expensive trains in the world, we now learn that we also have the fattest dogs. Should we rebuke ourselves about this, or regard it as a cause for self-satisfaction and national pride?

From another survey we learn that American university students have more or less abandoned the ancient American practice of dating, the name given to a system of serial monogamy. Instead of forming couples, casual sex after drinking bouts is now the norm. What will Tony and his New Labour friends make of this new fashion when it reaches Britain? Obviously they will not approve of the drinking element, but how will they stop it?

An even odder survey, conducted in Vienna, claims to have established that women, when fertile, are attracted by the smell of ugly men; when they are infertile they prefer the smell of handsome men. The theory is that they intuitively suppose that ugly men will make more faithful husbands, more reliable fathers for their children.

It is hard to know where to go from there. Readers will be happy to learn that the annual general meeting of the Sydney Smith Society, held in Combe Florey Village Hall on Saturday evening, was a resounding success.

Neither Noddy nor Big Ears attended, nor any of the Spice Girls, nor Teletubbies, but a schoolteacher from Yorkshire gave an interesting imitation of Smith in the Church of St Peter and St Paul, Combe Florey, after the meeting.

8 September 1997

Moment of Doubt

Among my friends, as I sometimes boast, I have a lady of modern
views who has a cook or secretary or nanny – I forget which –
who reads the *Guardian*. When I rebuke her for allowing this
sort of thing in her house, where the stupid opinions and bad
advice might influence the children and other servants, she looks
whimsical and says we must move with the times. On Saturday
she found her employee sobbing quietly; presuming the woman
had succumbed to the great national mawkishness, my friend
ignored her. In fact it turned out she had been reading an article
in the *Weekend Guardian* which confirmed what I have been
saying for years, that margarine is not only less healthy than
butter, but actually contains dangerous poisons. *Guardian*
readers, as I say, could have learnt this 20 years ago, if they had
taken the *Telegraph*, but no *Guardian* reader would ever dream
of reading the *Telegraph*, just as I imagine it would need a
weeping woman to persuade a *Telegraph* reader to take a look at
the *Guardian*. What convinced the *Guardian* writer of the truth
about margarine was a book by the Canadian biochemist Udo
Erasmus. Erasmus not only shows that deaths from heart disease
and cancers have increased at a rate parallel to the increased
sale of margarine. He demonstrates that there is a biochemical
connection between the two phenomena. Vested interests in the
food industry have united in recommending margarine for the
profits involved. So now it is official. Margarine is bad for you.
Where will *Guardian* readers go next? How will they be able to
convince themselves of their moral superiority and greater savoir
faire? In these moments of desolation and in the new spirit of
charity I feel we should take pity on them and offer them
chocolate souffle, foie gras and suckling pig to eat.

10 September 1997

Animals Preferred

Yesterday was apparently celebrated in hundreds of churches and cathedrals as World Prayer Day for Animals. At Ripon Cathedral they sang hymns and said prayers for whales, dolphins and porpoises, while recorded whale sounds were played throughout the service. In St Asaph Cathedral the Archbishop of Wales blessed dogs, cats and other pets during the service, larger animals outside.

Thirty years ago, I wrote rather a good novel, *Consider the Lilies*, about an animal-hating Church of England clergyman who feels obliged to conduct this sort of service. Critics at the time complained that it was exaggerated and nearly blasphemous. Now the Rev Andrew Linzey, honorary Professor of Animal Welfare at Birmingham University, explains: "The churches have been morally backward when it comes to animal welfare but there is a mood of change." In the same week, one observes, the London-based National Trust, once a beacon of hope in our Mickey Mouse culture, settled on its new role as an animal rights enforcement agency, at whatever cost to the countryside which was once entrusted to it.

Yesterday was chosen for these folderols because it was wrongly thought to mark the feast of St Francis of Assisi (1181–1226), one of the most remarkable figures of church history who celebrates his feast on October 3. St Francis is often endowed with a passion for animals, although the evidence for this is slight. He once rebuked some swallows at Alviano, and told them to shut up. By Lake Trasimeno, he found himself followed by a rabbit which refused to leave him, but this is the embarrassing sort of thing which might happen to any of us. The story of the tamed wolf at Gubbio is plainly intended to be taken allegorically.

While we concentrate on introducing pet animals to church, the Basilica of St Francis in Assisi, one of the great monuments of European civilisation, has been virtually destroyed by a series of earthquakes. Even those who disdain to take an interest in old buildings and despise history might have been moved by the plight of 30,000 Italians who have been made homeless in addition to the 100 monuments destroyed.

Time and again this week, the terrible news from Italy has been relegated to a few paragraphs on an inside page, while all our attention was focused on such ludicrous non-events as the Labour Party Conference. It will take Mr Hague 10 years to decide whether or not he wishes to lead us into full participation in the European Union. I shall be surprised if our European neighbours still consider us fit to join.

6 October 1997

Say It in Brum

I am sorry and surprised to learn that so few people decided to watch Channel 4's ambitious new series *A Dance to the Music of Time*, based on the series of novels by Anthony Powell.

I would have thought it might have gone down well on television since viewers rather welcome slow-moving stories and character stereotypes they can recognise, even if they are distracted or fall asleep. Moreover, the 12 novels have been reduced to four episodes, which must be a good idea. As novels, of course, they are harder work, although many people I know claim to have enjoyed them.

Sadly, I did not watch the first episode myself, because they eccentrically decided to show it at dinner time. In fact I practically never watch television and am in no position to preach, but if I had the job of producing the series, I think I would have cast it in a Birmingham accent throughout. There are three reasons for this.

In the first place, as a paper to the British Psychological Society conference explained, actors who speak with a Birmingham accent are most likely to be disbelieved. Without some such device, the irony which is an essential part of the author's technique might be lost on a television audience.

In the second place, as I observe, people often find a Birmingham accent funny. This would be a great help in the *Dance* series, the 12 novels of which are usually rationed to one or two good jokes apiece.

Finally, a good regional accent would make the series more acceptable in the homes of ordinary people all over the country who react to the sound of an upper-class or public-school voice with hatred and rage. It would be a pity if the whole £10 million enterprise failed ignominiously, as it seems set to do, as a result of this small mistake.

I cannot believe it is too late to dub the remaining three episodes in Brum. Channel 4 need not fear: I shall make no charge if it adopts my suggestion.

13 October 1997

Was Humphrey Murdered?

In the 1950s, more than a million copies of the comic *Dandy* were sold to British children every week. Now that sales have fallen to 125,000, I would be interested to know how many of its readers are middle-aged.

Few British 13-year-olds are up to reading it, I imagine. Desperate Dan is miles above their heads, as the publishers, D.C. Thomson, acknowledge, "Children aren't interested in cowboys any more. They are more interested in television cartoons and computer games."

In an attempt to keep people reading, the Sun has announced that it will be publishing old runs of Desperate Dan cartoons every day until *Dandy* decides to put him back. It is all great fun, I suppose. But there is a genuine desperation behind it, too. A responsible couple in Hook, Hampshire, have decided to send their 13-year-old son back to Ghana to receive a proper education.

It is sad to learn that children are now turning against pet animals, preferring to play with cyber-pets, another form of electronic toy. I wonder if this explains the disappearance of Humphrey, the Downing Street cat, said to have been sent to live in the country because of a kidney complaint. If people believe that, they will believe anything.

Humphrey was the last inhabitant of that building with any business to be there. Now, I suppose the Blair family can play with their Tamogotchi cyber-pets uninterrupted. I do not like to think what Gordon Brown gets up to when he is alone in his Downing Street palace.

17 November 1997

Hurry, Hurry

As Christmas approaches, I have noticed that more and more readers feel the urge to write to me, often with 40-page descriptions of some on-going legal action. If I read them all, I would have no time to do anything else. Please desist, at any rate until after Christmas, when things may return to normal.

To those correspondents who are still worried about Christmas presents, I must recommend the new, handsomely bound edition of *Way of the World* by Auberon Waugh (Illus: William Rushton) at £15.99 in the bookshops – Waterstone's is giving it a fine display – or for slightly more (£18.49 inc p&p) from Telegraph Books Direct (tel 0870 155 7222).

I have seen two reviews of it so far – in the *Spectator* by Helen Osborne, and in the *Highbury and Islington Express* an affecting tribute by Ion Trewin.

Nearly everybody who has seen the book agrees that it is the best one published this year. But you will have to move fast, and be prepared for a disappointment. Century have only 600 copies left to sell. All the rest have been taken home by literary editors to gloat over in the unbelievable squalor of their north London abodes.

24 November 1997

Isn't it Fun?

One of the few mysteries of the present Government – apart from those attaching to Mr Mandelson, the deeply mysterious Minister for Millennium Domes – concerns Tessa Jowell, the hyperactive minister responsible for making us all eat more salad: why is she described as "Miss Jowell" as if "Jowell" was her maiden name, rather than the surname of her first husband, Roger Jowell?

She could quite properly call herself Miss Tessa Palmer, or Mrs Tessa Mills, after the man who has been her husband since 1979. The preference for Miss Jowell probably has nothing to do with any desire to cover her tracks. It could be a simple confusion over timing, which seems to be one of her problems. Thus she launches her great drive for salads at exactly the moment that scientists are discovering how many poisons are contained in raw salad, how children really need a diet of chocolate and chips.

Only she could choose to announce that 16-year-olds will be forbidden to buy cigarettes at exactly the moment when New Labour is proposing to reduce the age for homosexual acts to 16. Tobacconists will have to say to their 16-year-old customers: "No, I'm sorry, son, I can't sell you any cigarettes, but I can sodomise you, if you like."

We shall all need to carry identity cards explaining what, if anything, we can do. But isn't it fun?

29 November 1997

Nation of Hermits

I was not able to stay until the very end of last week's party for *Literary Review*'s Bad Sex in Fiction award in the Irish Club. But when midnight struck, the band stopped playing and remaining guests were gently ushered out into the cold night air of Eaton Square, they all turned out to be beautiful, un-accompanied, single women: about 30 or 40 of them (or so I have been told).

When I was younger, they would all have found someone to take them home – even if it was a rude young cad who had to be rebuffed at the door. Much has been written about the sad state of single women in Britain – how they are looking for a committed relationship, impatient of casual acquaintances, demanding a perfect companion with whom they can develop their personalities and explore themselves.

I was moved by the evidence of Lauren Booth – Cherie Blair's sister – in Tuesday's newspaper. She went to a two-day California-style singles workshop in west London to discuss her problems as one of the 37 per cent of the adult population in Britain who live alone.

Nearly all of these single people were attractive, she told us. Many came to the conclusion that they are quite happy living alone. They do not want to make the effort of adjusting to another person. Another reason, I suspect, is that there has been a great revulsion from sex, especially among younger women. Men, as a result, have lost their self-confidence. For fear of a snub, or accusations of sexual harassment, they quietly retire to their solitary quarters, trying to look sensitive.

Many have noticed how sex has nearly disappeared from the English novel. Social scientists and literary experts attribute that to the influence of the *Literary Review* prize, intended to discourage oafish and redundant descriptions of the act. It would be a terrible thing if it is also responsible for the nation of hermits we threaten to become.

6 December 1997

In the Courts

A major breakthrough in Jack Straw's war on crime emerged this week. Ernest Masson, a 59-year-old disabled man, was fined £50 in Great Yarmouth, for being drunk in charge of an electric wheelchair. The incident occurred after Mr Masson had been out with friends celebrating the birth of his first great-grandchild, according to Anglia TV.

It seems very young to have a great-grandchild, but that is not the point. He could not be prosecuted under the normal drink-drive laws because he was in a wheelchair, not a motor vehicle, and he was not even on the road, but in a park. So they did him for disorderly conduct.

In other words, he nearly got off. The lessons of this episode are clear. It is quite wrong that police should be able to arrest someone for drink-driving only if the offender is in a motor vehicle or on the road. Drink-driving must be an absolute offence. Police should be able to arrest anyone who is suspected of being over the limit and who is within 20 yards of any wheeled object, even within the so-called privacy of the home.

Police must be given powers to enter any house or dwelling place where they have reason to believe that drinking has occurred, or even where they have no particular reason to believe that drinking has occurred, on a random check. Many armchairs have wheels, and could be used with devastating effect against young children if the police do not get there first.

Perhaps Mr Straw is prepared to take the risk, but when he has a dead child on his hands he will have some explaining to do. The public expects action before it is too late.

13 December 1997

Keep Your Hats On

One of the great stupidities of modern Britain is that even in the vilest weather very few men wear any sort of hat. Hats make an enormous difference to body warmth, as well as protecting the head from the possibly fatal effects of rain, wind and frost. People fear that any choice of headwear will be making some sort of personal or class statement, and choose to freeze instead.

It was puzzling, then, to read that the Prime Minister told the American magazine *Newsweek* that he takes his hat off to "new" Britain. I have never seen Tony in a hat, and I suspect he does not have one.

His explanation was even more puzzling. Britain, he said, was no longer "living in the world of a hundred years ago, when guys wore bowler hats and umbrellas, all marching down Whitehall".

The crassness of this remark can be explained either by deliberate self-parody, or by some softening of the brain. His further explanation would seem to support the second theory. He told *Newsweek* that films such as *The Full Monty* about unemployed Britons trying to make money as male strippers reflected the new mood.

"There's a great sense of confidence and adventure and greater sense of comfort with ourselves," he said. The country was discovering an "exciting" view of its future which was "look, what we're actually good at is being inventive, creative, dynamic and outward-looking".

I yield to no one in my admiration for *The Full Monty*, and perhaps it does reflect the new mood among unemployed Britons in the North of England, but however good they may be at being inventive, creative, dynamic and outward-looking, it does not suggest they have much of a future as male strippers.

In the same way, when Harriet Harman urges that welfare

payments should be axed in order to persuade young people to work, I imagine this means that unemployed young women will be encouraged to find work as prostitutes. The great fear is that they won't be any good at it, either. They will cause nothing but embarrassment and distress.

My advice to Tony is that when he eventually acquires a hat, he should keep it firmly on his head.

24 December 1997

New Year Resolution

In the course of his thoughtful essay on "The lost souls of capitalism", which appeared in Monday's newspaper, Sir Peregrine Worsthorne perceptively remarked that the decline of religion in this country has produced a violent and depraved underclass. How true, I thought – one sees it everywhere. Even as I found myself beginning to clap, he proceeded to suggest that the same influence has produced a new heartlessness and greed among the affluent.

This requires pause for thought. Is the greed of the rich really a new phenomenon? In earlier times, before it became fashionable to introduce religion, it was assumed that the two great incentives to human activity in a free society were the carrot and the stick – greed and need. Welfarism, which might well have been inspired by religious charity as much as by political prudence, removed the stick.

This would seem to leave avarice alone as the great motivational fuel for the political economy, but another one soon emerged. Socialism may have appealed to some as a substitute religion, but for most, I think, its appeal was to the simple emotion of envy.

Envy is another form of greed. Socialism was discredited when people discovered that in making the well-to-do poorer, it did not make anyone any richer. So we are left with the forces of avarice and envy, unharnessed to any particular ideology, as the main political choice available. But even when you can continue to work only for as long as capitalism continues to deliver the goods —the richer you are, the more things to enjoy.

Reading a long article about the lifestyle of Bill Gates, the richest man in the world, earlier this year, I decided that capitalism was a busted flush. Who wants a house where the piped music changes electronically to follow you from room to room? Where every door has its own digital lock? Although he may have a hundred thousand times more money, I live in a finer house than he does, and in prettier countryside, eat better food and drink nearly as good wine as he might be able to afford. I do not have the slightest desire to own a private aeroplane or communicate instantly with people in Brazil, Singapore and Greenland. Bill Gates has an unhappy face and is plainly a very dull man.

Contemplating his photograph, I resolved to work less hard in 1998. If others adopt this resolution, the economy may easily collapse, but under those circumstances we must agree that it deserves to do so.

31 December 1997

1998

Peril of Bedsores

Christina Corrigan, the 13-year-old California who has become a martyr in the anti-fattist cause, died among hamburger and fried chicken wrappers weighing slightly more than 48 stone. Police decided to prosecute her mother, Marlene, for child abuse because Christina was found with bedsores on a dirty sheet, but I defy any mother of a 48-stone daughter to protect her from bedsores or keep her clean if she does not want to be kept clean.

A more sensible course would be for the mother to sue the hamburger manufacturers and chicken friers. It was plainly their duty to put a warning about the danger of bedsores on their wrappers – or better still, to put some ingenious drug into their products which protects their clients from bedsores in the event of gross over-consumption.

Now that California has virtually banned all smoking we must expect an enormous rise in obesity, with its attendant problem of bedsores etc. The main anti-fattist organisations of America are all based in California. I was interested to learn in a long report on the subject that they have been infiltrated and taken over by lesbians.

I have never seen it suggested that hamburgers cause lesbianism or any other form of homosexuality, but it is an interesting idea. Only 35 per cent of adult Americans are reckoned to be clinically obese, but of course the figure will be much higher in California.

Anybody in California who is not grossly obese can usually be reckoned to be suffering from Aids, which is what makes it such an exciting place to visit.

5 January 1998

Everyone is Very Nice

Cardinal Bernard Law, archbishop of Boston, won an instant apology from the *Boston Globe* after complaining that a cartoon in it was a "deep insult" to Irish Americans because the two men in it were depicted as shiftless drunkards. The *Globe*, which is owned by the worst and most boring newspaper in the world, the *New York Times*, said it meant no insult to the Irish people or their many descendants in the greater Boston community.

In Britain, my colleague A. A. Gill is being investigated by the litigation department of the Commission for Racial Equality for describing the Welsh as "loquacious dissemblers, immoral liars, stunted, bigoted, dark, ugly, pugnacious little trolls".

His article, which appeared in a Sunday newspaper, prompted many complaints to the commission's Cardiff office. I do not know whether his criticisms will be upheld. There may be many Welsh who are taciturn, truthful, well formed, open minded, handsome and peaceful, even if no particular individual immediately springs to mind.

But the interesting thing is that Gill, in the same article, also described the people of Newcastle as being "drunk, violent and obsessed with football", those of Liverpool as being "serial adulterers and sexually incontinent". I can think of many criticisms which might be made about the people of Liverpool, but I have never found them exceptionally prone to adultery or sexual incontinence.

It seems unfair that there is no Urban Equality Commission to crack down on this sort of thing. There will be no equity in these matters until we are all taken over by the *New York Times*.

5 January 1998

Question of Taste

I did not wait up until 4 a.m. yesterday to watch the launching of Britain's first homosexual channel, Gay TV, which promised "the very raunchiest in gay entertainment", so I cannot comment on the decision of Chris Smith, Secretary of State for Culture, Media and Sport, to approve of it.

But I cannot help noticing that Mr Smith has applied to ban a heterosexual channel called Eurotic Rendezvous. The Independent Television Corporation is prepared to license a number of "soft porn" satellite channels, available only by subscription, which feature nudity and simulated sex. It maintains that Eurotic Rendezvous, which shows explicit sexual acts, is pornographic and Mr Smith, who has seen them, agrees.

The standard to be applied is whether such programmes "might seriously impair the physical, mental or moral development of minors". I would have thought that endless nude scenes of simulated sex might confuse them and impair their development more than a sight of the real thing, but that is not the main question.

Are they more likely to have their development impaired by explicit heterosexual demonstrations or by "the very raunchiest in gay entertainment"? In an age which has repudiated the old cruelties of queer-bashing, we must decide it is simply a question of taste. Smith, as the minister responsible, is in a position to impose his own preferences. That is his privilege. If we prefer some other solution, we can always arrange to be elected a Member of Parliament, work our way up to being Secretary of State for Culture, Media and Sport, then reverse his decision.

Smith has made no secret of his preferences, and should not be mocked for them. As the official token "gay" in Tony Blair's Cabinet, he must be expected to represent the gay community. If, in addition to that, he succeeds in putting a complete set of Everyman's excellent library of classic works in every state secondary school, he will have done more to save the nation than any other politician alive. When I come to power I will put tasteful nude statues of him everywhere.

7 January 1998

Ill Considered

A don at Cambridge university who tried to make a joke in his *Who's Who* entry has uncovered exactly such a hornet's nest as poor Tony Blair may have released with his ill-considered remarks about the inability of the Japanese to grow beards. George Salmond, professor of molecular microbiology in the university's department of biochemistry, listed among his recreations: "daily avoidance of assorted professional beggars, alcoholics and deranged individuals in the streets of Cambridge".

This little joke has apparently outraged the homeless of Cambridge, who have little to do but read the latest edition of *Who's Who* just out at the amazingly reasonable price of £105. Although Prof Salmond does not actually mention the homeless, they have decided he was getting at them when he listed professional beggars, alcoholics and deranged individuals as people to be avoided.

Ruth Wyner, director of a charity for the Cambridge homeless, says she is absolutely horrified. "This sort of statement from someone who has some standing is very unfortunate. I can't believe *Who's Who* can print things like that. It is really ghastly . . . Homelessness is not funny. It is literally a matter of life and death . . ."

Poor Professor Salmond, who comes from Strathclyde. That will teach him to make jokes in Cambridge. I wonder if his plight explains the mystery of Billy Dunne, whose 100th birthday we all celebrated on Friday.

Dunne has been shut up in a mental hospital for the last 75 years. Nobody remembers why he was put there in the first place – all the doctors concerned are long since dead, and his early medical records have been lost. No family ever claimed him, but for the last 75 years he has been a much-loved figure in the hospital, always cheerful and running around with a happy smile on his face. He smokes 15 cigarettes a day and is as fit as a fiddle, enjoying his 100th birthday immensely.

But still nobody knows why he was shut up all those years ago. The most likely explanation seems to be that after the Great War, where he may have served in France, he went up to Cambridge for his degree. At the university he was considered a brilliant student and also, after his experiences in the army, something of a hero. And then he made a joke . . .

12 January 1998

Youngest Father

As editor of a literary magazine, I spend large parts of my time correcting other people's spelling. Nothing they say about the inability of Oxford undergraduates to spell can surprise me. There are those who proclaim that spelling does not matter, it is elitist, it can all be done with digital spell-checkers. In fact, spell-checkers can only make a wild guess at what you are trying to say, and often get it wrong. Even if the spell-checkers worked perfectly, the question would arise: quis custodiet? Who will check the spell-checkers?

There must obviously be some model of correct spelling, or we will eventually lost all ability to communicate with each other through the written word. Spelling people spell easily, others don't. There is no need for anyone who is good at spelling to feel conceited about it. Those whose job it is to correct other people's spelling are not paid very well for it. Even so, one can't help feeling that correct spelling should be encouraged, and that education might play a part in this.

Our children may be becoming more and more difficult to teach, but I can't help feeling we should try. When I read that Britain's youngest father, 12-year-old Sean Stewart, had been allowed the day off school to attend his baby's birth, I almost despaired. It may have been reasonable to allow the 15-year-old mother a day off to have her baby, although this is her school's third pregnancy in 18 months – but to allow a 12-year-old boy off school to attend his child's birth seems frivolous.

How will our children ever learn the rudiments of spelling if they are always being given time off to have babies? Soon they will be asking for days off to conceive and beget them. I am sorry to sound old-fashioned, but there must be a moment when spelling comes first.

25 January 1998

Sorry Development

In Sydney today, where they are celebrating Australia Day at the height of their glorious summer, they will also be launching the idea of a National Sorry Day, to be observed on May 26. Australians will be asked to sign "Sorry Books" apologising for their treatment of the Aborigines over the years. These will then be handed to the various Aborigine community groups and everyone will feel a lot happier.

It would be sad to have to decide that this magnificent young country is already beginning to go soft at the edges. Sentimentality is an unattractive self-indulgence among individuals. I often feel, with sentimental people, that their sentimentality is the exact measure of their inability to experience genuine feeling. Under popular democracy, whole countries, adopt it as their chief claim to morality and self-respect.

It is most particularly an American disease, and will spread wherever American television is allowed to be shown, American magazines are allowed to be read. One sees it in Tony Blair's nauseating readiness to apologise for the Irish potato famine and anything else he can think of.

The most recent example comes from New York, where Hallmark, the greetings card firm, is to market a "suicide" card to send to those who have recently lost a child, spouse, brother, sister or "loved one" through suicide. These suicide cards will be available in Britain within a few months.

The first card, we are told, will show a sailing boat with a message about someone fleeing from life and the impossibility of understanding their pain. For its combination of sentimentality, commercialism and gross insensitivity, it might epitomise the popular culture of America which threatens to take over the world.

I would like to think that in Britain these suicide cards will sent only as a bad-taste joke to people who are not bereaved but who have annoyed the sender in some way. I would dearly love to think this will be so.

26 January 1998

Exciting, Handsome Man

This week found me in Suffolk, escaping the road pollution of London in a health clinic near Ipswich. Switching on the television to see if it worked, I found Polly Toynbee, the *Guardian* columnist, talking about newspaper prices.

On this occasion, the dreaded Toynbee seemed to be making rather good sense. She pointed out that the American business-man, Rupert Murdoch, was taking advantage of profits from his international tit-and-bum empire, and his television concessions in this country, to produce copies of *The Times* on certain days of the week at very much under the cost price. This was unfair trading, and threatened to close down small rivals like the *Independent* and, eventually the *Guardian*, she said.

The point had been well made in both Houses of Parliament, some of whose members were alarmed at the prospect of a future limited to tits and bums. But since Labour and Conservative leaders remain mesmerised in their sycophancy towards Murdoch, we can obviously hope for no help from that source.

Afterwards, several of my fellow guests at the Shrubland Health Clinic – they are *Telegraph* readers to a man, although one or two of the women read the *Guardian* – asked why there was no *Telegraph* writer to put this newspaper's point of view on television, particularly since Murdoch has told friends that his main purpose is to destroy the *Telegraph*.

I explain this phenomenon with reference to the exciting new arrangement by which all *Telegraph* writers, even those who have been writing for the newspaper over 37 years, are retained on a contract which lasts only 12 months. Personally, I have always found Mr Murdoch rather a pleasant man. He is quite handsome, too.

14 February 1998

Posh Talk

Oddly enough, Shrubland Hall had recently been the subject of a hatchet job in *The Times*. The Health Clinic – a former country seat, converted to its present use in 1931 – stands as a monument to an older England which was more efficient, more comfortable, more honest, better mannered, pleasanter and gentler than the boastful, incompetent television culture which has replaced it.

Such a notion is not acceptable to the all-powerful Rupert Murdoch, of course. Perhaps that is why *The Times* Saturday magazine sent Will Self to trash the place, describing its mild, polite, director as "ineffably fragrant, a wafting old bit of posh spice who was clearly used to being obeyed in matters of 'health' and deferred to by her supposed inferiors". Self, I should explain, is a writer who thinks it helpful to pretend to be working class, although in fact he is as middle class as any of us, being the son of a university professor, the grandson of a thrice-knighted civil servant, Sir Henry Self (1890–1975) and the great-grandson of Sir John Lonsdale Otter (1852–1932) knighted rather mysteriously in 1917 after being Major of Brighton for three years.

What, one wonders, can this exhibitionist bore teach us about the gentle arts of relaxation as taught in the beautiful surroundings of Shrubland Hall? Very little, I fear. Having met a barmaid who said she had stayed there and enjoyed herself very much – "everyone wears a dressing gown so you don't know whether they're posh or not" – Self adds: "I didn't like to point out to her that by the same token it means you don't know who isn't posh – presumably a great source of comfort to the arriviste hypochondriac."

If Mr Murdoch, at the age of 66, really thinks that this is a clever point to make, then it seems to me that we have nothing to fear, and old England can go on as it always has done, without looking to right or left. That is a comforting thought.

14 February 1998

How We Are Different

It seems curious that the Government can be bothered to pass a law against corporal punishment in private schools more than 10 years after it was banned in state schools. Since only toffs are beaten nowadays, it might even have approved.

In fact the proposal has been put into an amendment in the Schools Bill by a Liberal Democrat, but the Government is giving it a free ride. Perhaps it was troubled by the rumour that schools which allow caning do better, academically, than schools which do not. This would raise the spectre of elitism, of which nobody approves.

Dan Foster, its proposer, is right to point out that Britain is the only country in Europe where children are still beaten. In fact there has never been much of a tradition for it outside Britain. I have often wondered whether there might be something about young English males which requires occasional beating, or whether it is our teachers who are somehow different.

It was my proudest boast as a boy to hold the school record for the most beatings in a single term. Anyone can see it did me no good, but neither did it produce a taste for being beaten in later life, as it is said to do. In fact the only people I know with that particular taste were never beaten at school. A recent survey shows British children as the most selfish in Europe – rejecting their families, materialistic and friendless, interested only in being rich. I don't know why this should be so, but doubt if beating them will do the trick.

14 March 1998

At Our Best

If I had to choose any field in which the British were worse than any other, I think I would choose the manufacture of vacuum cleaners, pop-up toasters and almost any other electrical equipment, much of which does not seem to work at all.

Yet Mr Blair has decided to fill his two plastic mushrooms on Horse Guards Parade with exactly this trash and some children's models in the hope of convincing foreigners that modern Britain is "an island of fizzing creativity", as the Department of Trade put it. Why must we all be insulted by such an obvious lie?

On Saturday, I went to the wedding of Jan Fletcher to an old friend, Dr R. M. Posner, former secretary of the Academy Club in Beak Street. It helped that the bride, dressed by Sylvia Bancroft, was a figure of shattering, earth-shaking beauty and the bridegroom, a man some years older, was plainly transported by happiness and hope for the future. Even without that bonus, 120 guests sat down to a magnificent four-course dinner, with excellent and plentiful wines, followed by Scottish dancing at the Irish Club in Eaton Square, chosen because the bride was Scottish and the bridegroom Jewish. Here, I thought, was a glimpse of Britain at its warmest and best.

On Wednesday I went to the memorial service for Woodrow Wyatt – Lord Wyatt of Weeford – in St Margaret's, Westminster, to hear a medley of Gilbert and Sullivan tunes, including the peers' chorus from Iolanthe: "Bow, bow, ye lower middle classes! Bow, bow, ye tradesmen, bow, ye masses" played fortissimo, sing some stirring hymns – "Praise My Soul", "Mine Eyes have seen the Glory" – and listen to Mr Rupert Murdoch read from Matthew xxv, 30: "For unto everyone that hath shall be given, and he shall have abundance: but from him that hath not shall be taken away even that which he hath."

Weddings and memorial services – these are where Britain shows herself at her best, as Tony Blair knows perfectly well. So does his wretched crony, Chris Smith.

4 April 1998

Woodstock-Style

Meanwhile, American scientists claim to have discovered that rats are capable of laughter. I think one is right to be suspicious of anything presented as a discovery by American scientists. There are so many of them. It appears that one called Jaak Panksepp has spent his time at Bowling Green State University, Ohio, tickling rats. He claims it made them laugh.

But Robert Provine, a laughter researcher at the University of Maryland, doubts whether the noise they make can be equated with mirth. I agree with Provine. Some animals enjoy a joke – one of my pekingese has an outstandingly elaborate sense of humour – but the suggest that rats can join in must be made with the intention of discrediting the whole idea of humour.

American culture, by and large, is not well adjusted to the concept of irony, but among American scientists, in particular, there is also a defective sense of the ridiculous. How otherwise could they spend their time tickling rats, and think they were doing something useful?

This humourlessness is something Americans can handle, by keeping everything in its appropriate compartment, with one compartment for humour. Europeans need to be careful before embracing it. Vatican plans for the Millennium, according to the secretary of the Pontifical Council, who is appropriately enough called Archbishop Gioia, include a revival of the "modern concept of pilgrimage" as embodied by Jack Kerouac in his novel *On the Road*.

Kerouac is the most humourless writer in American literature. If Roman Catholic pilgrims start imitating his hero, Dean Moriarty, they will be the laughing stock of Europe. The Pope should keep a more careful eye on what his archbishops are reading. But perhaps Archbishop Gioia was playing a practical joke on us all.

2 May 1998

Royal Occasions

Surprised and delighted as I was to be asked to Wednesday's grand reception for the Arts at Windsor Castle, I could not help feeling there might have been some mistake. It seemed a long way to go for a drink; no doubt the police, in the new spirit of the times, would insist on breathalysing all the guests as they left; and I could not imagine that smoking would be allowed in the State Rooms, magnificently restored at a cost of £37 million after the disastrous fire of 1992.

On reflection, however, it seemed not only rude to refuse, but also conceited, pompous and wet. I had heard that unspoken oaths of secrecy attach to all Royal hospitality, and nobody is allowed to mention anything about it. All that has changed, apparently, in the new cultural revolution, and I was told that acerbic comments in the newspaper were expected. Perhaps to that end, guests were supplied with printed lists not only of the 650 people who were attending, but also of the 320-odd who had refused or neglected to answer the invitation.

No doubt many of the actors and actresses on the list as "also invited" had stage engagements which prevented them attending. Equally, I can well understand that some celebrities might see themselves as too grand to go to a drinks party with the Queen and Prince Philip, if too many other people were invited. But what of Nicholas Serota of the Tate Gallery, and Trevor Nunn, of the National Theatre? Did they have more pressing engagements?

In fact the restoration of the State Rooms at Windsor would have justified twice the journey. Completed before schedule and under budget, they may prove the last public enterprise in which the English can take pride. At present, we whinge and whine about having to spend a couple of hundred thousand pounds to restore the Lord Chancellor's apartment in the Palace of Westminster while the Government plans to put plastic mushrooms in Horse Guards Parade. My happiest discovery at Windsor Castle was that although smoking was obviously not encouraged after the fire (caused by a spotlight), an ashtray was put in each of the state rooms, with three in one of them. Great actors and artists stood around them, puffing like steam engines. This strikes me as the height of consideration and hospitality. God bless the Queen.

2 May 1998

Wise Old Men

Can it really be true that in 1928, only 70 years ago, the Prime Minister of the day, Stanley Baldwin, conspired with the Home Secretary, W. Joynson-Hicks, and the Chancellor of the Exchequer, Winston Churchill (not to mention the Director of Public Prosecutions, whoever he might have been) to suppress a novel?

We had something rather similar the other day when the Prime Minister went out of his way to make a public statement denouncing Gitta Sereny's interesting and informative book on Mary Bell. Anything to do with children has a hysterical effect nowadays, but in 1928 the subject which stirred these anxieties was lesbianism.

At the time when Radclyffe Hall first tried to publish *The Well of Loneliness* in Britain, practically nobody had heard of lesbianism, and many thought it impossible. There was certainly a fear that if women were ever to discover the delights which men had taken for granted all these years, they would never look at the male sex again. As leaders of the nation, Baldwin, Churchill and Joynson-Hicks may have worried about the survival of the British race. As males, they would have had more personal anxieties. Whatever their reasons, they managed to delay publication in Britain for 20 years.

I had been around at the time, I have no doubt I would have joined with E. M. Forster and Virginia Woolf in defending the author's right to publish. If we writers do not stick up for each other, nobody else is going to stick up for us. Seventy years on, I begin to have a terrible feeling that Baldwin, Churchill and Joynson-Hicks may have been right.

Lesbianism may not have yet achieved the stranglehold on this country which we see in the United States, but its younger sister, feminism, has much the same effect on relations between the sexes in the long run. Nobody can ignore the epidemic of male impotence which this has brought about. American women (perhaps rightly) despise their menfolk, and men cannot perform under those circumstances, even if the women let them. The age of Viagra is a pathetic illusion. Viagra is not an aphrodisiac, merely a cure for impotence. The men's problem is psychological, not physical, and Viagra affects only the physical aspect. At least we are 20 years behind the Americans in the matter of impotence, thanks to those wise old statesmen in 1928.

13 May 1998

Australian Puzzles

By the time you read this I should be more than half way to Australia. All my previous visits to that beautiful and unusual country have been connected with wine, but a second, hidden agenda has been the hope that I might get a chance to eat a koala. I have eaten most of the indigenous fauna in most countries I have visited, but Australians always throw up their arms in horror at the thought of eating their sacred koalas. Now I learn that many English zoos and game parks sell off their redundant specimens for the exotic meat market. We may soon be eating it in Somerset. Next time I visit, perhaps I shall bring some jointed koala to give my Australian friends, but that will not be quite the same thing. It would be interesting to see how a diet of eucalyptus affects the taste.

British visitors are warned not to allow themselves to be drawn into conversation about the republican movement, where passions run high. To many Australians the movement represents little more than a desire to dissociate themselves from modern Britain, with its pop music and creative cushions designed by Sir Terence Conran. To everyone else it seems hopelessly adolescent to want to have an Australian president at this late stage. The present system works very well; if they must change it, they should elect a koala as representing kiddies, etc.

Australian athletes who wish to remove the Union Jack from their national flag, leaving only the Southern Cross, are being babyish as well as rude, it seems to me. The Southern Cross is a collection of stars which look exactly like the ones you see in comics when a character has been hit on the head, or is drunk. Is this the image they want? Now I must learn to shut up on these matters.

13 May 1998

International Understanding

When I mentioned the distressing level of anti-Americanism I found in New South Wales earlier this week, space prevented me from describing the valiant efforts being made to overcome these unworthy emotions.

With their passion for history, they have founded a society dedicated to the study of less celebrated US Presidents. Called the Chester A. Arthur Society, after possibly the dimmest of them all, it attracts politicians, lawyers, journalists and academics who meet under chairmanship of the State premier, Bob Carr, to read each other papers and propose toasts.

Arthur became the 21st President in 1881 when President James A. Garfield, whom he was serving as compromise vice-president, was assassinated. Arthur, a Republican, made his fortune as a customs collector for the port of New York, and did practically nothing during his four years in the White House.

Mr Carr, who is an extremely active Labour premier of New South Wales, feels that the best way we can understand the Americans is to study their dimmest chief executives. I have been changed with founding an English branch of the Chester A. Arthur Society. Does anyone know the tune of "Hail to the Chief"?

30 May 1998

A Small Recompense

"Heat kills 713 in India," announced a melancholy little headline in Monday's newspaper. One cannot help wondering who counted the victims of the heatwave in that country, who collated the figures, added them together and presented them for the rest of us to ponder. Above all, we are bound to ask ourselves what we can do to help.

Then, in the same newspaper, we read that W. F. Deedes was celebrating his 85th birthday that day, and the answer became clear: send Deedes. No Third World disaster can be said to have taken place until he has told us about it.

We learn that this beautiful and blameless man joined the old *Morning Post* in 1931. When I first joined *The Daily Telegraph* 38 years ago, he had already become deputy head of the Peterborough column, a dignified post for a man who was also an MP, a decorated war veteran, a former junior minister.

I was the most junior reporter on the staff of Peterborough, but those were wonderful days to be a junior reporter. Before the newspaper industry decided to spend vast sums of money on cost analysts, executive consultants, administrative overseers and other efficiency experts, every journalist, however junior, travelled everywhere by taxi and first-class train or air ticket. Nowadays, of course, they are lucky to get a free bus ticket to go and report on the Ideal Home Exhibition at Olympia.

Even so, I was rather shocked to learn that my old friend Bill Deedes, on one of his fearless trips to some Third World danger point or other, was being required to travel economy class. As a former editor of *The Daily Telegraph* and cabinet minister, a Privy Counsellor of more than 35 years' standing and a newly appointed Peer of the Realm, might he not perhaps qualify for club class? One does not wish to interfere with the efficient running of the business side, but now Lord Deedes is 85 some readers may feel we should have a Way of the World appeal to upgrade his tickets wherever he goes. Perhaps he prefers to travel rough. I shall do nothing until I hear a word of encouragement from him.

3 June 1998

Protection Money

For what I fear may be the 28th year running, I have neglected to attend the Glastonbury Festival, although it takes place only about 25 miles from my front door, and is said to be very much enjoyed by young and old alike.

A hatred of pop music may have kept me away in the past, but now I am almost deaf, I might not hear it. The acute discomfort of sleeping under canvas in a mud bath could be avoided by coming home. The *Guardian* advertises the pleasures of Glastonbury by saying, "Here crusties and sallow youth get within dancing distance of one another."

I suppose it might be fun to dance with a crustie. The organiser, a local farmer called Michael Eavis who, at 62, has 17 grandchildren, is a totally amiable man and a credit to Somerset.

What prevents me from rejoicing with all these excited people from Birmingham and London, is the thought of the police overtime involved. You can't hold any event of this sort without police permission which is dependent on hiring an enormous number of policemen at overtime rates.

I have forgotten what each policeman receives by the hour, but this year the police are receiving £500,000 protection money from the festival. It is too much.

1 July 1998

The Guidance We Need

The Pope did not send me a copy of his apostolic letter *Motu Proprio Ad Tuendam Fidem*, so I have not read it and cannot really comment on it, although I think I may be coming round to his view on women priests. I do not take it amiss that he neglected to send me a copy. He is a very busy man, and must have many people on his list. Or perhaps he was ashamed of his rather babyish Latin.

Now we learn he has written a second pastoral letter, *Dies Domini*, due to arrive tomorrow. This will simply urge us all to go to church on Sundays, as popes, bishops, priests and deacons have always done. They would, wouldn't they?

Perhaps he does not expect replies to these pastoral letters, but if he has sent me one, I shall answer that it would be much easier to go to church on Sunday if he, as Pope, had put a stop to the ghastly Mickey Mouse liturgy instituted by his two predecessors.

It is one thing to argue that modern congregations do not understand Latin. In fact, they never did. They always took it on trust, for the most part, that the priest was saying the right thing, whatever that may have been. It is quite another to expect congregations to watch grimacing celebrants and listen to feeble, patronising jokes designed for five-year-olds of moderate intelligence. This is as bad as watching television.

Television, as we all know, not only increases your blood pressure, makes you blind and gives you cancer. It is also destructive of morals. If the Pope really wishes to offer guidance to the modern world, he should forbid Catholics from owning or watching a television set. I will happily compose an encyclical for him to that effect.

6 July 1998

A Bastard Nation

"Why bastard? wherefore base?
When my dimensions are as well compact,
My mind as generous, and my shape as true,
As honest madam's issue?"

Edmund, the bastard son of Gloucester, who asks this question in the second scene of *King Lear* is, of course, a scheming villain, one of the worst in the Shakespeare canon. It is not fashionable nowadays to treat children who have the misfortune to be born illegitimate any differently from other children, but social workers often express concern at the high proportion of offenders in this category.

The latest news is that throughout large parts of this country, illegitimacy is the norm, legitimate children in the minority. Figures just released by the Office for National Statistics show that in addition to places such as Liverpool, Manchester and Knowsley, which have always had a high illegitimacy rate (in Liverpool it is 57 per cent, in Knowsley nearly 60 per cent), the bastard majority now extends to Nottingham, Middlesbrough, even the former Welsh mining communities of Blaenau Gwent and Merthyr Tydfil.

The Government, we are told, is planning a national campaign to discourage teenage pregnancies. No doubt Tony Blair hopes to appoint a Teenage Pregnancy Tsar. While he is about it, he might appoint a super-tsar to supervise the whole business and encourage married couples to have babies.

Not that it will make any difference, of course. We who are not tsars, let alone super-tsars, may be at a loss for what to do. Can we help in any way? The unworthy thought occurs to me that the only sensible response for the private citizen might be to avoid those areas – Liverpool, Knowsley, Merthyr Tydfil – where bastards are in a majority.

8 July 1998

246

Two Wise Men

I would not have believed that Lord Rees-Mogg was due to celebrate his 70th birthday yesterday, if he had not assured us all to this effect. I am amazed he is so young. When he was my editor on *The Times* nearly 30 years ago, I always assumed he was at least 70, and treated him with appropriate respect.

It is true there was always a playfulness, a gaiety in his approach to the world, which is sometimes associated with the young. He uses the occasion of his 70th birthday for a paean to old age. Not only are the old wiser, cleaner, and more competent than the young, he points out, they are also richer and more numerous, at any rate in Europe. We should never forget that at the last election, half the voters in the United Kingdom were aged 55 or over. What Lord Rees-Mogg calls the grey army of oldies is growing by the year.

The only thing the young have to recommend them to advertisers and politicians is their comparative stupidity. When people realise this, we may see an end to the moronic teenage culture of television and advertisements. The grey army will have come into its own.

I have been pointing it out for many years, and am delighted to have my theories confirmed by such a distinguished colleague. Now we can go forward and solve the rest of the world's problems. When I suggested an all-woman priesthood as the best solution to excessive damages being awarded to molested choirboys in America, I did not mention the alternative possibility of all-girl cathedral choirs. This solution is opposed by various organists, and strongly criticised in a report of the Friends of Cathedral Music. Many, of course, are opposed to the idea of women priests. I do not know. What does Lord Rees-Mogg think?

15 July 1998

Hate Lists

Jolyon Connell, founder and editor of *The Week,* which summarises everything worth reading in the press, approached me at a party on Wednesday and asked for my list of 100 top novels of this century.

I groaned. Have people not read enough of these bogus lists? In any case, we now learn that reading is out of fashion. Although only three schools refused point blank to accept a free gift of all the classics, handsomely bound by Everyman and worth £2,500, many if not most of them were resentful of the offer and grudging in their acceptance. They did not want children to be bothered with books.

Against this we have hundreds of adults solemnly assuring us that the best book written this century is James Joyce's *Ulysses,* a book which is so incomprehensible as to be effectively meaningless. I told Connell he should ask people for a list of books to be avoided.

Here is mine: first and second, *Ulysses* and *Finnegans Wake* by James Joyce. If people must try Joyce, they should read *Portrait of the Artist* when they are 16, then throw it away. Next, children should be discouraged from reading J. R. R. Tolkien's *Lord of the Rings* and *The Hobbit.* This is because the whimsy prepares its readers for nothing beyond the grosser stupidities of Disney and advertising cartoons. Finally, I would put an absolute ban on A. A. Milne's disgusting *Winnie the Pooh.*

Children tempted by Tolkien should be encouraged towards *Alice in Wonderland* and *Through the Looking Glass.* Those hankering after *Winnie the Pooh* should be redirected towards Beatrix Potter. If Connell would like to extract these reflections for his brilliant magazine, he is free to do so.

25 July 1998

The Best Advice

Full support has been given to the British Airways pilot who locked up 148 passengers and crew on the Milan runway for 40 minutes because he suspected someone had been smoking in the plane's lavatory and nobody would own up to it. He was working at the time for a low-budget section of British Airways called Go, whose spokesman said: "We are 100 per cent behind him. There is a serious no-smoking policy on all our flights."

Eventually the pilot, Captain Brian Bliss, had to be removed from the plane by Italian police before the passengers could be released. Perhaps experience teaches BA that this is an acceptable way to treat low-budget passengers – possibly the best way – but even as a high-budget BA passenger I have noticed a patronising attitude among cabin staff which inclined me to avoid the airline long before it launched its "serious no-smoking policy".

I suspect that Captain Bliss is not a *Daily Telegraph* reader. Perhaps he was worried by the ludicrous American claim that smoking "shrinks the manhood". If he had read his Way of the World, he would know that this regrettable effect is achieved by excessive reliance on salad in the diet, not by smoking.

At least there are signs that this column's medical advice is reaching the Professional Association of Teachers, at whose annual conference grave concern was expressed at the number of pupils carrying mobile phones and using them in class. A delegate drew attention to the health risks in terms of memory loss, confusion, cancer and brain tumours. Mobile phones were not available when I was a schoolboy, and I feel sure if they had been, the master or teacher in charge would simply have told us to stop using them. This would have spared him having to bring the matter up at the next annual conference of the teachers' union on medical grounds. But the medical advice was sound. I hope everybody read Dr James Le Fanu's brilliant column in Tuesday's newspaper, where, in the process of complaining about bad medical advice and reckless prescribing, he described the case of a patient in Cheshire called Thomas Patten, who suffered pain in the muscle of his legs after being persuaded to switch from butter to margarine. On reading in Way of the World that margarine is a poison, he promptly switched back to butter: "Within days, the pain had ceased, and I have had no further suffering of that particular kind. I can only conclude that the pains were caused by margarine."

1 August 1998

Good News at Last

So much for the bad news. The good news is that the nation's career women – defined by the BBC programme *Watchdog* as professional single women in their mid-twenties to early thirties – are drinking too much. Three million of them drink as much as two glasses of a wine a day, we are told.

According to Sarah Jarvis of Alcohol Concern, this is too much. It jeopardises their fertility in later life. Half a million women, or nearly one in 50, drink five glasses of wine a day. I have the feeling that this information is supposed to shock us.

It is kind of Dr Jarvis and her friends to worry, and I am sure that their motives are the purest and best, but, for myself, I rejoice to think that the career woman in her office can enjoy life as much as any ordinary woman. Babies can be a great comfort, of course, but by no means all of them are. As Kipling might have said, a baby is only a baby, but a bottle of wine is a drink.

12 August 1998

Keeping Our Cool

Many years ago I decided to join the Dennis the Menace Fan Club, in honour of the *Beano* character who had given me such pleasure in my youth, and who seemed to represent some sort of national reply to Mickey Mouse, Minnie Mouse and Donald Duck. There are said to be more than a million paid-up members of the Dennis Fan Club, which must indicate some residual surviving pride in our national achievement.

Now I learn that Tony Blair has accepted honorary membership, and they are going to introduce a sister for Dennis in order to please women readers. I think I will resign. The appeal of Dennis the Menace is essentially masculine. His sister (as yet unnamed) can only cause confusion. And I do not think it proper that a Prime Minister nominally in charge of the country's collapsing education system, should interest himself in a weekly comic paper which well brought-up children are normally discouraged from reading at the age of eight.

We hear much that is truly terrifying from the universities – how they "mark up" hopeless students in order to improve their image etc. But the primary schools are the worst. The daughter of a friend, who achieved three "Es" and one "U" in her A levels, was quite properly refused a place in any university. Then she was accepted for teacher training at primary level. By contrast, another friend of my children, with an impressive string of degrees, was refused a place in any teacher college on grounds, apparently, of discouraging elitism. There is a conspiracy afoot to make Britain as ignorant and dumb as possible. Perhaps this is what Mr Blair means when he talks of "cool".

19 September 1998

A Great Thinker

There is something distinctly comforting in the way Alan Clark, the 70-year-old show-off and bore, is beginning to emerge as an elder statesman and Grand Old Man of British politics. Cynics will suggest this is an apt comment on the present state of British politics, but I prefer to think it is a sign of Britain's enduring affection and respect for the public school system. Anybody who went to public school will have recognised Clark as the sort of Old Boy who returns to his old school in some veteran or vintage car to impress the smaller boys. Many will have been touched to discover him playing the same tricks more than 50 years on. But now he is 70, he wishes to be seen as a serious historian, and plans to publish a history of the Conservative Party to replace the standard work by Lord Blake and to challenge the authoritative new study by Professor John Ramsden, *The Appetite for Power: A History of the Conservative Party*, to be published by HarperCollins next month.

Clark has even persuaded one of our more frivolous and susceptible daily newspapers to serialise his book. The same newspaper printed a two-page interview conducted by one of its most gifted writers who was so impressed by Clark's claims to be an elder statesman that she even asked him about his sex life. Needless to say, he had nothing to tell her. The new, serious Clark had more important things to talk about: "The extent to which I'm going to be remembered by posterity or incur feelings of gratitude from my descendants, or best of all from fellow-countrymen; these are the achievements one seeks." To counter this pompous drivel, the writer gave us some examples of his earlier bons mots. On Adolf Hitler: "No truly objective historian could refrain from admiring the man." On himself: "I am never flamboyant on purpose. I am just what I am. Never forget, I am very clever."

For my own part, I am constantly reminded of Clark because, oddly enough, I have a large nude portrait of his famous father, Lord Clark of Civilisation, posing as Michelangelo's *David* on the wall of a downstairs lavatory in my Somerset house. The most shocking of Alan's bons mots is on the subject of apologising: "Only domestic servants apologise for what they have done."

Presumably he has no domestic staff at Saltwood and his poor wife has to do all the work. His statement is the exact opposite of the truth. Anybody with any experience of domestic workers would know they practically never apologise, never admit they are wrong. Perhaps this accounts in part for their humble position in life. Only the best and gentlest people apologise. But I don't suppose Clark knows many of them, either.

21 September 1998

Thoughts On Education

On Monday, when I congratulated the preposterous Alan Clark on his new role as an elder statesman – at the age of 70, he seems to have convinced *The Times* that he was once a cabinet minister – I suggested that his promotion testified to an enduring affection and respect among all true Britons for the public-school system.

Now we learn that Madonna has taken steps to enter her daughter, Lourdes, for the Cheltenham Ladies' College. Lourdes, who will be two years old next month, will have to pass her entrance exams first, but it seems safe to suppose that if any sort of public-school education survives in this country, it will survive in Cheltenham Ladies' College.

Many delightful friends went to Cheltenham, although I do not think that Virginia Bottomley is among their number, as *The Times* claimed on Monday. Virginia, as I remember, went to the equally distinguished Putney High School. But Cheltenham is just the place to give the daughter of an American strip artist and her former fitness trainer the necessary self-confidence in life.

Five or 10 years ago, America seemed to have forgotten about Britain. Now we are all the rage. I hope it lasts, and we do not disappoint them. It would be nice to think that in 68 years' time, Lourdes will be recognised as a serious historian of the women's movement, her idle thoughts serialised in *The Times*, which will write of her "wisdom", "broad vision", "wide sympathies" and "acute judgment". It is wonderful what a public-school education can do.

23 September 1998

From Now On

I am less depressed by the miserable, godless "prayer" appointed to be read in every British home for the New Millennium than by the suggestion that it will replace the singing of "Auld Lang Syne" at midnight on December 31, 1999.

One can object to "Auld Lang Syne" that nobody knows the words, or what they mean, but it has a beautiful tune and is practically never sung sober.

But perhaps that is the new objection. Perhaps the new British Way is best represented by Douglas Morgan, 62, who was given a lift to the shops by his son, Robert, 35, and reported him to the police for driving erratically.

Magistrates in South Wales were told that Douglas Morgan regarded it as his public duty to inform the police that his son was still inebriated after a drinking session the previous evening. The father turned up in court to see his son banned from driving for three years.

Douglas Morgan must be seen as a hero of the New Britain. It is to him that we lift our glasses of elderflower cordial at midnight on December 31, 1999, as we listen to some effeminate, non-denominational clergyman read his dismal list of platitudes: "Let there be respect for the Earth, peace for its people, love in our lives, delight in the good, forgiveness for past wrongs and from now on a new start."

12 October 1998

Grounds For Hope

Normally, one would listen with great respect to anything said by Margaret Jay, as the daughter of a former Prime Minister, former daughter-in-law of a memorable former President of the Board of Trade, and former wife of a distinguished BBC employee. But I am afraid that something may have happened to her judgment, as sometimes happens to the most qualified people at a certain age, when life seems to be passing them by.

When Lady Jay (as she has inexplicably become) advances the fact that something has worked well for 700 years as sufficient reason for abolishing it now, the time has surely come to ask her whether she is having difficulty procuring the necessary quantity of aspirins.

When she addressed the House of Lords in what was described as a "taut, quietly menacing speech" against the hereditary peerage, I was not present to take her pulse or offer smelling salts. But it is worrying to read of a contemporary making such a fool of herself. Who will be struck down next?

I do not happen to believe her statistic that 45 per cent of the hereditary peerage went to Eton, and 37 per cent to Oxbridge, suspecting that the true figure is considerably lower in both cases. But what a splendid advertisement it would be for the hereditary peerage if it were true. They are obviously the people who should be running the country.

17 October 1998

Against Hitler

I do not think I have ever seen an original work by the late American painter L. Feininger, although one might judge from the examples shown in Friday's newspaper that they are pretty good rubbish. Now he is being feted in Germany as one of the great artists of the century but largely, so far as one can make out, because Hitler condemned his work as degenerate and featured it in an exhibition of degenerate art in Munich in 1937.

Perhaps the Germans are anxious to show how much they have changed, but I fear they are in danger of making fools of themselves again. They claim that more than 100,000 people have visited the Feininger exhibition in Berlin and I suppose that is just possible, if they are making some sort of political demonstration about it. But they should not forget that some two million turned up to jeer at the degenerate art in Munich 60 years ago.

The point being made is that Hitler favoured realistic works and regarded all forms of modern art as subversive and immoral. Its implication is that anyone who does not favour modern art must be like Hitler, wishing to invade Poland and to inflict genocidal mass murder on the Jews.

My own objection to what is called modern art is not that it is subversive or immoral but that it is ugly, boring and a waste of time. On the other hand, I do not wish to invade Poland and have no desire to harm the Jews in any way. The suggestion that anyone who is unprepared to waste time on this rubbish must have Hitler tendencies is the latest development in a gigantic hoax which started half a century ago. It assures some that they are extra-sensitive, intelligent and artistic; others that they are philistine, unintelligent and reactionary. The hoax has worked, as we can see from the fact that nearly all the monuments or memorials put up by local authorities, however philistine, are in the "modern" style. The new millennium stamps threaten another celebration of this victory.

After Munich, Hitler locked away the degenerate art and tried to concentrate attention on his own "authentic" or realistic variety. Nowadays, Hitler's "authentic" art is itself locked away in airless, underground rooms. Everybody agrees it was pretty indifferent stuff, but we are not allowed to see it. I wonder why not. Are they frightened that people might prefer its mediocrity to the hideousness and stupidity of modern art?

26 October 1998

Even Better Joke

Last week, when commenting on the decision of Bradford University Association of University Teachers to discontinue the playing of the National Anthem when handing out degrees, I quoted the local branch president as saying: "We have to remember that the ceremony is a celebration of academic excellence."

Some might think it rather a joke, I suggested, that Bradford University should wish to celebrate academic excellence. This annoyed a few Bradfordians, who were tempted to the usual boastful rejoinders, but just how good a joke it was emerged over the weekend in a survey of Britain's 98 universities.

I do not think it entirely invalidates the University Guide that it was commissioned by the *Sunday Times*, since the information came from respectable sources. Although the league table somehow managed to place Bradford in 59th place out of the 98, it came bottom of them all in quality of teaching, where it scored a total of 0 points out of a possible 250. This cannot be explained by an accident of geography, since York University, to the northeast of Bradford, which came fifth in the league table, scored 227 points out of 250 for excellence of teaching, second after Cambridge.

No subjects at all are taught excellently in Bradford, despite its handing out more than 1,000 university degrees next month. Perhaps it is the best joke of all to play the National Anthem on these gruesome occasions.

11 Novenber 1998

Celebration

As one gets older, one begins to appreciate that the approach of winter is not dreaded only because it means the end of all sunshine and happiness, the encroaching cold, the bare trees, the hard ground, the frozen, out-of-doors face. One of the main reasons for dreading it is that it also signifies the approach of Christmas.

There is nothing new to be said about Christmas. For the past 10 years at least, I have tried to ban all mention of it from the December edition of *Literary Review*, but occasional references slip through. Perhaps it is worst of all for journalists, but it is pretty bad for parents and grandparents, too, required to produce mountains of plastic bricks which are all that young children nowadays want or understand. They clutter the house for months.

In fact, fewer and fewer people in Britain are having children. The British birthrate has fallen to an all-time low. Perhaps we should concentrate on our pets. An advertising feature in the *Telegraph* Magazine recently offered a made-to-measure tartan kilt for dogs, at £99.95. I don't think it would do for either of my beloved Pekingese, who would feel they were being mocked.

But the same issue offers silver-gilt doggie bowls from Asprey and Garrard at £1,150 apiece. If one cancelled all other presents and celebrations, I feel this might be a good way of marking the Birth of Our Saviour in present circumstances. At least the Pekingese would wag their little tails.

14 November 1998

1999

Animated Bust

One can sympathise with the authorities in the University of Edinburgh who ordered the removal of a bust of Arthur Koestler when female students complained of "feeling uneasy under its gaze".

They are too young, of course, to have been aware of how Koestler's intelligent, humane, anti-communism acted as a breath of fresh air on the Marxist-besotted intellectual scene for nearly 40 years after the publication of his masterpiece, *Darkness at Noon* (1940), to be followed by his study of socialism's failure: *The God that Failed* (1950).

One may doubt whether they have even had time to read the recent biography of Koestler by David Cesarani, *The Homeless Mind*, but it was serialised in this newspaper and they may have heard rumours that it shows Koestler to have been a hard drinker who sometimes raped his women.

Hence the uneasiness of female students in the presence of his bust, put up in acknowledgement of a £500,000 bequest from his estate. In former times, the university authorities might have assured the students that they were in no danger of attack or sexual abuse from the bust, which has been standing on the site for ten years without attacking or abusing anyone.

Nowadays, one cannot treat students like that. Many of them come from broken homes, few have the intellectual equipment which was once considered necessary to read for a degree, and all expect instant obedience from parents and grown-ups. They must be given their way immediately. The chair in parapsychology which Koestler set up should be taken down, and the money given to Women Against Rape.

But it must not stop there. Richard Nixon is on tape as saying that women in government are a "pain in the neck". There will be no public monuments to him, in any case, but I look forward to the time when all mention of his name is removed from the American history books. Horatio Nelson was most inconsiderate to his wife, Frances. His statue in Trafalgar Square should be taken down as soon as possible, before other men decide they can get away with that sort of behaviour.

2 January 1999

Stand Up for Snobs

A friend characterised my strong desire for greater European integration as being inspired by snobbish motives, and this seemed fair enough. The word "snob" – at any rate since its original meaning of "shoemaker" – has always been used pejoratively, and we must agree that when it described an excessive regard for the peerage, or for social aggrandisement, it may have been justified as a term of abuse.

Nowadays, however, it is used in the proletarian culture to describe anyone who reads the *Telegraph* rather than the *Sun*, and in the great cultural battle between snobs and yobs we should be all proud to call ourselves snobs.

The difference between the two cultures was well illustrated on Friday night's television, when Jeremy Paxman, on BBC2, introduced a version of *University Challenge* with two teams, one from the tabloid and one from the broadsheet press. My point is not that the tabloids showed themselves in a poor light. In fact both the tabloid team, led by the *Mirror*'s Tony Parsons, and the broadsheet team, led by our own Boris Johnson, struck me as brilliant – very quick and impressively well informed.

Then half an hour later, ITV showed a new series: *Who wants to be a Millionaire?* This was presented by Chris Tarrant and sponsored, needless to say, by the *Sun*, promising up to £1 million for anyone who could answer a number of general knowledge questions correctly.

A fat, expressionless man called Jason with an unrecognisable accent was brought on and asked eight general knowledge questions of an easiness which made everybody present gasp. Refusing the ninth question, he was told he had won £16,000 and led away. Another, almost equally fat man, this time with a northern accent, was brought on and started the process again.

The contrast between the two cultures could not have been plainer. We are all snobs. This is not quite the same thing as saying we must all support the common currency, only that those who don't support it have some explaining to do.

4 January 1999

Whinge

Ever since Mary Chipperfield was found guilty of mistreating a chimpanzee called Trudy at her circus, the country seems to be swamped by hysterical sentimentality about these creatures. One tabloid has been running a Save Trudy campaign, regardless of the fact that Trudy is now safely lodged with Alison and Jim Cronin in Monkey World, the 40-acre sanctuary for apes they run in Dorset.

Sadly, I must own up to finding chimpanzees the grossest and most revolting animals, of unpleasant appearance and disgusting habits, as they grimace, scratch and show their bottoms. I would not mind in the least if they were removed from the face of the earth tomorrow, although that is no reason to mistreat them, of course.

Now my feelings are more complicated, having had the opportunity to watch BBC2's *Chimpanzee Diary*, a six-week serial every Sunday evening, presented by Charlotte Uhlenbroek. She spent four years in a hut in Gombe National Park, Tanzania, following and observing a group of 43 chimpanzees in order to make the series.

From a recent interview in *Radio Times* I learn that she rises at 5.15 in the morning and heads off into the bush in pitch dark, with a torch, because she likes to be with them when they wake. "Morning is a very exciting time when they establish their relationships." Then she follows them on their daily hike of around four to six miles, watching them feed, groom, mate and play.

"Sometimes they plunge off into the thickest undergrowth and I have to crawl and wriggle after them, always mindful of deadly snakes like the black mamba."

Uhlenbroek not only has a very pretty voice, but as anyone

who has watched the series will be aware, she is also a vision of loveliness. Her face in repose is beautiful enough, but when she espies one of her apes – Fifi, Frieda, Freud or Frodo the delinquent – it glows with radiance, vitality, saintly understanding and pure love.

If ever I have the good fortune to meet her she can convert me to an enthusiasm for her apes in a matter of seconds, but I doubt she will wish to have me as her friend. However much I grimace and scratch and show my bottom, her eyes will be elsewhere. It is a curious business to find oneself, in middle age, consumed with jealous hatred towards a group of chimpanzees more than 4,500 miles away. The bitterest irony of it all is that they appear to regard the heavenly Uhlenbroek with complete indifference.

1 February 1999

Lost Pleasures

I thought it rather tough of the Duke and Duchess of Northumberland to release pictures of their 14-year-old son and heir, Lord Percy, showing him in the pink and gold kit of a Royal page. But when I read that the lad wept when his uncle died because he did not want to be a duke, I was even more moved.

There was a time when nearly everyone in this country wanted to be a duke or a duchess, with a couple of million pounds to dispose of, living in a castle like Alnwick. It was one of the things which held our great country together. However, looking at last week's pictures of Alnwick, on a cold winter's day, I suddenly realised that I no longer want to live there at all. Nor did I want to be the Duke of Northumberland. Poor boy.

Later in the week, I found myself watching a BBC2 programme about Lady Tavistock, called *Country House*. Apparently it plans to run for almost as long as *One Man and his Dog*, but I had never heard of it before. Lady Tavistock, who is married to the Duke of Bedford's immediate heir, probably hopes to publicise Woburn, their stately home open to the public, but on this occasion the programme was chiefly about her eldest son, Lord Howland.

Although perfectly presentable, and eventual heir to a large fortune and huge estate, as well as one of our finest stately homes and grandest dukedoms, Howland told us that at 36 he had had various girl friends but could never find a woman prepared to marry him.

Forty years ago, half the women of England would have swooned with pleasure at the thought of becoming a duchess, even without the rest of it. All that has been lost. The sadness is that nothing has taken its place.

22 February 1999

Difficult Decision

I was alarmed to discover this week that none of the people who work in my office at *Literary Review* had ever heard of Jeremy Thorpe, who is rumoured to be bringing out some sort of autobiography in May. Admittedly, they are all rather young. When I told them about him, they were fascinated. My conclusion is that if one wishes to address the young, one has to observe the tiresome convention of introducing everyone named: "Prince Philip, who is the husband of the Queen", "Jeremy Thorpe, a former leader of the Liberal Party, who was acquitted of conspiracy to murder a male model in 1979."

As events grow more distant, the explanation tends to grow longer. I wonder how many Members of the House of Commons, even, had any memory or knowledge of Anthony Nutting, once famous as the best-looking Member in his days there (1945–1956) who died this week at the age of 79. As those who read the obituaries will know, he was Minister of State at the Foreign Office at the time of the Suez invasion in 1956. He resigned from his job on principle, and also from the House of Commons. Apart from one unsuccessful attempt to re-enter Parliament in 1966, and a few books which caused little stir, he disappeared from public life, retiring eventually to manage the sheep on his Sutherland estate.

At the time of Suez I was a schoolboy, and a vociferous supporter of Eden's initiative, much to the annoyance of my older, wiser teachers. Anthony Eden, I should explain, was the Conservative Prime Minister 1955–1957, dying as Lord Avon in 1977. I rejoiced in the fact that France and Israel were with us, and thought it absolutely right that troops should be sent to reclaim a canal which we had built and which belonged to us.

Neither the British nor the French case was stated in these

terms – we had to pretend to be imposing a peace between Israel and Egypt – and the whole thing was a disaster. Now we can see that Nutting was right. The great lesson of the episode was that Britain no longer has a world role. We could do nothing without American approval, even then.

I wonder if the lesson has been learned. It strikes me as crucial to the great debate of our time, whether we should follow Tony Blair into Europe or stay at home with William Hague. Nutting became a fervent European, of course, but that was before Hague had emerged as a great national leader.

27 February 1999

Headless Memories

There must be few people around today who remember the great Argyll divorce case of 1963, when the 11th Duke of Argyll alleged that his wife, Margaret, had had 88 lovers, including three members of the Royal Family, various film stars and two cabinet ministers.

The case revolved around two photographs of the Duchess in a bathroom, wearing nothing but some pearl necklaces, pleasuring a man whose head was missing from the photograph. There was much speculation about the identity of this Headless Man, and now a biographer threatens to reveal it.

Lord Denning established that it was not John Profumo, the war minister, and the biographer, Michael Thornton, now says: "Actually the man in the photographs was someone much more famous than that. I have the greatest admiration for the man, and there is no question of persecuting him."

Who can he be thinking of? There is talk of legal action threatened by the man about to be named, but it is hard to see where the action will lie on a 36-year-old indiscretion if Thornton has his facts right. I can see much more trouble coming his way from all the men who claimed at the time that they were the Headless Man in question. I was definitely among their number. Few of us are in any mood to have our proud moment called into question by some pipsqueak biographer.

10 March 1999

Unusual Gifts

Tuesday's newspaper carried a handsome obituary of an old friend of mine, Bobby Corbett, who has died at 58. In size and prominence, it might have been the obituary of a dead Cabinet Minister. Those who had not heard of him will have been even more puzzled by a caption to the appropriately huge photograph: "Corbett: gift for placing unusual information into conversational banter."

In truth, Bobby did nothing else. Born with prodigious gifts of discrimination, intelligence, imagination and memory, he devoted them simply to amusing himself and his friends. He left no children, which is sad, but he also left no books, no paintings, no new laws, no proposals for the reform of society. There are those who would describe any life dedicated to the unswerving pursuit of pleasure as a wasted life, but it occurs to me that his was probably the most intelligent approach to all the problems of existence.

After Oxford, our paths diverged, as I accepted the undignified necessity of earning a living, and he embarked on his magnificent pretence of being a rich man (which he wasn't) and having inherited a great fortune (which he hadn't).

No doubt any books he wrote would have been excellent, but by now, they would be no more than an additional piece of clutter on the domestic scene. Journalism is forgotten in a day, as any good journalist knows. A new history of the *Spectator* edited by Simon Courtauld, is due to be published by Profile Books at £20. At first glance, I decided it attached insufficient importance to my own contribution as a regular columnist for 32 years. It was a dull book, and I would not read it. But who on earth is going to read any of these wretched books in a year or two? Bobby Corbett, with his infinitely superior intelligence, showed us what fools we all are.

13 March 1999

The Wrong Moment

One wishes the Vatican had not chosen this particular moment to soften its attitude towards masturbation. Preaching against this was a harmless way of spending time for thousands of clergymen who might otherwise have been up to mischief, even if nobody paid the slightest attention. Psychologists claim that a few people were made to feel guilty, but unreasonable guilt seems quite a healthy attitude to life when compared with the selfishness and self-satisfaction taught by psychiatric counsellors.

There are now more counsellors in Britain than there are members of the Armed Forces, all of them urging their victims to masturbate. This may seem as harmless as urging them not to do so, but the important aspect of the new Vatican approach is that it will weaken Cardinal Hume's opposition to the Greenwich Dome.

The real objection to the Dome, which Mr Blair proposes to use as a young person's boutique for the sale of cut-price condoms, may be different, but the Church's opposition to contraception is based on the same biblical story of Onan as its opposition to masturbation. Softening one softens the other, and we desperately need reasons to forbid people from visiting Mr Blair's shameful exhibition of British mediocrity. Come along, Basil. Give us the leadership.

22 March 1999

Wasted Evening

Last week I found myself attending a lecture given at the Royal Society of Literature (whose secretary is Maggie Parham) by Alan Howarth, Minister for Arts in Chris Smith's famous Department of Culture, Media and Sport. His subject, broadly speaking, was government policy on literature.

In a long Catholic education, I found myself being required to listen to a weekly, hour-long sermon, mysteriously called a Sodality. The result of this is that as soon as anyone starts making a speech, on any subject, I find I have switched off within a matter of minutes; after five minutes I am in a semi-comatose state not easily distinguished from death. Political speeches were the worst of all, which caused me some trouble when I later became a political correspondent on one of our more thoughtful political weeklies. Although Mr Howarth started with some well-chosen remarks about the Royal Society of Literature, founded by George IV and dedicated to excellence, he soon relapsed into the familiar tones of the ministerial speaker, and I found myself nodding off.

What shocked me was the attitude of the audience, all of whom appeared to be begging for more government subsidy. I was woken up by a resounding cheer for the minister when he mentioned the Oxford University Press decision to stop publishing contemporary poetry – certainly one of the most helpful literary developments of our time – then I went back to sleep again.

The chairman was Michael Holroyd – married to the great Margaret Drabble, and himself a writer of books about Lytton Strachey, Augustus John, etc. He did not allow me to ask the minister whether subsidies paid to writers might do more harm than good. Nor was I allowed to ask why, if the minister approved of the Royal Society and its work, he had not yet rescued it from the loss of its premises. Its lease in Hyde Park Gardens has run out but it only needs a tiny amount of money (by government standards) to save it from being turned out on the streets. I am afraid it was rather a wasted evening.

29 March 1999

Busting the System

The harm of subsidy to writers is that it encourages little committees of pseuds and their sycophants to form cliques and promote their own second-rate ideas and friends. The present state of British poetry is the result of this.

The Arts Council, sensibly enough, devotes only one per cent of its huge budget to literature. Where literature does need subsidy – at the reading end – it comes through the public libraries and the Department for Education. The idea of a payment to special, approved writers who could perfectly well survive on the dole is odious and counter-productive. No doubt it was to avoid charges of favouritism that the judges of the National Poetry Competition required people to send their entries anonymously. They chose a poem in the Caribbean dialect, apparently written by a black Rasta shark-fisher, for the £5,000 prize.

> Jigharzi an me stand in de
> water
> warm an friendly
> for de world smell like snails
> ooozing on hot charcoal . . .

No doubt they hoped to encourage West Indians generally, but unfortunately for their purpose, the poet turned out to be a middle-aged, middle-class, white Englishwoman from Flushing in Cornwall who had never been published before. Well done Caroline Carver, the 63-year-old former journalist concerned. It is not easy to beat the system.

29 March 1999

Don't Say 'Me', Say 'I'

An important new survey into contemporary behaviour and attitudes reveals that the "me" generation of the 1980s, characterised by the immortal slogan "I'm all right Jack", has given way to the "I" generation. If there were a slogan to celebrate this exciting new development, it would probably be along the lines: "I am a deeply interesting and unusual person."

Self-fulfilment is the goal of this female-dominated philosophy. Its adherents tend to turn their backs on their families: four out of 10 are happier living alone, and eight out of 10 think men and women should negotiate domestic tasks equally. Two-thirds of the entire population maintain that men are just as capable as women of bringing up children and the same proportion feels that "mothers should fulfil their own needs and not just their children's".

Perhaps to disguise the naked selfishness of this programme, they have decided to call it the "i" society rather than the "I" society, with the suggestion that the small "i" stands for individuality, independence, identity and interactivity. Melanie Howard, a director of the Future Foundation and author of the report on the "i" society, explains that it is about individuality rather than individualism, self-actualisation rather than self-esteem.

All of which is absolutely fine as a summary of every sub-feminist cliché that has been appearing in every woman's magazine for the past 30 years. The only thing that is at all surprising is the extent to which this tendentious twaddle has become the received wisdom of our culture. The two-thirds who say they believe that men are just as good at raising children as women (or just as capable, as Ms Howard puts it) rise to three-quarters among the under-30s.

There is nothing peculiar or even disreputable in the way women have allowed themselves to be brainwashed into following their more selfish instincts. Previous brainwashing tended to lead them into a life of misery and toil. The most interesting thing is the way that men have allowed themselves to be brainwashed into unselfishness. They remain of course, the physically stronger sex. The major difference, in a world of selfish women and unselfish men, is that the women will tend to despise the men.

10 April 1999

Memorial

It is exciting news, I suppose, that the Teletubbies have been singled out as representing the best of British creativity and design for exhibition in the Greenwich Millennium Done. On Sunday, we also learnt that the Christian churches had won the right to hold daily services in the building, although there is no suggestion that they will be given a part in the dreaded New Year's Eve celebration.

On the same day, Cardinal Hume broke the sad news of his impending death. For some time I had been criticising him for his failure to condemn the Dome outright, and ban all Roman Catholics from setting foot inside it. Now, one understands he may not have felt strong enough.

In fact his gentleness towards this shameful enterprise has been saintly. I feel it should be commemorated somehow. Perhaps they should change its name to the Basil Hume Dome in memory of him. If that seems something of a mouthful, perhaps we should take a leaf from the late Sir Alec Douglas Home, who always pronounced his name as if it was spelled Hume. If we pronounced the name of the Millennium Dome as if it was spelt Dume, this might be a suitable memorial to a man who will be fondly remembered in so many walks of life.

21 April 1999

Horrors of Travel

I had an unpleasant experience in the London Underground on Thursday morning, when a woman of perhaps some 40 summers came and sat beside me. That is a most attractive age for women, of course, but this one had done nothing to make herself pretty. She sat in a shapeless grey jersey, her coarse, short hair un-brushed, wearing large brown plastic-rimmed spectacles as she studied her copy of that morning's *Guardian* supplement.

Having no desire to look at her, I read it, too. The first three pages were entirely devoted to supporting the teachers' vendetta against Chris Woodhead, with a larger-than-life portrait of him on the cover, captioned: "The naked public servant: How the past caught up with Chris Woodhead."

A headline over the main 1,500 word article by Decca Aitkenhead summed up the argument: "His ex-wife says he's a liar. Teachers hate him. Few people believe his version of events. So why is the government so determined to save Chris Woodhead?"

One can understand that the *Guardian* will always feel tempted to support any former wife against any former husband – or, indeed, any woman against any man in sexual matters, but this time it is surely going too far. The teachers' union may be clamouring for a criminal prosecution against Woodhead for allegedly making a false affidavit, but anybody can see that the Crown Prosecution Service, at its most demented, could not claim the beginnings of a case against him.

Mrs Woodhead says she remembers a 23-year-old conver-sation with her former husband in which he described an affair with a schoolgirl. Both alleged participants have sworn it did not happen at that time. All the rest is gossip, tittle-tattle and malice. Perhaps some of these people who are rushing forward to give the *Guardian* their "inside information" genuinely do not understand the difference between a relationship and an affair. Certainly the dreadful *Guardian* woman sitting next to me on the Underground gave the impression of knowing nothing about either. I had no doubt, from the self-satisfied expression on her ugly face, that she was a teacher.

The key sentence in the *Guardian*'s crusade against Woodhead is, of course, that "Teachers hate him". Almost singlehandedly, he has taken on the job of tackling the plummeting standards of state education. On his appointment he called for the sacking of 15,000 idle or incompetent teachers – I should have thought 25,000 was nearer the mark – with the naming and shaming of bad schools.

How they wriggled and spat, those teachers, but the public had begun to realise that all their idealistic talk about the virtues of child-centred education – long since discredited – was no more than a cover-up for their own laziness.

The teachers' behaviour is contemptible, but then one has forgotten how hypocritical and unpleasant these "progressives" are. And rude, too. As I left the train, the wretched woman did not even look up when I apologised for kicking her on the shin.

24 April 1999

Ovine Defence League

Some years ago, to my great joy, I was appointed an honorary patron of the National Canine Defence League, along with the Queen and other noted dog-lovers. My own appointment came as a result of my having stood as parliamentary candidate for the Dog Lovers Party in the general election of 1979 in North Devon. The DLP, I should explain, was an ad hoc body formed to protest at the indifference shown by North Devon Liberals over the fate of a Great Dane, called Rinka, which had been shot in mysterious circumstances by a hired gunman on Exmoor.

The Liberal candidate – who was also sitting member for North Devon – was so worried by my intervention that he sought a High Court injunction to prevent me from publishing my manifesto. This was thrown out by the Lord Chief Justice of blessed memory, Lord Widgery, but he took it on appeal the same day to Lord Denning, who was already 80 years old, and who agreed that I should face the votes of North Devon without being allowed to explain to them why I was standing.

But throughout this curious episode, the behaviour of the NCDL and other dog-lovers in the constituency was entirely admirable and although, with no manifesto, I secured only 79 votes, I should like to think that our combined activities helped unseat the Liberal candidate. A book called *In My Own Time* by Jeremy Thorpe (published last week by Politico's at £18), gives an alternative view of these events.

The episode convinced me that the NCDL was something which should be supported, and I rejoiced to learn last week that it had received a surprise £7 million from the will of an elderly widow who died in November.

But now we learn that the NCDL has demanded changes in Richmal Crompton's Just William stories on the grounds that

William has an incorrect attitude to dogs, complaining in particular about a scene in which William's dog, Jumble, chases some sheep: "Jumble was deaf and blind to everything but the ecstasy of chasing those foolish white creatures." This is a brilliant description. It is the greatest joy in a dog's life to chase sheep, and the only taste of excitement a sheep ever has. A spokesman for the NCDL, Siobhan Lavelle, says: "The publisher should seriously consider the change in social mores and the unacceptability of cruelty or ill-treatment, especially as fun, by today's readers." What nonsense. It would appear that, like the National Trust, the NCDL has been taken over by bossy, ignorant urbanities who wish to destroy the life of the countryside. That is bad enough. The attempt to censor one of our greatest children's classics is unforgivable. I propose to resign as patron and strongly advise the Queen to do the same.

8 May 1999

Observer Folk

People sometimes ask what has happened to all those well-to-people who used to describe themselves as socialists now that socialism has been discredited. The answer would appear to be that they spend their time trying to convince us that they worry more than anybody else about the poor.

I was reminded of this when I saw a seven-column top-of-the-page headline in the *Observer* this week: "Room to swing a cat? The poor can't even afford the cat." The article, by Will Hutton, opened with a searching question: "Should the poor be allowed to keep a cat when it costs £3.28 a week?"

The question is presumably addressed to cat-lovers in positions of responsibility. Should they forbid the poor to own cats? We may be glad that the radical bourgeoisie has lost none of its authoritarianism – Tony Blair's war in the Balkans is a shining example of it – but the question, of course, is nonsense.

Anybody who has had anything to do with cats knows that it costs absolutely nothing to keep them – unless you decide to give them the disgusting tinned food produced for the suckers' market. A saucer of milk a day is enough to keep them at home. If they need anything more solid, they can catch mice or help themselves to all the delicious things to be found in the neighbours' dustbins.

There might be something amiable about this concern for the cats of the poor. The *Observer* is, after all, quite an expensive newspaper. But a glance at the readers' letters suggests that it is read by some of the nastiest and stupidest people in the country. One, presumably from a teacher, starts: "I read with interest that Prince Charles has states his support for Chris Woodhead. Given the Prince's record on morality, this is rather like Idi Amin expressing his support for President Milosevic's record on human rights."

Another letter, presumably from a bearded person, can be quoted in full: "Isn't it time you or your sub-editors put a stop to the insistent, irrational, ad nauseam repetition by Richard Ingrams of his gratuitous insults to bearded people, many of whose lives are as successful as those of anyone else."

Ingrams happens to be a friend of mind. I wonder if he appreciates the sort of highly successful people he is addressing.

12 May 1999

Awkward Subject

I wonder if this tendency for young womanhood to turn its back on the opposite sex is slightly older and more widespread than we may suppose. The thought is prompted by a letter in Monday's newspaper from a nurse who was in Africa for the first appearance of Aids. She describes how the disease developed from the practice of men in Central Africa who have sexual relations with a particular type of green monkey.

"Presumably humans had had sexual relations with these monkeys for a very long time," she writes. "So why was it only in the 1950s that the monkeys contracted the virus and passed it on?"

She explains that the monkey was particularly attractive; while other monkeys were hunted and eaten, these were adopted as pets, and even venerated. Their green sheen was thought to have mystical powers. She writes: "I was taken aback to learn that men copulated with them."

But why does she suppose they had been doing so for a very long time? Could it not be the case that Congolese women suddenly saw their menfolk adopting whatever might be the African equivalent of baseball caps, near-beards and earrings, and decided to withdraw their favours?

The men, in their frustration, would then have turned to the pet monkey in the house, with all the dire consequences we now see in California and elsewhere. One does not like to discuss these matters, but it would plainly be wrong to shirk them.

19 May 1999

Remembering the War

Surveys of "young people" in this country nearly always provide distressing information and we should not be surprised by the latest survey of 15- to 30-year-olds, conducted for a video company, which reveals more or less total ignorance about the last war.

Six out of 10 young people approached did not know its dates and three out of 10 could not get close by guessing. Four out of 10 were not aware that Winston Churchill was prime minister at the time. Even more impressive, 12 per cent of the 450 young people interviewed did not know which side had won.

What makes these fairly predictable figures worthy of comment is the remark by a spokesman for the Department for Education who said schools and teachers were not to blame: "The Second World War is a compulsory part of the national curriculum for 11- to 14-year-olds, and has been since 1991," he explained.

This statement, if true, tells us more about current standards of teaching than the earlier discovery taught us about young people's lack of curiosity. An even more widely held error is suggested by the British Legion spokesman who commented: "Such a level of ignorance is very disappointing. It is vital for children to be well-versed in their nation's victories over dictators."

We did not go to war because Hitler and Mussolini were dictators. That was fortuitous, and in any case both enjoyed democratic support. Nor did we go to war, as nine out of 10 Britons seem to believe, through any moral or high-principled reaction to Hitler's persecution of the Jews. We went to war because we felt threatened by Germany's take-over of Czechoslovakia and Poland.

Although Hitler's anti-Semitism was abundantly clear by the autumn of 1939, the real persecution, in the sense of mass extermination or holocaust, did not start until nearly four years later, in 1943 – nor could it conceivably have occurred except in the circumstances of war. Far from being fought to prevent or punish the holocaust, the Second World War effectively caused it.

I mention these unwelcome facts only because the myth that we went to war for moral reasons – and to rid the world of ethnic cleansing – now encourages twerpish young would-be Winston Churchills like Tony Blair to indulge their power fantasies at our expense. The lesson we must all learn from Blair's disastrous interference in Yugoslav affairs is that the money British tax payers pay on defence is designed to defend ourselves and our essential interests against anyone who threatens them.

Nato may or may not have outlived its usefulness, but its purpose was never to impose decent standards of behaviour on the rest of the world. That sort of thing must be left to the Americans, and if the Americans bomb us, we will bomb them.

7 June 1999

Making Friends

My last column for a week seems to be entirely about books. If it saves a few people from the television for an hour or two, it will have done well. Christina Foyle, who died last week at the dignified age of 88, must have sold more books in her lifetime than other human being in the history of the world. There can be no doubt that she has gone straight to Heaven.

But it is not for her enormous bookshop in Charing Cross Road that she will be chiefly remembered as for the famous, monthly Foyle's Literary Luncheons which she started in 1930 at the age of 19.

I first met her in 1960 when she invited me to be guest of honour (as a 20-year-old) to celebrate my first novel – much to the rage of my contemporaries and rivals in the literary world, some of whom have been seeking revenge ever since. Immediately afterwards I joined the Peterborough staff on the *Daily Telegraph* and attended nearly all her lunches for about three years in that capacity. Sometimes she would forget I was there as a reporter and absentmindedly called on me, out of the blue, to make a speech. It would have needed a very brave man to refuse.

The greatest achievement of these lunches, over nearly 70 years, was to introduce writers to each other. Many were relieved to find their colleagues less disagreeable than they had supposed. It is a major discovery. Perhaps she was the spiritual mother of the Academy Club. Not all writers are awful. It is only the poets who let us down.

12 June 1999

Never Again

Last week, I found I went to eight parties in London, starting with one for Henry Kissinger's riveting final volume of memoirs *Years of Renewal* (Weidenfeld). Kissinger told me that he always reads the *Literary Review* and had been particularly gratified by our review of his book in the June issue, by Paul Johnson. No wonder he got so far in American public life.

On one night, I went to three parties – first that of the *New Statesman*, in Carlton House Terrace, full of well-mannered, attractive, elderly people, then the *Spectator*'s, packed, as always, with shouting young men, and finally to the American Embassy residence in Regent's Park, celebrating the 223rd anniversary of America's Declaration of Independence.

I was pleased to be asked to this as I had not yet met the new ambassador, and have many happy memories of the house and garden there. On this occasion, however, about 2,500 guests had been invited. We were welcomed by "people greeters", and then everybody stood close to each other in a huge marquee, talking in American. There was not a single person in that number whom I knew or wanted to know, and nobody who appeared to know or want to know me.

It was a humbling experience for a London occasion. My conclusion must be that it was a great mistake to go. We should commiserate and sympathise with Americans over their independence, but never pretend to celebrate it. That is too cruel.

5 July 1999

Social Insight

On the subject of health scares, I feel I must be one of the few people in Britain who sincerely hopes that mobile phones do not disappear from the scene as a result of the present scare about loss of memory, brain cancer, etc.

Cynics will say that this because I do not care whether mobile phoners lose their memories or suffer from brain cancer or not. It is not the real reason.

What fascinates me about these mobile phones is the insight they provide into contemporary society. We hear unattractive, apparently ignorant men bellowing into them in common accents, and realise that these are the people who run Britain nowadays.

There is a cruelty about them, as well as an arrogance, which explains much of what is going on in the country, from the sadistic incompetence of arrangements at Paddington Station to the endless rudeness addressed to the Queen and Royal Family. One expects this in the Murdoch newspapers, of course, but there was a good example in Thursday's *Guardian*.

Far easier to listen to the New Britons shouting at each other on their mobile telephones than to read the rubbish they write, or to try and talk to them ourselves.

10 July 1999

Fatal Mistake

My economics tutor at Oxford, the late Sir Roy Harrod, said I would never make an economist because I was reluctant to believe anything I was told. He was quite right. The whole of economics, as it was then taught (and no doubt still is) seemed to be based on a number of obvious and easily exposed errors.

On one thing they were all united: that gold was a waste of time, its use as a monetary guarantee no more than a deference to quaint superstition. Even business friends, whose judgment I respect, have always advised against investment in it. The settled wisdom is that gold has had its day, being replaced by the ability of national governments to manage their currencies without it.

Perhaps it depends on how much we are prepared to trust our national governments. No British government has yet dared to sell our gold reserves, whether to "invest" in paper money or spend on daft, semi-sadistic schemes to prolong the lives of the poor. What has changed?

It is possible to meet twerpish young Lefties, looking for something to feel angry or bitter about, who will blame Churchill's return to the gold standard in 1925 for the unemployment of their alleged grandfathers in the Thirties – that and the fact that Churchill was an Old Harrovian, of course. On this occasion, I feel it in my bones that I will be proved right: that when Blair, Brown, Cook, Dobson and the rest of them finally end up dangling from ropes, it will not be because of their having provoked civil war over hunting, nor for their murderous bombing of Yugoslavia, nor their abolition of private property in order to suck up to "ramblers", nor, even, because of their deliberate alienation of the country's 10 million smokers. It will be because they have destroyed the economy by printing worthless banknotes.

14 July 1999

Not a Bad Woman

On Thursday, I went to claim my lunch with Jackie Ballard, the Liberal Democrat MP for Taunton, which I had won against heavy competition at a charity event in Taunton's famed Brazz restaurant. We lunched in the Stranger's Dining Room in the House of Commons where the food, to my amazement, is now very good indeed.

Friends criticised my readiness to be entertained by such a vociferous opponent of hunting – the only political issue of any importance in Somerset – but I have always maintained that women should not be despised if they disapprove of hunting. Women are among the fiercest members of any hunt, but others are troubled by the thought, as might be expected in the gentler sex.

One could argue that there is a big difference between disliking the hunt and trying to ban it, but this is no more than the difference between normal human beings and MPs. Having met a number of MPs, I must testify that, as MPs go, Jackie Ballard is a humorous, sporting, intelligent and attractive woman, and I hope she wins the leadership of the Liberal Party.

Male opponents of hunting are an entirely different kettle of fish. These men can easily be identified as bitter, power-mad crypto-perverts, who should be denied any promotion in their jobs and ignored at all times. Their greetings should not be acknowledged even by the tiniest nod of the head.

17 July 1999

Tourist Attractions

According to the International Gay and Lesbian Association, based in Florida, the United Kingdom attracts 500,000 gay visitors annually. This does not seem to be a tremendously high number when we reflect that the British Tourist Authority claims we receive 26 million foreign visitors every year. Nobody can believe that only one in 52 foreigners is gay. This may explain why the authority is so keen to attract more gays to this country. Another reason may be the one given by Louise Wood, of the London Tourist Board, which has produced a brochure for distribution in America, describing London as the "Gay capital of Europe". She explains that "American gays are frequent travellers, long stayers and big spenders".

No doubt her intentions are good, but I wonder if she is really being kind to these American gays. Has she given any thought to what they will find in our crooked, overpriced, incompetent country? The British Tourist Authority's 12-page brochure lists gay clubs, hotels, shops and bath houses, and draws attention to "London's Soho" as a gay Mecca.

But this is not the view of Paul Burton, author of *Queen's Country*, a travelogue on gay Britain. Soho, he says, is becoming an attraction for "gawping heterosexual tourists. You feel you're a zoo animal."

As someone who works in Soho, I must agree with him that the tourists – no doubt most of them heterosexual – are a pain in the neck. But it is not only Soho. The whole of west London and all the tourist sites in Britain are ruined by coachloads of young foreigners who walk very slowly in impenetrable groups. These people spend no money at all. I refuse to believe the BTA's claim that our tourist industry is worth £53 billion a year, but even if it were true, it would not be worth it.

This country is a democracy. We must all ask ourselves what benefit we receive, as individuals, from this monstrous invasion. I certainly receive none, only endless nuisance.

If, as I suspect, we are in the majority, we must demand that the Government closes down its tourist boards and forbids all foreigners – gay or otherwise – from entering the country unless they have relatives to visit or can show at least £2,000 in spending money.

26 July 1999

Best Image

Ffion Hague seems to be an attractive and pleasing person. She is understandably anxious to change her husband's public image and I would dearly love to help her, but I am not sure she has quite the right ideas. She appears to believe that Hague is unpopular because voters regard him as a remote, elitist and bookish figure, an over-privileged southerner with an unhealthy interest in politics.

Ffion and her friend Amanda Platell are striving to promote him as a physically fit family man from Yorkshire, the product of a comprehensive school, an action man as witnessed by his interest in judo and outdoor activities.

This image might recommend him to some of the voters, but scarcely to all. Many readers of this column might decide not to vote on that basis. So far as we know, he has not yet started a family, and few of us really care about his physical fitness. The idea of being a Yorkshireman does not command instant admiration in the south, and many of us doubt the benefits of a comprehensive school education.

For my part, I will promote him to Way of the World readers as a quiet, bookish Home Counties figure from some respectable minor public school like Shrewsbury, reasonably adept at croquet but with a loathing of football and popular music. He will be swept to power.

My motive in this is to secure a knighthood for my Editor, a good man who richly deserves it, if only for publishing this column week after week.

14 August 1999

The Best We Can Do

A correspondent writes to ask whether it is normal for the newspapers to give the details of school examination results, day after day, throughout the entire month of August. I have to answer, no, I do not think it is normal. It is an innovation. Since the end of the Cold War destroyed all interest in international news, we might have hoped to spend August learning a bit more about Posh Spice and Tara Palmer-Tomkinson. Instead we were given daily statistics, breakdown and commentary on GCSE and A-level results – whether girls were on top, or boys were on top, whether they managed it better in single-sex or in co-educational schools, etc. etc.

The wonderful thing about this year's results is that they have never been better. More people have passed at higher levels than at any time since education began. The figures have made huge numbers of teachers, children and parents very happy. They might even have helped us all in our sadness over the death of Diana, Princess of Wales. Nothing could be more reassuring than to learn that our children are intelligent and highly motivated, our teachers are brilliant, our parents capable of breeding such good offspring and providing them with a suitable home background in which to pursue their studies. Only a cynic could suspect it is all a great, unspoken conspiracy to hide plummeting standards all round.

I would be happier, myself, if a teacher had not sent me a copy of the GCSE English Literature paper, involving a passage from Nadine Gordimer. It contains five spelling mistakes – "venders" for vendors, "women" for woman etc. When she wrote to the board to complain, they replied that several of the mistakes were to be found in their version of the original text, while acknowledging two of their own, which they insisted on calling "typographical errors". Their letter would have been more impressive if it had not itself contained a bad spelling mistake, no doubt to be described as a typing error.

30 August 1999

Unsuitable for Adults

I have not seen and do not intend to see the 10-part BBC2 series *Adult Lives* which starts this week and describes itself as a serious and restrained look at ordinary people's sexuality. Nor, I suspect, had Polly Toynbee, the 52-year-old thinker, seen it all when she denounced it last week as "a sexy freak show". But Toynbee had a good point when she objected to use of the word "adult" to mean sexually explicit or indecent, although the *Oxford Concise English Dictionary* allows this meaning. *Collins* is more cautious, suggesting "regarded as suitable only for adults, because of being pornographic".

Both Collins and the BBC are hopelessly out of date, as anybody who has read the newspapers will know. Sex has nothing to do with adulthood nowadays. It is something that happens chiefly between pupils aged between 10 and 15 at schools where they are taught how to do it in the vain hope that it will discourage them from having babies.

There is every sign that adults are having less and less sex, as the youngsters take over. If the BBC really wants to attract viewers to its sexy freak shows, it should put them on in *Children's Hour* with a special warning for adults like Miss Toynbee not to watch.

6 September 1999

Slough Motion

When Betjeman wrote his famous poem about Slough, most people agreed with him that it was a pretty dreadful place. Nowadays, of course, it is little different from anywhere else. Most of provincial urban Britain has become an extended version of Slough. A number of our fellow-citizens, if not a majority, lives in the sort of surrounding which saddened Betjeman to the point of exclaiming: "It isn't fit for humans now."

Perhaps this awareness is what has inspired people in Slough to ask the new Poet Laureate, Andrew Motion, to write a poem extolling the town's glories, or at any rate looking at its brighter aspects. They made the same request to Motion's predecessor as Laureate, Ted Hughes, but he refused, reckoning that Betjeman had got it about right.

I dare say Motion will shrink from the task, too. The bad reception given to his rotten poem for the TUC Conference might have discouraged him. Perhaps I should set it for the New Year *Literary Review* Poetry Competition.

> Come friendly folk who live
> in Slough,
> There is no need to say
> "bow-wow".
> We can see you're humans,
> now,
> Same minds, same breath.

22 September 1999

Pooh Corner

There seems to be nothing more to say about the renewed campaign to discredit P. G. Wodehouse, except to question the motives of those involved. In fact, I do not think there was malice behind last week's moronic headlines announcing that Wodehouse had yet again been exposed as a Nazi agent by MI5. It was just ignorance.

There may have been an element of malice in the original attacks on him during the war immediately after the Germans allowed him to make some humorously anti-German broadcasts to America. Bill Connor (Cassandra of the *Daily Mirror),* who was put up to it by Duff Cooper on Winston Churchill's suggestion, did not have much time for Wodehouse or his upper-class buffoons. Cooper, who had written a book about Talleyrand, had literary pretensions of his own, as did Churchill, who might well have been moved to jealousy by the success of a younger acquaintance and fellow-member of The Other Club.

But Connor, who made his peace with Wodehouse after the war, was a decent man and had no reason to be jealous. Many years later, when I got to know him, he agreed he had probably been in a state of journalistic over-excitement, as many of us are from time to time.

Among the many inferior writers who joined in denouncing Wodehouse was A. A. Milne, author of *When We Were Very Young* and *Now We Are Six*, whose loathsome exploitation of his unfortunate son, Christopher Robin, would surely land him in prison nowadays.

If often upsets me to see how many apparently intelligent 60-year-olds persist in reading this sentimental rubbish. Approaching my own sixtieth birthday, I am delighted to learn that John Murray, the publisher, plans to bring out a full-length parody,

Now We are Sixty, by Christopher Matthew. It is a bit ribald in places, but beautifully produced to look like the 1927 original. It will make a wonderful birthday or Christmas present to 60-year-olds:

> "They're changing sex at Buckingham Palace."
> Murgatroyd mutters with undisguised malice.
> "Roger is marrying one of the guard –
> Bugger whose bearskin reeks of pomade,
>   called Alice."

22 September 1999

Good News

Wednesday's party to launch the sale of tickets for the Greenwich Dome might have been a scene-setter for the grand New Year's Eve party which has been promoted by the Dome's organisers as the biggest and best party in the world that night.

On Wednesday, the world's media were invited to arrive by the exciting new Jubilee Line Extension, as the public is expected to do after January 1. Unfortunately, the Tube broke down, so guests spent the evening stranded in the Underground. On the great night itself, when 10,000 guests will look forward to mingling with the Queen, Prince Philip, Tony Blair, the Archbishop of Canterbury and other VIPs, nearly everybody will have to take the Tube because the Government has decided to close all bridges across the Thames in London.

If, as seems quite likely, the new Jubilee Line Extension breaks down again or is on strike, guests will simply have to swim across the Thames – a difficult and dangerous thing to do at midnight, in winter. On this occasion it will not be made easier by the decision of a government minister, called Nick Raynsford, to set the Thames on fire at the crucial moment with 60 metre flames.

As I reported on Wednesday, Raynsford has appropriated five badminton courts in Victoria to serve as a mortuary for the 1,000 fatalities he anticipates as a result of this bit of fun. If one adds to that figure the number of guests drowned while trying to swim to the Party of the Millennium, then it is obvious he has not made nearly enough provision. The best solution must be to turn the Dome itself into a giant mortuary. It is so big there would be plenty of room for it to serve as mortuary, emergency medical centre and ballroom/reception area for the partygoers simultaneously. This would also have the advantage of freeing the badminton courts for those who wish to play badminton. The good news may well be that practically nobody will buy the tickets. Figures are to be kept secret until next year, but everything suggests a massive lack of enthusiasm. Perhaps we are not such fools as these people thought. The poor are often said to be less intelligent than the rest of us; they will be spared temptation by not being able to afford the £20 admission charge.

Organisers hope to sell enormous numbers of tickets to foreigners, and it is true that west London in particular is full of gangs of young foreigners, most of whom look pretty foolish. But few of them can speak a word of English, and none of them, I suspect, has £20 to spend on visiting Mr Blair's £758 million mortuary.

25 September 1999

Grounds for Hope

At literary parties like the one mentioned above, I seem to spend most of my time advising people of every age and sex – most of them attractive women – not to write novels. I was interested to read in Tuesday's article by Jonny Geller, the noted literary agent, that he tends to give the same advice.

Few enough first novels can find an agent, let alone a publisher, and publishers seem to have the greatest difficulty in getting their books into the bookshops, unless they are guaranteed best-sellers. But literary parties are a major part of the London social scene and publishers are happy to pretend they are on the look-out for any sort of thriller or romantic trash. It requires an act of faith to believe that there might still be a readers' market for intelligent fiction. At the same party, I met a man who told me he had started a small firm of publishers, called Arcadia Books, determined to make no compromises. As I prepared my face in a sympathetic smile, he said that last year he published a novel by a first novelist called Richard Zimler: *The Last Kabbalist of Lisbon*, about Jews living secretly in 16th-century Lisbon. Before I could get out a handkerchief, he said that after advertising it in the *Literary Review*, he had sold 25,000 copies – 1,000 alone in Hampstead's Waterstone's, where it was a best-seller for many weeks. It seems to me there is hope for Britain yet. The morons have not take over completely. And London cab drivers are still the best in the world.

2 October 1999

Best Poet

Tomorrow is National Poetry Day, an event not normally celebrated in my part of Somerset, but it was interesting to learn that friends of the Poet Laureate are planning to inaugurate an Andrew Motion Fan Club.

Or so Peterborough informed us on Monday. I suppose there is always a hope he got it wrong. There is something inexpressibly gloomy about the thought of an Andrew Motion Fan Club.

By coincidence, the Betjeman Society, of which I am proud to be a vice-president, celebrated its 11th birthday last week with a reception in the Council Room at King's College. That huge, magnificent room was packed by lively, intelligent people determined to have a good time, with delicious food and wine and practically no young people present. We discussed how Betjeman, a man who detested the company of bores and fools, was driven by his natural sanctity to try to popularise the idea of proper poetry on television. He was criticised for this by his friend Evelyn Waugh, who felt that any contact with the mass culture was not only wasted effort but also bound to degrade and dehumanise. At the time, we all thought Betjeman was doing a splendid job trying to bring happiness and civilisation into people's lives, but after all these years I begin to think that Waugh was right.

Motion, by contrast, will spend tomorrow under the auspices of the Poetry Society, debating whether Bob Dylan, the American singer, is as great a lyric poet as Keats. Everybody finds this thrilling. Personally, I do not think I have read any of "Bob's" poetry but I doubt if it can be as dull as Motion's last poem to the TUC.

6 October 1999

Hatred of Toffs

Nobody will be surprised to learn that Cambridge University students, as undergraduates are now called, have launched a campaign to have Prince Philip dismissed as Chancellor, calling him an "obnoxious and anachronistic figurehead". If it upsets Prince Philip, who has been its chancellor since 1976, he should learn that these "students" are not the people they used to be.

At one time they were thought to be chosen for their academic ability but now, we learn, this is discouraged in case it favours the more intelligent, many of whom may be middle class. Nor can they be chosen from the working class, in case this discriminates against the very large number of unemployed or single parents who have never worked. In order to qualify for government grants, colleges now feel they have to favour the most underprivileged, those most in need. While theoretically studying the media, domestic science, leisure and politics in order to prepare themselves to rule the country, these people in fact have enough time on their hands for other things – to campaign for a new chancellor, for instance. This may seem a rather pointless exercise, since the chancellor has no relevance to any aspect of their lives. They declare that Prince Philip is a "bigot", citing his harmless little joke about the standard of electrical installation in India – a criticism well borne out by anyone who has travelled on the sub-continent.

But I do not think these louts are really interested in electrical fixtures. They claim that this "gaffe" has made him unfit to be chancellor of their wretched university, but what they are really saying is that they do not want a toff in the post. Hatred of toffs is among the few things which hold young Britain together. I don't think it is a healthy development. These young people should be looking for jobs, instead of shaving their hair, wearing earrings and scowling at everyone else. It has replaced redistributive socialism and even xenophobia as the great consolation of the underprivileged. Now it is the toffs who need consoling. The Queen, as chief toff, should give us a lead, but she has chosen to ignore my friend A. N. Wilson's advice, and Anthony Powell has not yet received his OM.

Powell, whose novels deal exclusively with the upper-middle and upper classes, is now 93 years old and probably not in the best of health. The Queen must move fast to show us whose side she is on. It would be a noble gesture.

9 October 1999

Good Excuse

Can it really be true that seven million plastic toys representing an alien foetus have been sold in this country? They are about 4ins long and slimy, curled up in an egg. The makers, H. Grossman of Glasgow, hope to sell as many again before Christmas.

This may tell us more than we really want to know about the new generation of British kids. One of these objects was found on the platform at Blackhurst Hill Underground Station by a cleaner. Police closed down the station and rushed the doll off in an ambulance with an escort. In the hospital, they said the plastic object was in no danger. A spokesman for the London Ambulance Service said: "Police were taking no chances, and neither were we."

This seems an entirely sane and reasonable reaction to the object concerned. But why did they close down Buckhurst Hill Underground? Did they think the foetus would explode? It seems to me that the Tube and railways alike will use any excuse at all to close down a station, a line, even a whole service. The reason has nothing to do with safety, or even with idleness. It reflects a general misanthropy, a hatred of clients, a desire to inconvenience them.

If it is really true that 14 million of these plastic objects will soon be in circulation, we cannot reckon on any Tubes or trains at all.

6 November 1999

Unsporting

The Prime Minister is oddly shy about letting the world see what a good tennis player he is. Photographers who sneaked shots of the PM practising his top spin at the Durban summit were warned that, should they publish any, they'd be barred from future Commonwealth meetings. "They were only allowed to take photographs of heads of governments relaxing with their permission," says a Downing Street spokesman with no perceptible sense of the ridiculous.

When the Royal Court theatre returns to its Sloane Square home, will it resume a tradition? "We used to have a nude cleaner," says artistic director Ian Rickson.

"He vacuumed in the middle of the night with no clothes on. We don't know why he did that."

Sir Peregrine Worsthorne offers ringing support to my call for Auberon Waugh to be knighted. "I shall certainly propose him," he says. "It would be only to return a favour." "Bron" successfully campaigned over 10 years for "Perry" to be knighted.

18 November 1999

Too Modest

On celebrating my 60th birthday earlier this week, I heard a rumour that I can claim a third off all rail fares if I wave my passport at the ticket seller. I have not tried it yet, having mislaid my passport, and am reluctant to join the company of those who hold up the queue at every ticket office arguing about the price of their tickets.

It is true that the ordinary second-class return fare from Taunton to Paddington must, at £84, represent some sort of attempt at genocide. Others pay less than £25. If only British Rail would charge a reasonable fare for everyone, I would happily forget my status.

Now I am 60 all my friends are also urging me to accept the knighthood they feel I am bound to be offered by a government desperate to ingratiate itself with people like us. I feel sadly indisposed to do so, not so much because I grudge Tony Blair any credit he can claim for my birthday, but because I feel it might affront the many people who have paid good money for their knighthoods, or spent their lives in some boring job in order to secure this form of recognition at the end.

I think particularly of an acquaintance who, after many years of public-spirited service in the City of London, was awarded a knighthood on retirement and bought himself a small country property to enjoy the fruits of his labours. Rumour has it that he lost all his money in Lloyd's, which continues to ignore my advice against trying to do business in America. Now he counts his few remaining sheep, with only his knighthood to enjoy. It would not be a charitable act if I, too, accepted a knighthood as someone who has seldom set foot in the City of London and practically never eaten any of the disgusting luncheons they had to eat day after day, year after year.

20 November 1999

Same Again

It has been a wonderful week to be in England, with Cherie Blair's pregnancy, Neil Hamilton's most enjoyable libel action – which would be enough to keep the entire nation happy for a month or so – and Mohamed Fayed's defence.

Blair's hint that his baby was conceived at Balmoral may raise further anxiety about his suspected designs on the monarchy. It is no good pretending that William Hague rings the same bells with his announcement that he and his wife will delay starting a family, as having a baby is called in their circle, until Ffion has secured a grotesquely overpaid job recruiting other overpaid people. But the Tories are doing their best to keep us amused, what with Hamilton's libel action and Jeffrey Archer's disclosures about the *News of the World*.

Having dithered over the matter for some time, I have decided that were he to stand for mayor of London, after all, I would definitely vote for Jeffrey Archer – if only to register my disgust at the behaviour of the *News of the World* and the *Daily Star*, and the revolting hypocrisy of my colleagues on the *Observer* and the *Guardian*.

It would be nice to think that it was all the result of a simple mistake by the tabloids, confusing the identities of Monica Coghlan, the honest, hard-working prostitute, hired by the *News of the World*, and Andrina Colquhoun, the popular society figure and former friend of Lord Lucan, who worked as Archer's personal assistant. One can understand that the distinction between Coghlan and Colquhoun might be too difficult for these overworked people.

But even if the *Daily Star* made an honest error, that is no reason why it should be repaid any of the £500,000 in damages or £700,000 in legal expenses which this incompetence has cost it to date. Its motivation was to titillate its disgusting readers by raking over the private life of a public figure. If an element of malice can be deduced, even at this late stage, the newspaper should be prosecuted for criminal libel and fined the same amount again.

24 November 1999

Cheering Thought

Many years ago I used to see the occasional French film: long after all other film-makers had moved to colour, they were generally in black and white, very serious, and seldom with a cast of more than two or three. Perhaps they have improved since then, but I will never know, having given up going to the cinema altogether – with about 30 per cent of other cinemagoers – since they introduced the idiotic no-smoking rule. But one must fear the worst for the present standard of French films when one reads that their makers are demanding a ban on bad reviews in the French newspapers. Artists have always been sensitive to criticism but now they have banded together to denounce French reviewers as a "sadistic, arrogant, treacherous and cruel bunch of scribblers". Already heavily supported by their state, the French film industry is demanding a ban on any reviews appearing until the films are on release. They think this will attract more people to the cinema.

We may sympathise with them, but I fell they are being over-sensitive, as well as over-optimistic. The crucial perception which they lack is that nobody of any intelligence pays the slightest attention to anything which appears in the newspapers. This great truth was dramatically confirmed on Wednesday night, among the huge crowd who turned up at the new In and Out Club in St James's Square, to celebrate *Literary Review*'s seventh Bad Sex in Fiction Prize, lavishly sponsored by Hamlet cigars. It was awarded to A. A. Gill for an extract from his disturbing novel *Starcrossed* (Doubleday £9.29).

I had chosen as presenter of the prize a man who has been reviled in the tabloid press as a "cad", a "love-rat" and as "the most hated man in Britain", although my theory has always been that Major James Hewitt was the victim of social and sexual jealousy rather than genuine concern for the Royal kiddies. Be that as it may, and perhaps the crowd was not typical, consisting of the country's three or four hundred top literati and liberal intelligentsia, but when I announced his name as presenter, and Major Hewitt stepped forward, a cheer went up such as one normally hears only at football matches in the north of England.

27 November 1999

A Woman's Lot

When Glenda Jackson reveals that she has never been in a relationship with a man in which he hasn't raised his fists to her, I don't know whether this tells us more about the contemporary male or about Glenda Jackson.

Perhaps it is perfectly normal for men to punch women nowadays. If so, that is an example of things getting worse, like the trains, the roads, etc. On Monday, I listed three things which had definitely improved in my lifetime to set against all the things which have got worse: cars which start in the morning, watches which work and telephones. To this list I think we should add washing machines, which definitely make life easier.

But there can be no doubt that the woman's lot has got worse. Nowadays women are expected to earn money as well as having babies, rearing children, looking after the home, et cetera. They were cunningly allowed to persuade themselves that this was what they wanted to do. Next it appears they are also regularly punched by their menfolk. I imagine these developments are connected. Ms Jackson is right to complain. She would have been much better off as a respected housewife and mother in the old days.

1 December 1999

End of Oppression

The National Secular Society has declared January 1 a National Day of Lamentation to mark "two millennia of oppression from Christianity", and for the first time I begin to feel a certain sympathy.

Religion seems to be getting out of hand, although I have not yet heard Sir Cliff Richard trying to win his way to the top of the pops with the Lord's Prayer set to the tune of "Auld Lang Syne". I rather doubt that it is possible, since the words don't fit.

But in America things are much worse, with two presidential candidates vying with each other on the depth of their religiosity. One, George W. Bush, of Texas, is also a fanatical enthusiast for capital punishment. Last week he had an unconscious paranoid schizophrenic prisoner taken from a life support machine to be executed by lethal injection. Recently he entertained guests with his imitation of a condemned woman unsuccessfully pleading for her life.

We don't really want Bob Geldof or Sir Cliff Richard in any position of great power, but Malcolm Maclaren may be exactly what the nation needs for Major of London. Everything he says is sensible – that London has the worst public transport system in the world, and is one of the dullest places to live.

He proposes legalising brothels, decriminalisation of cannabis and selling alcohol in libraries – all admirable ideas, but I feel the churches could help by throwing their premises open as places for people to meet each other and pick up partners. Let this be their New Year message.

2 December 1999

2000

A Bad Idea

One piece of solid news which managed to break through the 10-day orgy of self-congratulation and parlour games strikes me as particularly gloomy. The Dutch are to ban non-European prostitutes in Holland.

For years I have been a keen supporter of the European idea, hoping it can save us from the animal lovers, child welfare experts, road safety enthusiasts, anti-smoking fanatics and other groups of screeching busybodies whom British politicians hold in such high esteem, as being the only people who will take them seriously.

But if the European Community proposes to follow Holland down this particular path, I will have to start listening sympathetically to all the saloon bar bores who tell me they are seriously worried about the euro. Those who have studied these things assure me that whereas English prostitutes are the worst in the world, when it comes to greed for money, offhandedness to their customers and the grudging inadequacy of their services, German and Dutch prostitutes are very close behind. Some of the best "sex workers" in the world, as well as the most reasonably priced, come from Africa and Asia, especially the Dutch East Indies.

It was in order to save our womenfolk from making fools of themselves in this way that we invented so many millions of jobs in child welfare, sanitary inspection, penal counselling, et cetera. Is all this good work to be undone through the crude demands of a few thousand greedy Dutch prostitutes?

3 January 2000

Not Inspired

Of all the various exhortations we have heard over the last week, I found Dr Carey's the least impressive. It was his opinion that the worship of fame is the predominant error in our society. Is that why fellow-prisoners planned to drug Jonathan Aitken, strip him naked and photograph him in compromising circumstances to sell to one of the popular newspapers? Is that why John Lennon was shot, George Harrison was stabbed and any successful popular entertainer has to surround himself with armed guards like some wartime quisling?

"Blessed are the famous, for they will enjoy the praise of men; blessed are those who are rich, because they will inherit the earth; blessed are the mighty, because they will become more powerful yet," intoned Carey, in what he obviously thought was a clever parody of the Sermon on the Mount.

In fact he is totally wrong. It is true that advances in communications and entertainment have created a large number of "celebrities", but these people are not particularly admired or even liked, let alone worshipped. Envy and hatred are more usual.

By pretending the opposite, Dr Carey may seem to be setting his cap at the spiteful, the envious and the unsuccessful in our midst, but I doubt that they will be much impressed by his string of local government platitudes.

"Love, then, rather than being wishy-washy and sentimental, is down to earth, relating to building community and caring for one another."

I am sorry, but there are hundreds of thousands, possibly millions of public employees trying to organise us into communities so they can patronise us and boss us around inside them. That is not the church's function.

5 January 2000

Lesson in Mercy

But is it, perhaps, what the Christian Church is reduced to in an age of unbelief? Islam has other problems but I was impressed and even rather moved by the story of the Iranian teenager who was left standing with a noose round his neck on a scaffold in Teheran while his family pleaded for mercy. Eventually, the father of his victim, who decided to exercise forgiveness, was carried away on the shoulders of a cheering crowd.

In Britain we no longer have public executions, of course, although there may well a certain demand for them. I wonder if a British crowd would be so merciful. One of the recognisable features of our new proletarian culture is its apparent lust for punishment. Any tuppenny ha'penny Tory MP can see his photograph grinning out of the newspapers, if he recommends a life sentence for some driving offence. No doubt the cheers would be even louder if he urged the death penalty.

The Iranian teenager's offence was that he had stabbed a 22-year-old Islamic militiaman who had ordered him to stop smoking in the street during Ramadan, when Muslims are expected to refrain from smoking and eating until sunset. A gallows was erected on the spot where the incident took place on December 13.

Many in the 3,000-strong crowd who had turned out to watch the execution in Imam Hussein Square joined the pleas for mercy. They cannot all have been fellow-smokers, although they may have agreed that anti-smoking fanatics can be intensely irritating. That is no sufficient reason for killing them, of course, but I feel we should all be grateful to the victim's father, Ali Mohebi, whose merciful decision is a credit to his family, his religion and his people.

5 January 2000

Lest We Forget

It was Charles Spencer, theatre critic for *The Daily Telegraph*, who spotted the notice inside Blair's shameful Dome and reproduced its wording for the benefit of those millions and millions of fellow-citizens who have no intention of going anywhere near the place: "Smoking is not big, is not clever, and is not allowed".

Nothing could better sum up the desire of the event's organisers – or, indeed, the desire of the entire new governing class – to treat the public as if it were composed of naughty 11-year-olds. Incompetence may seem to have been the main hallmark of the dreadful opening ceremony, but bossiness was also a key factor.

It was bossiness which required all the guests to be scanned or searched, creating three-day delays, and bossiness which ensured that all the bars were closed by the time guests arrived.

Even beyond the incompetence and bossiness which marked the opening, this monument to our national second-ratedness must be seen as a permanent reminder of the follies of over-government. The most glaring recent illustration of this was the great CJD scandal, almost unreported, where 2.5 million cows were slaughtered on the recommendation of "health experts" in the public service. There was never the faintest danger of a major CJD epidemic from BSE. The 48 deaths claimed in the past three years – including that of at least one vegetarian – have had another figure of "up to 10" further deaths added by the CJD industry, but this must be compared with the total of 153,037 deaths from pneumonia in the three-year period between 1997 and 1999.

The problem of what to do with about two million unnecessary public employees remains, but the cost of unemploying them would be prohibitive. Some might suggest they could be quietly put to death, but the answer to that is "no". Any political solution which involves killing people is wrong, as Mr Blair should have realised before he started bombing Kosovo. The only thing to do with this vast army is to ignore it. But then we have the ludicrous Greenwich Dome as a permanent reminder, lest we forget, lest we forget.

5 January 2000

What To Do With Them

Not many people seem to be much impressed by the billionaire Bill Gates's suggestion that every pupil in Britain should own its own laptop computer. Perhaps this lack of enthusiasm derived from the unworthy suspicion that Gates has other motives than pure philanthropy – he is chairman of Microsoft – but I think there is also a dawning awareness that the usefulness of these machines will be much smaller than has been claimed. Internet sales are already falling dramatically, and everybody is losing money on them.

Computers can be useful for reference purposes but they take a long time to concentrate on a particular inquiry – much longer than it would take in an ordinary library equipped with *Britannica*, *Chambers*, *Who's Who* and a score or so of other volumes. When used in administration they are capable of gross and potentially disastrous errors, as anybody who attempts to fly into Heathrow airport is liable to discover. My own feeling is that children should be kept away from these machines as much and as long as possible, but this hardly answers the great question of what should be done with the children. Someone has suggested that a million of them should be sent to the Dome, but that seems a cruel and unnatural punishment for unspecified crimes. Perhaps David Blunkett's 20,000 unemployable "mentors" could be sent on a course to teach them to spank teenagers, but one may doubt whether they would be any good at it.

I was interested to see a recent suggestion that children should be forcibly restrained in special seats whenever they travel by aeroplane. The official reason for this is that it might improve their chances of survival in the event of an air crash, but I can think of other reasons. On my recent trip to the Leeward islands by Air Jamaica, there were no children – the excellent Sandals chain of hotels refuses to take them – and it was a blissful experience. I wonder how many marriages have been ruined by this convention that children must be taken on holiday.

Perhaps they could be banned from aeroplanes altogether. If it is absolutely essential for them to travel, they could be put in the hold, where they might play happily with the passengers' pet animals who are also cruelly excluded from the main cabin, even when they are allowed to travel at all.

5 February 2000

From Outer Space

News of a secret union pact with the Labour Party to ensure that new Labour MPs are working class was apparently contained in papers leaked to a daily newspaper, although I have not seen the document concerned, and would dearly like to scrutinise its wording.

After the experience of Tony Blair, Old Labour may well insist that all ministers – if ever there is another Labour government – should be working class, too, speaking in pronounced regional accents which are incomprehensible to most of their fellow countrymen.

Even Conservatives generally agree that the working classes are best. Hitler, Stalin and Dr Harold Shipman were all from the middle classes, they say, while Jesus was a worker. There is no end to the nonsense people are prepared to talk on this subject. As for the English working classes, they are absolutely superb, unquestionably the best in the world. Labour has always been funny on this subject, as a study of *Who's Who* will reveal. Genuinely working-class ministers often given the impression of coming from a higher level of society while those from professional or privileged backgrounds are anxious to hint at humble origins.

Some ministers are reticent about their backgrounds to the point of secretiveness. Looking up David Blunkett, Blair's controversial Secretary for Education, to discover where he was educated, I was not particularly surprised to find that he mentions no schools by name, referring to "night school and day release" before settling at the Shrewsbury College of Technology. He then lists four places of further education, including the East Midlands Gas Board, before his glittering political career started on Sheffield City Council, at the age of 22.

What are we to make of this? He gives no indication of where he was born, or what his parents were called, if he had any, while also neglecting to name the woman he married and who bore him three sons. My own conclusion is that Blunkett may not have been of woman born, like the rest of us, but probably comes from Outer Space. Even so, and even if he came from Mars, I would be quite interested to know whether he was an upper-, lower- or middle-class Martian. It might decide whether I vote for him or not.

7 February 2000

Policy Statement

For as long as I can remember I have vaguely supported the idea that possession of cannabis should be decriminalised, but I have never much liked the stuff, and now the Police Foundation has come out with the same opinion I am beginning to have doubts.

We are often told how harmless it is, but I can only testify that those of my friends who have smoked a lot of it generally seem to be rather stupider than those who haven't.

They tend to talk in an irritating, affected way and much of what they say does not seem to make sense, although I do not know whether this is the result of the drug, or whether it merely tells us something about the sort of people who are drawn to it.

Mo Mowlam is plainly the most celebrated former marijuana smoker in the country. When she was asked on GMTV for a policy statement on decriminalisation, she said: "I never cancel anything in or anything out."

The *Guardian* interpreted this as holding out the prospect that cannabis could eventually be decriminalised, but I do not see how they reached this conclusion. Perhaps she was talking in a language comprehensible only to marijuana freaks, but I do not see that she is a good advertisement for the habit.

9 February 2000

Flags Needed

I wonder how many of us, as we talk about our daily business, have the faintest idea whether we are within 400 yards of a school. Yet this is to be the deciding factor on whether people go to prison or not when they are found carrying cannabis, if Mr Hague has his way.

Might we decide that he worries too much about children? Perhaps it is time he had some himself, or "started a family" as he would prefer. When I was his age, I already had four children and certainly did not spend my time fretting about the danger of people carrying cannabis within 400 yards of their various schools. He is not alone in this absurdity. The Government's White Paper on road safety proposes a 20 mph limit to be imposed around schools between 8.30 a.m. and 9 a.m. and from 3 p.m. to 5 p.m., when children are thought to be travelling to and from school (or not as the case might be). Nobody explains how the ordinary traveller between these crucial hours can know whether or not he is near a school.

The only solution must be to equip every school with a flagstaff – perhaps 200ft high – which motorists and cannabis carriers will be able to see before judging how far away it is. It should carry a huge flag saying "SCHOOL" or perhaps "KIDS" with a picture of a child, so that everyone will understand.

The reason Britain has one of the worst records for death and serious injury to child pedestrians is that British parents are unable to keep their children in order. Instead they form parents' groups to demand action from the Government against everyone else. One day the Government may realise how fatuous and oppressive these parents' groups are, but nobody dares point it out.

12 February 2000

Au Secours

British troops still shivering in tents through the terrible Kosovo winter for Mr Blair's little moment of folie de grandeur may take comfort from learning of a report in this week's *Lancet* which condemns the traditional British Army training run as outdated, pointless and dangerous.

These involve alternate fast marching and running for five or six miles, and were easily the worst ordeal of my military service. They left me with a hatred of sergeants which survives to this day and a deep suspicion of anyone who parades his working-class origins when in a position of authority.

No doubt others have similar prejudices. These ancient antagonisms make any form of leadership rather problematic in modern Britain. The Army seems to have got round it by appointing leaders with names that appear to be French, as with General de la Billière. Those in charge of the Dome have faced up to the problem by appointing someone to run it – Pierre-Yves Gerbeau, the car-parking expert – who is, quite frankly, a Frenchman.

Perhaps that is the answer to our leadership problem. When our brave soldiers return from Yugoslavia they may want to stage a coup and overthrow the government but it is hard to think who they can appoint to lead the country. The only prominent politician with a faintly French name would appear to be Norman Lamont. We may not have thought much about him as a possible national saviour, but I am sure he would be better than Blair.

14 February 2000

Twite's Point of View

Of all the insults suffered by farmers as their livelihood is destroyed by the envious urban majority, one of the most nauseating is surely to be found in the suggestion that they should devote their time to finding and succouring rare birds for the benefit of town dwellers who wish to come and gape at them. Particularly singled out is a Eurasian moorland finch, related to the linnet, called a "twite".

I am not sure I have ever seen a twite – its name derives from the noise it is said to make – and would probably have mistaken it for a sparrow if I had, although the cock is said to have pink feathers on its rump. Experts reckon there are only about 225 pairs left in this country and farmers are to be paid an extra £15.5 million in subsidies to protect them.

These same experts claim that the twite's numbers have been reduced as a result of changes in farming methods, although since they live on heather-covered moorland, I do not see how farming methods can affect them. Nor do I believe that anyone has counted them, or has the faintest idea how many there are in the whole country. It is nothing but self-important, bossy waffle, and I do not know why we put on respectful, sentimental faces to listen to it.

From time to time my front door rings in Somerset and there is someone with a pair of binoculars at the door asking whether I mind if he looks for wild birds on the property. In fact, the idea fills me with disgust. If there are any, they certainly do not wish to be stared at by wild-eyed Jesus freaks. I always ask them how I can be sure they are not collecting birds' eggs – soon to be an imprisonable offence. But if they are refused admission, they will probably pass a law making it an imprisonable offence to refuse admission to bird lovers. It might provide a useful occupation for farmers in these bad times to train their cattle, pigs, even sheep, to attack anyone carrying binoculars. I am sure the birds would be grateful.

19 February 2000

Errors of Judgment

Everything about the new Archbishop of Westminster seems almost too good to be true – he has not even claimed to admire the English football team, so far as I know – but I was disappointed to learn that he kept a fat volume of T. S. Eliot's poems above his desk.

There need be nothing morally objectionable in this. Eliot was capable of some good jokes and sharp observation amid all the obscurantism and showing off. Some of my friends claim to enjoy him; they argue that no poet writing in the modern idiom has been any better.

All this is true, but by displaying Eliot in this way, a man makes a statement about himself: that he hopes to be thought clever, well educated and reasonably modern. In fact, he is more likely to be proclaiming himself unadventurous, insecure and intellectually inert. I would respect a Catholic archbishop much more who displayed Betjeman.

Perhaps we should put it down to his age. Bishop Murphy-O'Connor is 67, and when he was a young man it was definitely considered smart to pretend to enjoy Eliot. We should not mock him for failing to follow the fashion. In exactly the same way, it was considered smart to admire the IRA in the 1960s, when John Lennon was apparently giving them money. We shall never know whether the money helped them murder a few extra Britons. It was a long time ago, and we all make errors of judgment when we are young.

23 February 2000

Going Downhill

Accustomed as we all are to seeing New Labour steal any ideas the Tories produce, many will have groaned to learn that Mr Hague is now copying Mr Blair to the extent of sitting down to dinner with Madonna. Or so we learnt on Thursday morning about the leader of the Opposition's eating arrangements for that evening.

Strict secrecy surrounded the gathering, we were told, which was planned to take place in the upper room of a London china shop. It was due to be attended also by two famous footballers, one called Vinnie Jones, the other called Graeme Le Saux. I wonder if Graeme would make a suitable next leader of the Conservative Party. He has the right sort of name.

So secret was the occasion that although we were told that the guests would be welcomed with champagne served in multi-coloured hand-blown flutes, and even how much the dinner plates cost – £70 each – we are not told what they were going to eat. This seems a shame. None of us can be much interested in what Madonna said to Mr Hague, or vice versa, but British food has seriously improved in the past 10 years, and I am surprised that our politicians, who are always looking for something to boast about on our behalf – our football, our cricket, our Dome or what you will – never mention food.

Good restaurant food used to be a London phenomenon with few exceptions, but now it has spread nearly everywhere. Recently I learnt that the head chef of our local hostelry in Taunton – the Castle Hotel – earns something like £40,000 a year, plus a lavish expense account to eat in other restaurants for new ideas. He was in dispute with his proprietor, who complained he spent too much time performing on television for *Ready, Steady, Cook*.

There can be no doubt that we are becoming a food culture, as the French used to be. Parisians claimed to be very shocked when they discovered that a Scottish restaurant in Paris was serving deep-fried Mars bars with a cinnamon sauce. Perhaps that is what Hague, Madonna and the footballers chose. But the most interesting discovery, it seems to me, is that there is a Scottish restaurant in Paris. A much more disturbing piece of news is that Rome's famous and elegant Café de Paris is to become a hamburger bar. What has happened to the Italians?

26 February 2000

Exciting

In Somerset, where all these matters are energetically discussed, debate on the parents' historic vote in Ripon was somewhat obscured by a general uncertainty about where exactly Ripon is. Some said North Yorkshire, but a robust school of thought put it in Kent, and in the heated arguments which followed the point about selectivity in education was rather lost.

Most other discussion has centred on the question of whether Ian Brady should continue to be force-fed by a tube through the nose, or whether, after 35 years in prison, he should be allowed to die, if that is what he wishes to do. Of more immediate concern is the debate about whether men should be required to take off their hats when inside Exeter Cathedral. The dean has decided they should not, suggesting that St Paul's instructions (I Corinthians 11) are now out of date, since women no longer cover their heads:

"There are some kinds of headgear which are regularly worn at all times, notable among which is the baseball cap . . . We therefore instruct our stewards not to approach or remonstrate with people who choose to wear hats in church. In particular, they should not approach or remonstrate with people young or old who wear baseball caps."

The dean goes on to point out how embarrassing it would be if someone ordered to remove his baseball cap in church had been receiving chemotherapy, although this had never happened in Exeter. Perhaps he should insist that all men should be required to wear baseball caps in church. Isn't modern Christianity exciting?

13 March 2000

Lunch Time

Rather than brood about the terrible bus crash in Kericho, Western Kenya, where two buses collided head-on, killing 100 people, it is comforting and restful to read about the Prince of Wales's pillow-fight in Norfolk 41 years ago.

One can even learn with equanimity about the attack on Prince Philip in Tasmania with a badly aimed tomato. Compared with the excesses of the French Revolution, or the American War of Independence, this seems a fairly mild incident.

There is a huge comfort to be derived from the new acceptance of our beloved Royal Family. Perhaps they are all we have left of our extraordinary past when, as a small nation led by its aristocracy and educated middle class, we civilised half the world.

Even so, our Royals must bear in mind the tremendous responsibility involved in their position. When the Prince of Wales announced he was giving up eating luncheon for Lent, he probably thought he was setting a good example in Lenten observance.

Perhaps he was not aware of the alarming tendency to give up luncheon altogether. Those who went to work in the City of London traditionally did it for the luncheons. Now they do it for the money, and all power has shifted to faceless, incompetent accountants, many of whom may be vegetarians or worse.

That is why nothing works in England any more, the simplest proposals are frustrated by the stupidity, ignorance and bossiness of the accountants in charge. I hope I will not be accused of sensationalism if I suggest that this repudiation of lunch – one of the two most important meals of the day – threatens the end of civilisation as we know it. What else has life to offer? Wales must think again.

1 April 2000

Last Literary Lion

I met Alex Comfort only once or twice. He seemed a thoroughly genial person, and I enjoyed his son Nick Comfort's account of him in Thursday's newspaper – so unlike the run of "My father, a drunk and a bore" which seems to be the new fashion among children of my friends. Dr Comfort may never be named as a literary lion of the 20th century, but for at least a decade he had a profound influence on attitudes. Better than that, his *The Joy of Sex* (1973) gave us an optimism, a degree of hope, for which we should all be grateful. For a time at least – until bitter experience proved to the contrary – it seemed that the key to human happiness might indeed lie in free, uncomplicated sex (what is nowadays called sexual promiscuity) with anyone who felt in the mood.

While Dr Comfort was working on his first major treatise, *Sex in Society* (1963), his contemporary Anthony Burgess was completing *A Clockwork Orange* (1962). Burgess definitely has a claim to be considered as one of the last literary lions of the 20th century. The film of *A Clockwork Orange* (1972), which appeared a few months before Dr Comfort's magnum opus, *The Joy of Sex*, has just been revived in London.

When I went on Wednesday, the small theatre in the Odeon, Marble Arch, was less than half full, but I urge anyone with a strong enough stomach to go and see it. Never can two writers have had a more different message for the world. Where Comfort preached the hope of joy and renewal through sex, Burgess argues that sex is no more than one other outlet for the selfishness, brutality, power mania and often sadism which are the main characteristics of human nature.

They are both wrong, of course. But while we welcome Comfort's wishful agenda, knowing it to be false, we are reluctant to consider Burgess's more austere proposals. I feel we should confront both. There may be no ultimate truth about human nature, but it must part of a writer's job to search for it. Otherwise we are left with Jackie Collins and Anthony Powell.

1 April 2000

Prison Charity

It is not fashionable to show any sympathy for Jonathan Aitken, the former cabinet minister who is now recovering from six months in prison for perjury, after an unsuccessful libel action against the *Guardian*. Some of the antipathy may arise from the fact that he is a Tory, an old Etonian born into a famous and rich family. One must also admit that it was extremely foolish for a journalist to sue another newspaper. The libel law is designed to keep journalists in their place. If they think they have been wronged, they should seek their revenge by other means.

Even so, I feel that Aiken has acquitted himself well. Passages which I have read from his book *Pride and Perjury*, published by HarperCollins, make me rather admire him.

It is quite tough for white-collar offenders to find themselves locked up in prisons which are bursting at the seams to accommodate all the violent thieves, killers, rapists and other criminals who may be products of a less privileged background. The *Guardian*'s gloating vindictiveness must have turned at least a few stomachs among its dismal readers.

Even journalists are capable of human decency. I was strangely moved to learn that David Astor, 88-year-old former editor of the *Observer*, sends Myra Hindley a sum of money every month, largely because everyone hates her and he feels sorry for someone who has already served 33 years of a life sentence. Others might like to make a similar gesture to other prisoners in the same sort of circumstances. This would be an unpopular charity but a worthwhile one. If Mr Aitken will organise it, I would be delighted to help.

3 April 2000

Don't Laugh

It is gloomy news that laughter clubs, introduced to India as a way of keeping healthy five years ago, are to be set up in Britain. Various medical claims are made for the practice – that it lowers blood pressure, eases asthma and triggers the release of endorphins – so members meet out of doors in the early morning to have a good laugh together before going to work.

Artificial laughter may be available for radio comedians as a way of informing their audience that they have just make a joke, but real laughter, celebrating happiness, humour and friendship, has occupied a noble place in human relations until now – especially, perhaps, among Englishmen, as a way of breaking down their traditional reserve.

It will be a terrible shame if this sacred activity has been kidnapped, like so many others, to the grisly cause of health. If laughter is to be made available on the National Health, it must add to Frank Field's case for sending as many NHS patients as possible to India.

Alternatively, if these people are genuinely worried about their health, they should be told to eat lettuce and fruit and fresh vegetables, avoiding fat, sugar, red meat and excessive alcohol. That is all anyone needs to know about health nowadays.

My great terror is that people will start laughing on my weekly train from Taunton to London on Monday morning. Since First Great Western, the miserably incompetent company which is still allowed to operate trains from Penzance and Plymouth, allowed itself to be taken over by the prigs and perverts of the anti-smoking lobby, and since their trains are almost always late, when they have not been cancelled altogether, there might seem to be nothing for the unfortunate passengers to do but laugh. That will be the beginning of the end.

12 April 2000

Not To Be Encouraged

Damien Hirst deserves the support of us all when he announces his intention to boycott the opening of the Tate Modern next week. So shall I. It will celebrate the work of a group called Young British Artists (YBAs), among whom Hirst himself used to be numbered. With age, he may have learnt that these people are not to be encouraged. The Modern Movement in the arts enjoyed a short moment when people thought it daring and even exciting, but now it has become a crashing bore.

Even without supposing that British artists might be able to produce something worthwhile if they were not encouraged to produce drivel, we can see that Modern Art as it survives has become the currency of dishonest craftsmen, unscrupulous dealers and crooked academics.

Perhaps there might be room for a gallery in the Victoria and Albert to cover this painful and strangely drawn-out episode in the history of art, but the idea of building a new gallery, a new museum, to prolong its life must be seen as a betrayal of human intelligence.

Britain is not alone in this absurdity, of course. The Romans propose a 70ft high inverted ice-cream cone on the banks of the Tiber by a sculptor called Arnaldo Pomodoro, or Arnold Tomato. Let us show the world that we were the first to come to our senses.

6 May 2000

Just an Indication

Nobody has a good word to say for the May Day rioters, and it is hard to think of one. The defacement of Churchill's statue was as babyish as the defacement of the Cenotaph was unpleasant, but I cannot feel quite so indignant about the destruction of a McDonald's hamburger bar.

Perhaps the rioters felt that these burger bars represent the surrender of Britain and Europe to the American culture, but there is excellent food to be found in the United States; one need think only of the oysters of the East Coast or the soft-shell crabs. If we really wish to protest about the Atlantic takeover, we should destroy our television sets.

By some reports, the attack on McDonald's involved Matthew MacDonald, the Etonian son of a university professor. Poor man, one can see how, if he did not like the burgers concerned, he would have found the burger bars apparently named after him particularly annoying. I hope the counts are merciful. He is only a teenager.

Next we learn that Ely Cathedral had also been attacked by teenagers and children as young as 11. Three stained glass windows were broken in the 900-year-old building, and the bishop's greenhouse was destroyed. Next day, a youth smashed open a collection box. The Dean of Ely made light of these matters, describing them as fairly minor: "It is just an indication of trends."

No doubt he is right, but others may find it an alarming trend that so many young people feel the desire to break things, this urge to vandalism. It is not confined to this country. Even in Russia, we learn, vandals have attacked the huge state of Mother Russia which rises 230 feet above the mass graves at Stalingrad. Is there something seriously wrong with young people today?

Apart from putting them all in prison, the only thing we can do is try to direct their attention away from great works of art and historic monuments. There are plenty of shops selling baseball hats, beefburgers and that sort of thing.

8 May 2000

Women at War

When I last discussed the plinth in Trafalgar Square, which has been happily empty for 150 years, I urged that it should be left empty. This was unacceptable to the hyperactive philanthropists who seek to make their mark on every aspect of our society. They set up an "advisory group" to canvas opinions and make recommendations. John Mortimer, who led the proceedings, is a kind and good man whose influence on our times has been entirely benevolent, but on this occasion he has made a terrible mistake, preferring the worst of all the options.

This is to use the plinth as an outdoor exhibition, changing the objects displayed every eight months. We will have a procession of modern rubbish which is not only boring to look at but also, as often as not, quite ugly. Worse than this, it will encourage these lazy artists to suppose there is still vitality – and money – to be extracted from the dead embers of the modern movement. In fact, we have just opened Tate Modern for exactly this purpose.

During the debate, it was suggested that a statue should commemorate the women's role in our last war. I opposed this suggestion at the time, thinking that womanhood would not be flattered by a monument showing Land Girls, Wrens, Wracs or Waafs.

Then I fell to brooding. Most women did not wear uniform in the war. They stayed at home suffering from a shortage of food and clothing and also, although it may not be fashionable to say so now, from the absence of their menfolk. No subject is better for sculpture than the nude woman. Let us have a group of slim, unclothed women comforting each other in their husbands' absence. But of course nobody will adopt this suggestion. We are ruled by a dictatorial caucus of ignorant philistines.

15 May 2000

349

Transmogrified

With one thing and another, I have not had time to visit the Funeral Services Exhibition 2000 in Birmingham's National Exhibition Centre, and so cannot claim to have seen the much-maligned statue of Diana, Princess of Wales by Andrew Walsh which was unveiled there 10 days ago.

It will remain at the Bloxwich headquarters of Mr Walsh's company, called Walsh Monumental Masons, until they can find another home for it. Oddly enough, although the dress is unappealing and the overall design rather strange, it is beautifully carved – the sculpting was done in India – and would make an unusual but quite amiable decoration in a large white hall, such as we have at Combe Florey.

I would be happy to give it a home, but I think I would play down its connection with the Princess of Wales, for fear of offending the Spencers. Instead it would serve as a memorial to my beloved Pekingese, Leo, who died and was buried on Friday at the immense age of 15 (say 105 in human terms). On the next day, I observe that Cherie Blair gave birth to a son called Leo. If Leo Blair is a reincarnation of my Pekingese, as seems likely, his mother will find him intelligent, affectionate, loyal and utterly fearless, but she might be well advised to keep him away from cats.

22 May 2000

His Main Discovery

Many years ago, even before he became editor of the *Sun* in 1969, I once had lunch with Larry Lamb, who has just died as a knight bachelor at 70. I cannot remember why we had lunch together, or what he wished to discuss, but nothing ever came of it, and after this great gap of time I cannot even remember what we ate.

But Lamb certainly will be remembered – one might say he has won a place in the history of journalism – as the man who introduced bare-breasted Page Three Girls to the *Sun*, thereby ensuring the success of the newspaper and the continuing wealth of its proprietor, Rubert Murdoch.

Lamb himself was modest about his contribution to the social history of our times, saying: "If we hadn't emancipated the nipple, I'm sure some other paper would have done it before long."

Perhaps he is right, but one cannot help noticing that it is nearly 30 years since Lamb emancipated the nipple, and nobody yet has succeeded in emancipating the female groin, at any rate so far as the mass market is concerned.

One imagines that exactly the same objections would be heard as were raised when Lamb started showing bare breasts on a daily basis – that it insulted and cheapened womanhood, that it encouraged promiscuity, not to say sexual violence, and might have a terrible effect on children or young people. Exactly the same religious and women's groups would raise the objections, and the general public would show exactly the same indifference, with scarcely a single voice in support.

On that basis, as I say, Mr Murdoch has been able to show us his topless women for nearly 30 years. No doubt extravagant celebrations are planned for the 30th anniversary later this year.

But why have the topless ladies never made way for what we call, in the trade, the "full frontal"? The answer, I think, is that the full frontal has been tried from time to time, and it doesn't seem to work. Far from attracting male buyers, on balance it discourages them. Apart from a minority of enthusiasts, people are liable to be embarrassed by the sight of an unknown woman with no clothes on, while being quite happy to inspect her breasts.

I do not know whether this should be seen as a sign of chivalry, or whether it should be seen as the result of some psychological impairment. In either case, it is an interesting discovery to have made. Lamb's life was less pointless than many.

22 May 2000

Back to Work

Whenever I find myself in the comfort and ease of my favourite health farm, called Shrublands, near Ipswich, I make a determined effort to watch television and join the human race. It might also give me something to talk about if ever I meet Mr Blair, but unfortunately, it seems worse than ever. Independent Television appears to be staffed and presented by sub-humans, while the BBC has been Dyked down to a level of permanent Left-wing lower-class rubbish. Or so it seems.

Instead I turn to a study of *Time*, the unusual treatise by Alexander Waugh which has just been published in America by Carroll and Graf amid scenes of what can only be described at hysteria. The book, which is a masterpiece, sold more than 10,000 hardback copies from Headline in this country despite receiving only two or three notices – although one of them, admittedly, was by Patrick Moore in the *Literary Review*.

The reason why the English literary establishment ignored the book was only in part because literary folk tend to be timid and jealous and only quite intelligent. The main reason is that *Time* is an extraordinary book, unlike any which has been written before or since. It cleverly produces huge amounts of information in a witty monologue which is also highly enjoyable.

Since the death of the novel and the discrediting of poetry, this type of prose, using irony and wit to impart condensed information, may become the new literary art form. A pity if they say the Americans thought of it first.

31 May 2000

Edinburgh Man

Those few people in Britain who follow politics owe Gordon Brown a vote of thanks for his magnificently ill-judged leadership bid. The resulting outbreak of class warfare kept everyone happy and amused for a week, but I fear it spoilt any chances he might have had of succeeding Tony Blair as Prime Minister.

His argument, stripped of its fancy oratory, was that Blair had no business to be Prime Minister because he went to Oxford, a snobbish institution associated with public schools, whereas he, Gordon Brown, had been to Edinburgh University and was obviously the better man for that reason.

John Prescott, 12 years older and already Deputy Prime Minister, soon wiped the floor with him. Prescott, having failed his 11-plus, had to make do with Hull University, and obviously had more right to feel indignant about Laura Spence, the Newcastle teenager who was refused a place at Oxford. So he singled out Newcastle University for attack. Unfortunately, Newcastle had actually offered a place to Laura Spence to study medicine, but she had turned it down.

They have both got it wrong. The way to conduct a class war in this country is to say: "Oh, I say old chap, by gum," in a posh voice, and everybody will laugh and be on your side. It is a waste of time to look for serious points and reasons. If Brown and the rest of them have any interest in education they should address themselves to the fact that our state schools are a national disgrace. Nobody must be allowed to forget the devastating statistic that a child in an independent school is 10 times more likely to gain three "As" at A level than a child in a state school.

Otherwise, he should stick to his job of looking after our money. I observe there are not nearly enough £5 notes in circulation. I had to buy three new pairs of trousers on Saturday because the pockets had worn out. No doubt he makes smaller profits from printing £5 notes than the £10 or £20 variety. They probably taught him that in Edinburgh.

5 June 2000

Learn from a Dove

Every Whit Sunday for the past 510 years, the citizens of Orvieto, in central Italy, have celebrated Pentecost with a ceremony that involves a dove in a wooden frame representing the Third Person of the Holy Trinity descending from Heaven.

The dove is not harmed by this treatment, although it may suffer a brief moment of anxiety. In fact, it survives to be reserved as a semi-sacred animal for the rest of its natural life. Visitors to Italy may have been puzzled by the ceremony, but they have generally had the good manners to accept it as a quaint local custom.

Now, with the regrettable spread of foreign travel, it has come to the attention of an English group calling itself the Catholic Study for Animal Travel. They demand that the Italians stop this ancient practice or use an imitation dove. Orvieto has refused, from ordinary citizens to mayor and archbishop, Cardinal Grandoni. Townspeople are said to be arming themselves with eggs and tomatoes for use against these English *animalisti* on Sunday.

Deborah Jones, general secretary of the study circle, said: "I know people who are so disgusted that they are considering leaving the Catholic Church if it is not stopped."

Let them leave if that is how they feel. I only wish I had time to take some eggs and tomatoes to Orvieto to speed them on their way.

7 June 2000

Oh Susanna

It is curious how race relations seem to attract the most ignorant, as well as the stupidest and bossiest, people in Britain. Observing that a troupe of traditional Morris dancers in Carlisle plastered their faces with charcoal and animal fat in imitation of poachers as they have done for 200 years, the city council stepped in and ordered them to remove the charcoal.

"What if a black family visited Carlisle and the kids saw these gangs with their faces blacked up singing 'Oh! Susanna'?" demanded the complainant, who works for the Carlisle Council for Voluntary Services. The answer, I suspect, is that the black family would be absolutely delighted.

It was a good-natured occasion and the incident illustrates a happy marriage of two cultures. "Oh! Susanna" is a good song and familiar to everyone in this country. The make-up makes it jollier. Would it be forbidden for a black group to paint their faces white for a joke and sing "Drink to Me Only With Thine Eyes"? The complainant added that Stephen Collins Foster, who wrote "Oh! Susanna", was considered in his lifetime to be a pro-slavery writer. This may have impressed the Carlisle City Council, but it is absolute drivel. Foster, who died at 37, only visited the South once, in 1852, and spent most of his life in Pittsburgh, where he was born, attending Negro church meetings and minstrel shows, learning their songs also from Negro labourers at the Pittsburgh warehouse where he worked for a time. Which of his songs is supposed to show approval of slavery: "Swanee River"?, "Camptown Races"?, "Jeanie With the Light Brown Hair"?, "Beautiful Dreamer"?

I suppose there will always be some residual awkwardness between the races in our multiracial society so long as there is a race relations industry to create and foster it.

12 June 2000

Getting Away

I have never been to Paisley, and it is now on my list of places to avoid at all cost. Last week a 16-year-old girl in Paisley called Louise Burns found a £1,000 prize token in a packet of Golden Wonder potato crisps, and refused to share the money with her five brothers and sister.

Dorothy, her mother, who pointed out that she had paid for the crisps in the first place, ordered her to do so, and when she refused, threw her out of the family home.

"I couldn't believe my own daughter could be so selfish. She is not welcome in the house until she apologises."

But Louise, who has gone to stay with her grandmother, Jeanette, is standing firm. No doubt there is something to be said for both sides, but the reason she has given is that she wishes to take a trip to America with her boyfriend, and that is the real pathos of the story.

Why should a healthy 16-year-old girl from Paisley wish to go to a country that is crawling with terrible diseases, where she will be sexually assaulted and the police will simply laugh in her face and search her for drugs? Paisley must be a truly terrible place.

19 June 2000

Plugging the Dyke

Three-quarters of the population probably have only the faintest idea of who "Greg" Dyke is or what he does. He is not to be confused with Geordie Greig, who is editor of *Tatler* and has never done anyone any harm. Dyke is intensely irritating, partly because everything he thinks is nasty, stupid and wrong, and partly because of the way he says it.

As director-general of the BBC he tells us he is not going to abandon all factual programming or news on BBC1. "It's much more a case of shifting emphasis, rather than a fundamental shift," he explains.

"By the end of the decade, if the Government does what it says it's going to do, every home will be a digital home. We have to look at how people in digital homes behave once they get an electronic programme guide."

What on earth does this mean? Is any of us fully digital? If the question means anything, it means do we have all five fingers on each hand? As it happens I don't, having lost one in Cyprus, but that has nothing to do with "Greg" Dyke. If I had 100 fingers on each hand, I still would not wish to see any of his boring, lower-class rubbish on television.

Of course there may be room for Dyke in the BBC, as a canteen waiter serving horrible food with an oily smirk. But he would certainly ask too much money for the job and complain about the tips.

24 June 2000

Better Watch Football

Research commissioned by the Arts Council has produced the "surprising result" that Britain's working class now prefers the arts to football. Only the upper and middle classes are turning to football, they say. "Gerry" Robinson, chairman of the Arts Council, goes further: "Even in lower-income groups, half the adults participate in the arts," he says. Nobody will be surprised to learn that the purpose of this was to urge an increase of £100 million a year in government funding for the arts in general, and the Arts Council in particular. I am sorry to take what might be seen as a negative, even a philistine, attitude to this. Whether it is the result of the new working-class interest in the arts, or whether this was what attracted the working class to the arts in the first place, the sad truth remains that modern British art is nearly all rubbish.

To give it more money will be a crime against aesthetics as well as a further blow to our national pride. Anybody who doubts my judgment should visit the Turner Prize exhibits at the Tate.

A great anxiety is to see the same thing happening in the commercial world of letters. On Sunday we read of a nine-year-old Californian girl who had received an advance of nearly £66,000 for a book of poems, apparently on the strength of one called "Beautiful Girls".

"Beautiful Girls/ are the dwelling instruments/ of the human heart/ Girls are as beautiful inside/ as they are on the outer layer/ of their bodies." Can nobody in HarperCollins see that this is drivel? Will people really buy it? Would they not be happier watching football?

28 June 2000

A Worse Insult

A new academic study of the works of Enid Blyton, by David Rudd, *Enid Blyton and the Mystery of Children's Literature* (Macmillan, £40), argues that the gollywog was not originally intended to represent a black person. However the nation's professional "anti-racists" fastened on it as a symbol of racism, and once it had been given a new, negative meaning in the public mind, it had to be banned.

Of the children to whom Dr Rudd showed his gollywogs, none identified them as a black person. However, Mr Darcus Howe, the black television personality, takes a different line: "English people never give up. Gollywogs have gone and should stay gone. They appeal to white English sentiment and will do so until the end of time."

I have never had strong feelings about the gollywog, and would certainly not wish to offend Mr Howe or any other black Englishmen, however little they might resemble the child's doll.

In fact, the only child's character that ever caused me anxiety was Eeyore, the donkey in *Winnie the Pooh*. Anybody can see that he is intended as a cruel caricature of a Liverpudlian, with his permanent melancholy and his detachable tail. I do not know why A. A. Milne should have chosen to insult the citizens of Liverpool in this way – perhaps he had an unhappy experience there as a child – but it says much for the Liverpudlian generosity of spirit that they never demanded the book should be banned. Perhaps they never noticed.

Now I am off to Tuscany for a few days, and will not be appearing here until July 12.

5 July 2000

A Suitable Punishment

But would an alternative government be any better? Mr Hague can promise that he will reduce taxation until he is blue in the face, but no one will believe him. It is well known that the only thing which attracts people to government is the promise of exerting power and spending other people's money. Even if he manages to cut some services, he will find thousands of new ways to spend the money.

The only important policy difference between Tories and New Labour nowadays is in the matter of punishment. The Tories really believe in it, and we must ask ourselves how this enthusiasm can be brought to solve some of the problems we all face in New Britain.

I mentioned the horrors of air travel, but trying to move anywhere in London is just as bad. Stuck for nearly an hour in a cab approaching the West End on Monday, I was interested to hear the cab driver confirm my suspicion that these jams are deliberately created by the traffic authorities, using a combination of semi-abandoned road works and contradictory traffic signals, in order to discourage people from driving in London.

The Conservatives will have to do something about the fact that all traffic is at a standstill in central London for much of the day, but what can they do, the cab driver asked. They will have to identify the right people to punish, and then decide on a suitable form of punishment. The villains of the story are the chief traffic executives and their planing officers in local government.

"How should they be punished?" he asked. Stuck in the back of a cab with this boring, aggressive and rather unpleasant driver, I found the ideas flowed quite easily. The planners should be taken to Hyde Park Corner at rush hour and skinned alive, I said. Then they should be hung upside down by their feet and eviscerated so that their bowels droop over their faces and suffocate them. At any rate, that is what I told the cab driver, but I would not wish to press the suggestion, or Mr Hague might think I was after his job.

15 July 2000

Who Wants the Grammar?

It is all very well for the Lord Chancellor to demand that civil servants should use proper English in their public pronouncements and internal memoranda, but proper English has not been taught in many schools for a long time. The moronic orthodoxy has been that pupils should be taught to be creative, rather than literate. It was well summed up by the reaction of David Hart, General Secretary of the National Association of Head Teachers, who described the National Literacy Centre plans for a grammar textbook as "a waste of tax-payers' money".

He added: "I think the answer is for the Government to look again at its National Literacy Strategy and change it so it gives a greater opportunity to concentrate on creative writing. All we have is a Gradgrind literacy strategy which teachers will rebel against."

By "creative writing" he presumably means novels, short stories and "poetry", but the reason teachers will rebel against teaching grammar is that so many of them have never learnt it. Formal grammar disappeared from the curriculum in most places in the 1970s. Now the only hope is to recruit teachers abroad, where proper English is still taught and where they might not have heard about our teenagers or even our five- and six-year-old "kids". The problem with them is partly that all forms of discipline are completely alien to them, partly that any attempt to impose it is liable to end in violence from an angry father at best, criminal prosecution and a prison sentence at worst.

Who, under those circumstances, would wish to be a teacher? The truth of the matter is that there is a strong reaction in this country against any form of education or learning. Far better let the New Britons concentrate on sport, at which they are also rather bad.

7 August 2000

Don't Blame the Kids

The Chief Constable of Hampshire, Mr Paul Kernaghan, is happy to inform the world in general, and Americans in particular, that his own province of Hampshire and the Isle of Wight is "an extremely safe place to live". I have not heard anyone describe Devon or Somerset, where I spend my weekends, in those terms very recently. Taunton and Tiverton, in particular, are usually held up as centres of violent crime.

Mr Kernaghan, who was answering an American television claim that Britain is a "violent urban jungle", produced figures in support of his case, showing an average of only 48 violent crimes a day. That seems a reasonable number, but the area of West London around Shepherds Bush, where I spend my weekdays, has indeed become exactly such a jungle. It is hard to meet anyone without a friend or acquaintance who has been beaten up and robbed in the past six months. The chief trouble comes from gangs of teenagers who will first insult any pedestrian at random, then rob and kick the victim to the ground before running away. Locals complain that the police show little interest in these incidents, and it would be easy to attribute this to their over-riding anxiety about parking controls but I think on this occasion it would be unfair.

The police have only to lay hands on a teenager – especially a female teenager – in order to restrain its disgusting behaviour, for the whole area, led by the child's parents, to rise in arms. It may be hard to feel sentimental about the case of Jean Lyons, 19, and her sister Kelly, 17, who have just been found guilty of battering an 87-year-old widow who lived in the same block on their North London estate in the course of a robbery. The widow died six days later. They were caught because they bragged about what they had done.

But there is a general sentimentality nowadays about children or "kids" which I find as nauseating as it is incomprehensible. Travelling in the Tube recently, I saw a middle-aged couple stand up to give their seats to a boy and girl of about eight whom they did not appear to know. The two children sat down in the seats without a word of thanks. I wonder what those children will be like when they are grown up.

19 August 2000

Look at Kenya

Those of us who live in the gentler, more liberal atmosphere of southern England may have been distressed to learn that drunken Leeds United supporters were to be found giving the Nazi salute in Munich before the European Champions' League qualifying match on Wednesday. Thirteen Leeds United supporters were arrested and charged with drunkenness. Poorer Britons will always tend to get drunk whenever they go abroad, as I never tire of pointing out, because of the appalling cost of drink in England. Soon, they will not even be able to afford to drink the petrol in this country. If there is any comfort to be derived from this shameful episode, it may be in the assurance that Leeds United fans have studied European history. All too often people in the north of England will deny any knowledge of Hitler, let alone Himmler, Ribbentrop and the rest of them.

I wonder how many of our rulers have paused to reflect about the Boxer Uprising in China, which ended 100 years ago this week, when troops from Britain, France, Germany, Japan, Russia and the United States entered and occupied Peking. This was after gangs of Chinese had roamed the country for two years, killing all foreigners as well as Christian or English-speaking Chinese.

Rather similar conditions seems to be developing in Kenya at the moment. Our government expresses a great lack of concern about the British Kenyans, but many Britons have gone there on holiday at this time of year, and Gordon Brown might reflect that China was required to pay a huge indemnity at the end of the day.

The point about Kenya is not so much that white farmers are being expropriated by blacks, with the approval of the Kenyan government, and a few have been murdered. It is that more than three million people are facing starvation in an abominable drought. Incompetence and corruption prevent most of the aid getting through.

Politicians love sending troops and bombers to remote parts as a means of feeling powerful and important. Might they not win even greater glory for themselves by rescuing Kenya than by continuing to bomb Iraq for no reason that anybody can understand?

26 August 2000

Welcome Reminder

The terrifying power of organisations such as the RSPCA, which will soon take over every aspect of public life, is well illustrated by threats to ban the new Brad Pitt film, which shows a hare coursing meeting.

In the finished version, the hare escapes, but there were rumours that in the course of filming, some hares might have been injured or even killed. Columbia Pictures agreed to let the RSPCA see a preview, but the society complains it was not present at the actual filming.

In America, an organisation called People for the Ethical Treatment of Animals, or Peta – some sort of equivalent to our own RSPCA, I imagine – has started a campaign to discourage people from drinking milk. It is against the consumption of any animal product, but where milk is concerned, it has chosen to promote the idea that it gives you prostate cancer.

Rudolph Giuliani, the mayor of New York who withdrew from the New York senate race when he was diagnosed as suffering from prostate cancer, has been the particular butt of these ethical animal lovers. Posters in Wisconsin show him with a milk moustache over the message: "Got milk? Got Prostate Cancer?"

I have never much cared for milk myself, but I am glad things have not yet gone so far in this country. In fact I was delighted to learn of a restaurant in the East End of London which has started serving horsemeat – a welcome indication that we are still Europeans, despite the many charms of America.

28 August 2000

Attracting the Young

So desperate is Dundee University to attract new students that it has sent out 20,000 posters and postcards showing pictures of a bra, condom and pints of beer to possible applicants. The university's directory of admissions explains: "Our research focus group tells us it's what young people respond to."

I wonder if the research focus group has got it right. A different questionnaire sent to 2,250 13- to 15-year-olds at 21 schools reveals that many girls want the age of consent raised to 18. Nearly one in five boys has the same wish. There would appear to have been a general withdrawal, not to say revulsion, from sex among the young. It will be sad if the Dundee University campaign, on which they have spent £200,000 attracts only a handful of illiterate sex maniacs. A greater problem than finding students is to find teachers who understand English. Few of them, apparently, have been told about the adverb, and resent any suggestion that they should learn. The general secretary of the National Association of Head Teachers feels that Ofsted's suggestion for teaching grammar would be "a waste of taxpayers' money", and demands "a greater opportunity to concentrate on creative writing".

Meanwhile, would-be recruits have other obstacles put in their path. A woman in her late thirties with a very good English degree at a famous university was told that her application to a teacher-training college would not be considered unless she produced the actual GCSE certificates she had lost about 10 years ago.

The university which awarded the certificates claimed to have lost its filing system, while the university she attended, which had inspected her certificates at the time, refused to produce details of them, invoking the sacred words "data protection". Need anybody be surprised that we enter the new school year with an estimated 4,000 teaching vacancies in secondary schools?

11 September 2000

Now We Can Speak

It is sad that Lever Brothers plan to stop production of soap bars next year at their Port Sunlight factory on Merseyside after more than 100 years, although they will be made elsewhere, and the 125 jobs lost will be no more than a drop in the Merseyside ocean. But the reasons for this decision should be more widely known.

Apparently fewer and fewer Britons are taking baths, more and more prefer showers. Bars of soap are less convenient in the shower, so more and more people are buying gels and liquid cleansers.

Obviously, people are entitled to their different tastes, and nothing but fatuity can result from a bath versus shower argument, but I wonder if some are being turned away from baths – which I much prefer – by shockingly bad design of British baths and the shortage of bath racks.

The first means that there are no handles for people to use when they wish to sit up, and the second that there is nowhere to put the soap, which always falls off the side of these badly designed baths.

As I say, many people prefer showers in any case; if they can control the temperature and volume of flow one wishes them nothing but joy. But there remains a suspicion that people are being driven to showers by the inadequacies of English bath design, and this seems incomprehensible in an age when we have lost our former embarrassment in talking about such things.

16 September 2000

No Time for Tears

Does one think better or worse of Peter Mandelson on learning that he burst into tears when ordered to resign as Trade and Industry Secretary after details of his £375,000 home loan from Geoffrey Robinson emerged? A recent book claims that Alastair Campbell, the Prime Minister's press secretary, also wept:

"By the end of the conversation, tears were trickling down Mandelson's sepulchral white cheeks. A dark-eyed Campbell, himself blubbing, gave Mandelson a hug," writes Andrew Rawnsley, the journalist.

For a long time, it has been fashionable to argue that there is nothing unmanly about tears. Where great sorrows are concerned, like the death of a loved one, it is the sign of a proper, caring human being to weep, regardless of sex. The traditional male stiff upper lip is a denial of human nature, we are told.

No doubt this is true, but there is a difference between tears of sorrow at some great sadness or personal tragedy, and tears of pique at some setback to one's career. I am not sure we should encourage men in public life to break down in sobs at a setback of this sort. This is not so much because it might be thought unmanly to weep – the same objections would apply equally to a female cabinet minister who lost her job – but because it is the sign of a child to burst into tears when it cannot have what it wants, and we do not want to be governed by children. Kids, as they are called in politics, are used to show what big hearts we all have. They are not on the scene for politicians to emulate.

Of all the Cabinet places available I should have thought that the job of being Secretary of State for Northern Ireland was least suitable for a man who is prone to tears in this way. Something rather odd seems to be happening in the Government. I hope Mr Blair is not unwell. No doubt the journalist Andrew Rawnsley will explain it all to us eventually.

20 September 2000

A Greater Threat

Clive Aslet, editor of *Country Life*, has undoubtedly provided a useful public service with his survey of children's attitudes to the countryside. It involved a written questionnaire, completed in class by 250 children aged between seven and 14 in the Greater London area, and a national survey of nearly 400 children carried out by a market research company. The degree of ignorance revealed should surprise no one who has studied the young children of Britain. In fact there are probably few subjects on which they would be any less ignorant, although a questionnaire on pop stars and electronic games has been suggested. Only one in five of those asked knew what a gamekeeper was, while two-thirds did not know where acorns came from. One suggested they came from "the squiril" (sic), another that they came from cows.

Even so, I do not think Mr Aslet is necessarily right when he suggests it would be a good idea to teach them more on this subject. He does not appear to ask himself to what use they would put their knowledge, or which aspects would appeal to their teachers, who are probably nearly as ignorant as they are. It is easy to imagine that the only aspect of the subject which would prove of any interest to them would be the protection of wild life, and especially birds which are judged by the experts to be in short supply or threatened by extinction.

This might seem to be a worthy enough cause, but it does not take into account the extreme bossiness of these urban bird fanatics, or the nuisance caused to farmers. Already the Royal Society for the Protection of Birds has started calling for prison sentences to replace the current fines, and demanding that police be given powers to arrest anyone suspected of improper behaviour towards a bird.

It cannot be long, in the new spirit of zero tolerance, before landowners and farmers find themselves prosecuted for walking too close to a bird's nest on their own land. The RSPB may claim that 24 buzzards were poisoned or shot last year, 14 peregrine nests were robbed and four golden eagle nests, but the simple truth of the matter is that these birds have survived all these hundreds of year through the goodwill or indifference of farmers. They are a monument to the virtues of private property in the days before ramblers and public access. As soon as RSPB inspectors start demanding the right to barge over other people's land while they count the wild birds, both goodwill and indifference are lost.

14 October 2000

Stay at Home

The average Briton travels more than 6,800 miles every year, according to figures from the Department of Transport. This is an increase of 28 per cent since the mid-Eighties, and car travel accounts for 82 per cent of the total mileage, or 5,576 miles per person.

One can understand why nobody wants to travel by train. Even if you do not object to the no-smoking diktat imposed by the bossy and incompetent half-wits who have taken over Great Western, there is always the possibility that the train will be cancelled at the last minute, or subjected to intolerable delays while the company employees play out their power fantasies in the holy name of health and safety.

But one wonders why anybody wishes to travel at all in a world where work involving computers, internet, e-mail and suchlike can be done at home. The English countryside has been more or less destroyed by development. Whenever it is flooded, and possibly of some interest to look at, the trains are cancelled and all other forms of travel forbidden.

There was some joy at one time in going out for a drink with a friend, but nobody drinks any more, least of all when they are driving.

They say that air crews enjoy all-night binges before flights, but they never ask passengers to join them. Who wants to fly anyway when they could stay at home?

The main thing that drives people from the comfort and safety of their homes is the disgraceful standard of television programmes. They say the lower classes like them, but I don't believe it.

16 October 2000

An Unnoticed Moment

No doubt Nottingham is part of that other Britain about which we read from time to time. Police in Somerset do not carry guns. Last week in Taunton, a Mongolian fruitpicker suddenly ran in front of the car in which I was a passenger. Luckily it was travelling at under 20 mph. Within 30 seconds, there were three policemen on the scene.

Everyone was friendly and polite. The fruitpicker was as apologetic as the driver. The police were utterly charming. Anybody watching the scene would conclude that Britain was an extraordinarily nice country to live in.

The week before, I had spent three nights at a new hotel in St Mawes, Cornwall. It was quite expensive, but the seafood was excellent, the rooms and sea-views memorable, the staff were cheerful, welcoming and highly trained.

It occurred to me that Britain may have become the pleasantest country in the world to live in, especially if you can get out of London, Nottingham and other urban centres. If so, it has happened without anyone noticing. Obviously, it won't last. We read of plans to build 3.8 million new homes in the next 20 years, mostly in the countryside. But until they have succeeded in banning the hunt, chopping down all the trees and turning the Quantocks into a gigantic public lavatory, it is a glorious moment to be alive.

30 October 2000

Bloody but Unbowed

These exciting times are not easy for journalists to write about. I was impressed by the timing of a savage attack on the Queen Mother which appeared in Wednesday's *Daily Mail* under the by-line of Lynda Lee-Potter.

Declaring that the Queen Mother received £643,000 a year from the Civil List to pay her expenses, Lee-Potter wrote: "Possibly, somebody could point out that if she can't struggle through on around £54,000 a month, it might be time to make a few economies.

"The average old-age pension for less fortunate widows is around £67 a week. This has to be used to pay for rent, lighting, heating and food. It would just about buy one of the vintage bottles of champagne the Queen Mother is so fond of."

Ooh! I do not know exactly how old Lee-Potter is, but does she really believe the average old age pension of £67 a week covers rent, lighting, heating and food? I am prepared to bet she is at least 20 years younger than Queen Elizabeth, who celebrated her 100th birthday in August after nearly 80 years of public service. But it shows that your average, well-paid British journalist still has a keen sense of social justice.

Without these fearless middle-aged ladies like Lee-Potter around, we would probably have succumbed to a Nazi-style government under the late Duke of Gloucester about 40 years ago.

4 November 2000

Too Difficult

We are all expected to have opinions and make decisions on subjects about which we can know practically nothing, accepting the advice of one school against another which believes the opposite.

The list is familiar enough. For about 20 years we have been urged to eat practically nothing but fruit and fresh vegetables. Now we learn not only that women who diet become sterile, catch cancer and die young, but that cabbages and parsnips and such like vanities are actually bad for us.

Milk was one of the first to go and nobody wants that back. Attempts to restore beef have been upset by the BSE scare, despite wild promises of compensation for anyone who can actually catch the disease.

Acting largely on intuition, I took it on myself at quite an early stage to warn the world about mobile telephones. If you watched a mobile telephonist closely enough, I declared, you could see strange rubbery tubes and pieces of jelly hanging out of his ears. Nobody ever contradicted me when I pointed out that they can make you sterile as well as giving you German measles as well as pneumonia, chicken pox, gastro-enteritis, dizziness and itching.

Yet people continue to use them. It is almost as if certain sections of society wish to die. We are told that three out of four teenagers use a mobile telephone, which might give us a clue about the modern teenager's attitude to life. But then, in the next breath, we are told that absence of sleep gives you cancer, and most teenagers seem to sleep about 20 hours a day, presumably for medical reasons. Many will feel this should be encouraged.

4 November 2000

Too Easy

When I was a child, there were always one or two children in every age group who behaved worse than anybody else. They were liable to be more disobedient and aggressive, living in a state of constant war with the authorities. Perhaps their function was to remind us of the guilt of original sin, inherited from Adam and Eve's disobedience in the Garden of Eden. Few people believe in the Garden of Eden, and there is no such thing as a bad child nowadays, we are told, only a child who has been pushed into anti-social attitudes by inadequate parenting. The latest idea is to describe them as suffering from an attention deficit hyper-activity disorder.

This is not so much a psychological illness as a straightforward injury, like a twisted ankle. The growth of the health industry has taken so many forms in recent years that one can easily forget how much of it comes back to the simple choice of medicines. A new drug for misbehaving children, methylphenidate, sold under the name of Ritalin, seems to work quite well. It is not thought to be addictive. Of the 69,000 children in this country suffering from the most severe forms of "hyperactivity disorder", only 21,000 are taking it, but in the United States of America four million children take the drug.

Money is not the major factor, since it can cost as little as £150 a year to keep a child on Ritalin. The reason it arouses such hostility is rather complicated. If one forgets all the sociological euphemisms about attention deficit hyperactivity, the drug turns a nasty, neglected and resentful child into a contented and acceptable member of society. Can that be wrong? It might seem to hang on the point whether these American children are so rude and charmless because they are neglected by their parents, who have better things to do, and welcome the chance to neglect them still further. Or perhaps they are neglected by their parents because they are rude and charmless children in the first place. I find the assumption that unpleasantness of nature can be cured by a pill strangely frightening. In this country, our leaders are so overexcited by their new powers that they talk of wiping out the entire sheep population in response to the more or less imagined risk of a human BSE epidemic. If they are prepared to consider that, as well as giving children pills to make them better behaved, why should they not eventually decide to give children the sheep pill and solve both problems?

4 November 2000

Show It Again

I never knew Guy Burgess although I once met Donald Maclean, the diplomat who defected with him to Russia in 1951. I also met Anthony Blunt on several occasions. A film about Burgess's meeting with Coral Browne, the Australian actress, in Moscow 10 years later, brilliantly dramatised by Alan Bennett and repeated by BBC2 on Saturday evening, was bound to create powerful emotions of nostalgia among those who had anything to do with British Intelligence as it used to be.

At a time when the old public school elite who had run Britain so well for the previous 250 years was beginning to be driven out by the new generation of "classless" incompetents, the top public schools kept a very good hold on the Intelligence Services.

Many of them were homosexuals, but I do not think it was official disapproval of their homosexuality which drove them to become traitors. More than that, it was their rejection on class grounds by the new "meritocracy", under which Britain was rapidly losing any respect or influence it had enjoyed since the war.

Since the removal of Burgess, Maclean, Philby, Blunt (and others we have never heard about) British Intelligence has become a great embarrassment. Consumed by self-importance and obsessed with secrecy, it finds itself, since the end of the Cold War, with no useful role to play, and no secrets worth keeping.

However, politicians in power love the thought of controlling a secret service, and there seems no end to the amount of money they are prepared to spend on the pleasure. Just occasionally, we are allowed a glimpse of what this involves, as in the annual report of the parliamentary Intelligence and Security Committee, published on Monday.

This revealed that the cost of moving one half of the General

Communications Headquarters, as our spy centre is called, from one side of Cheltenham to the other, has more than quadrupled from the original £60 million estimate. The reason for this is that GCHQ intelligence is judged so vital it cannot stop work even for one second.

Which is quite a good joke when we reflect that we have no secrets to keep, unless we invent them for the purpose. How Burgess, Maclean and the rest of them must be laughing.

8 November 2000

Ordinary People

A letter in *The Times* on Thursday complained that few church guides contain more than a passing reference to their First and Second World War memorials. This is not surprising when one reflects that they are nearly always displayed prominently and often of quite ugly design. They seldom add to the beauty of the scene, and church wardens may feel there is no need to draw visitors' attention to their presence.

The writer of this letter, Lord Phillips of Sudbury, is a contemporary of mine (although I do not think I have had the pleasure of meeting him) and therefore too young to have fought in either war. "By contrast," he explains, "it is common to find extensive reference to the gentry and aristocracy, who usually died in their beds but could afford to erect memorials and monuments to themselves and their families. Yet many villages lost staggering numbers of their sons (and a few daughters) and it must be disappointing, to say the least, to their families and, indeed, all who remember them that, in all the talk of architectural splendours and the like, there is no space for the 'ordinary' people who gave their lives."

He is right, of course, that we should not forget the war dead, although fewer and fewer people will remember them personally. Most important of all is that we should not forget why they died. Lord Phillips is a would-be politician, having stood on numerous occasions as a Liberal Democrat parliamentary candidate, even if he has never been elected. He cannot conceivably be held responsible for either world war, any more than I can, because both of us are far too young. We should ask ourselves why they happened. Both were the result of the same cause, which is the tendency of politicians to take themselves too seriously. Just occasionally, the public decides to indulge them. As we have seen in our own time, the urge to give free milk to children – or not – is scarcely to be distinguished from the urge to bomb Serbs in the Balkans. Both are the product of what we might call the self-importance factor that persuades people to go into politics in the first place.

Perhaps it is of some comfort to the relatives of these "ordinary people" – as well as the gentry and aristocrats who gave their lives – to be reminded of these things, but if I were a budding politician, I think I would tend to keep rather quiet on the subject.

11 November 2000

Our New Hercules

Does anyone have an address for the Elton John Fan Club? I would be very happy to pay the subscription and turn up among the adoring crowds, even if I do not qualify for fully fledged membership. This would be because I do not think I have ever heard him sing or play the piano. I am not sure that I had even heard of him before this week, but that is true of most of the people one reads about in the newspapers these days and in Sir Elton, I feel, we have found a new national hero.

It would be nice to think there is a corner of Heaven reserved for the big spenders, who spread their wealth and happiness around the world, but everything about him is admirable. Coming from Pinner, in Middlesex, where he was known as Reginald Kenneth Dwight, he has entirely invented the character and role of Sir Elton Hercules John, greatest spender since the first Marquess Curzon. It needed a touch of genius to see that the country was yearning for someone with "Hercules" as his middle name.

On Wednesday, he appeared in court 17 at the Royal Courts of Justice to demand damages from some accountants. Their counsel put it to him that he had spent £30 million at an average of £1.5 million a month in the period under study: "Do you have any reason to think that inaccurate?"

"Probably not," he said.

"It says here that you spent £293,000 on flowers alone. Is that possible?"

"Yes, I like flowers," said Sir Elton. "I have no one to leave my money to. I am a single man. I like spending money." Our society is full of bores and prigs who will say he should have given the money to charity, probably involving children in Liverpool. For my own part, I think there is something truly wonderful about a man who can spend £293,000 on flowers. It shows that money can still bring joy. Let the kids of Liverpool grow their own poppies and pansies for a change.

Sir Elton also chose to spend £3,500 of his new money on a wig to celebrate his 50th birthday. This seems a good response to the melancholy event, although I notice he does not choose to wear it in court among all the lawyers who spend similar sums on their headgear to impress us with their importance. Never mind. Sir Elton is bigger than any of them. He can do no wrong, so far as I am concerned.

18 November 2000

Nightmare

On the other hand, it seems to me that Michael Caine has gone too far. When the Queen decided to dub him knight on Thursday, he chose to take the title under his real name, Maurice Micklewhite, explaining this was in tribute to his late father.

Caine is not a bad actor, as anybody who saw Alfie will remember, and certainly deserves a knighthood as much as most of them, now he has reached the age of 67. But we could have done without the endless self-congratulatory harangue about how he was born on the Old Kent Road and grew up in poverty, his father, of gipsy descent, working as a fish porter in Billingsgate and his mother as a charlady.

He has described himself as "every bourgeois's nightmare, a cockney with intelligence and a million dollars", but there is nothing paradoxical or even unusual in the son of a Billingsgate fish porter being knighted. Most of those chosen for knighthood nowadays seem to come from that sort of background.

The only Billingsgate porters excluded from the system nowadays would appear to be the confirmed bachelors among them, who have no children, but no doubt Peter Mandelson will do something about it when he wakes up to the obvious injustice involved.

I do not know whether Sir Maurice Micklewhite can qualify as every bourgeois's nightmare, but fear he might prove a bit of a bore.

18 November 2000

Our New Teacher

One can easily understand why government ministers favour the idea of patriotism. Patriotic citizens will support their country in whatever its politicians decide to do. On learning that the new office block for MPs that finally opened this month has cost £231 million, the patriots among us will cheer and clap our hands.

Even so, it seems slightly strange on Mr Blair's part to have written to all his Cabinet ministers telling them to be more patriotic, and even stranger to have appointed a Minister for Patriotism. He is Michael Wills, a former television producer who became Labour MP for Swindon North at the last election.

Presumably he will be paid the same as he was when a junior education minister. There may be those who find it odd that anyone should expect to be paid simply for being patriotic, but they may be comforted to learn that Mr Wills, whose father was Austrian and mother a New Zealander, appears very keen on the British indeed: "We would pick out openness, a sense of fair play and decency, and the work ethic as quintessentially British qualities," he explains. Than you very much, Sir.

27 November 2000

Hope for the Country

The gigantic figure of William Shakespeare will always tower above any attempt at creating a modern English literature, but I have always believed that our second-best achievement might be found in the series of light operas produced by William Gilbert and Arthur Sullivan between 1871 and 1896. They remain sublime in their musicality, their humour, their clever plotting and their quintessential Englishness.

It would be absurd for English parents to suppose they have given birth to a modern Shakespeare, although I am afraid this may be quite a frequent delusion, and it helps to explain all the slim volumes of "poetry" that continue to appear 14 years after the death of Betjeman.

Not so many people will be tempted to indulge the hope that they have somehow produced a new version of Gilbert and Sullivan, but I must admit that I confronted the possibility when I eventually went to see *Bon Voyage* on Wednesday evening. This is the new musical written by Alexander and Nathaniel Waugh, which ends its week-long run at the Tabernacle, Powys Square, Notting Hill, tomorrow. There are one or two tickets left at the box office (£16 for evening shows, £12 for matinees) on 020 8749 4750 but the best chance might be to turn up at the theatre. In the spirit of times, it may be found slightly rougher than anything that would have been encouraged at the old Savoy Theatre under D'Oyly Carte, but the same humour is there, the memorable, even breathtaking tunes and above all the same assurance that there is an intelligent, sceptical England surviving under all the rubbish we see on television. *Bon Voyage* is a delight and joy, and I am proud to have fathered the two geniuses responsible for it.

16 December 2000